CREOLE WOMEN AND THE MEN THEY LOVED

A NOVEL

BY

R. DOUGLAS OSBORNE RE

Copyright 2015 by R. Douglas Osborne.   re

All rights reserved. No part of this book may be reproduced in any form or by any means without the prior written consent of the publisher. This book is largely a book of fiction.

About the Author

R. Douglas Osborne lives with his wife, Debra, in Myrtle Beach, South Carolina. He is the author of the novels, An Unexpected Guest and A Train of Destiny; both available in Kindle and print at Amazon.

He holds a bachelor's degree from the University of Iowa and a Master's Degree from The University of Northern Iowa. He is recognized as an accomplished residential designer and has turned his passion for world class design to describing the human condition through compelling characters in story form in a manner which is thought provoking, easy to read, and nearly impossible to put down until the last page is turned.

Special Credit

Without John McCreary this book would be a jumbled mess sitting in the dark morass of a dilatory computer. He has spent untold hours arranging all the books I have written into manageable formats. John is a talented and decent human being. I have always believed the true and full measure of a man is the effect he has on those he encounters throughout life's journey. In that regard I know there are many who share my sentiment; I am a better man for having known him.

R. Douglas Osborne

Dedications

To My Aunt, Phyllis Agan

Until about ten years ago my last memory of Aunt Phyllis was at a family gathering at my grandmother's house in the little town of Deep River, Iowa. Unfortunately, as so often happens in families, we lost contact with each other for nearly fifty years. Thankfully, we were able to meet once again and begin correspondence. She is a kind and loving and most talented and remarkable woman. She has read and critiqued all of my books and been involved in the editing process of Creole Women. She was educated to be a teacher and has spent the greater part of her life in the service of others.

She is currently living in Davenport, Iowa near family and friends. Over the years, she has been an inspiration to so many. I often think what a better world this would be if everyone was blessed with their own Aunt Phyllis.

"Behind every good book is a better proofreader. Such is Phyllis Agan."

Aunt Phyllis, with my love, I dedicate this book to you.

To My Wife, Debra

My entire life is, and shall always be, dedicated to the love of my life, my wife, Debra.

R. Douglas Osborne

Table of Contents

Chapter One

Chapter Two

Chapter Three

Chapter Four

Chapter Five

Chapter Six

Chapter seven

Chapter Eight

Chapter Nine

Chapter Ten

Chapter Eleven

Chapter Twelve

Chapter Thirteen

Chapter Fourteen

Chapter Fifteen

Chapter Sixteen

Chapter Seventeen

Chapter Eighteen

Chapter Nineteen

Chapter Twenty

Chapter Twenty One

Chapter Twenty Two

Chapter Twenty Three

Chapter Twenty Four

Chapter Twenty Five

Chapter Twenty Six

Chapter Twenty Seven

Chapter Twenty Eight

Chapter Twenty Nine

Chapter Thirty

Chapter Thirty One

Chapter Thirty Two

Chapter Thirty Three

Chapter Thirty Four

Chapter Thirty Five

Chapter Thirty Six

Chapter Thirty Seven

Chapter Thirty Eight

Chapter Thirty Nine

Chapter Forty

Chapter Forty One

Chapter Forty Two

Chapter Forty Three

Chapter Forty Four

Chapter Forty Five

Chapter Forty Six

Chapter Forty Seven

Chapter Forty Eight

Chapter Forty Nine

Chapter Fifty

Chapter Fifty One

Chapter Fifty Two

Chapter Fifty Three

Chapter Fifty Four

Chapter Fifty Five

Chapter Fifty Six

Chapter Fifty Seven

Epilogue

CREOLE WOMEN

And

THE MEN THEY LOVED

Chapter One

Southampton, England 1854

Standing on the bow of the clipper ship, West Wind, Young Thomas Claiborne watched the Alum Bay Cliffs on the Isle of Wight disappear off the port side of the ship as they headed into the English Channel and the open seas, bound for Charleston, South Carolina.

Age 23, newly graduated from the university in England, with a new bride, of a marriage arranged to preserve the bloodlines of nobility, scheduled to follow him to America in several months, Thomas was assigned to succeed his father as the Lord and Manager of the family's vast agricultural empire in the Low Country.

He was well educated; always at the top of his class at the university, ambitious, and willing to accept challenges. He was full of confidence and not taken back by the prospect of assuming the management of the vast Claiborne plantations. Managing a labor force of a thousand slaves was another matter. He placed great value in the Claiborne family holdings, yet was repulsed by the notion of slavery. He realized that the immense quantity of rice produced on the plantations could only be sustained by slave labor and, somehow, he would have to find a way to balance his business responsibilities with his assessment of slavery as one of man's greatest inhumanities to man.

He could only wonder what the future would hold.

. . . .

Columbia, South Carolina – 2005

Peck's bad boy had graduated from law school and had passed the bar exam. Although branded as a classic underachiever as a youngster, he had always managed to climb through the ranks. Cantankerous as a toddler, mischievous in middle school, defiant in high school, and rebellious in the strict military system of the Citadel, no one was more amazed at his ascent to a position of prominence in the study of law than himself. His father, Joe, had nicknamed his recalcitrant child, Peck, and over the years, he had proven himself worthy of the moniker. Yet here he was an attorney; about to keep an appointment with another attorney of note; his Godfather, mentor, and Justice of the Supreme Court of South Carolina.

Mark ascended the limestone steps of the imposing Supreme Court building in Columbia, South Carolina, and passed between two of the towering stone columns on his way to keep his appointment with Justice Harold Sanders. Although Mark had known Harold Sanders his entire life, he was dressed in his lawyer's best suit out of respect for the man's office and his position in the legal community. The waiting area was nearly filled with people having business with the court, the clerks, and the justice assistants. Julia Meyers, the receptionist, noted his arrival and cheerfully said, "Good morning Mr. Bradley." With her voice lowered she said with a smile and a wink, "So you passed the bar exam. Good job." With her voice returned to normal volume and proper business decorum for the benefit of the other visitors in the lobby, she continued, "Justice Sanders is expecting you. I'll let him know you're here."

Harold Sanders was a mixed race African American who, along with Mark's father, had earned a Juris Doctor degree from the University Of South Carolina School Of Law. He had a sterling record as an attorney and judge and had distinguished himself during his five years on the bench of the South Carolina Supreme Court. Sanders and Mark's father, Joseph Oliver Bradley II, had maintained a strong personal and professional relationship since graduating from law school, with Harold returning to the Greenville area to practice law in a predominantly black community in the upstate hill country of South Carolina and Joe returning to the family law firm and the white upper crust social environs of Charleston in the Low Country.

The Justice warmly greeted Mark with a quick hug and a long handshake as he entered the Judge's expansive chambers replete with all the trappings: paneled walls, adornments, and furnishings one would expect for a Justice of the Supreme Court. "You certainly didn't waste any time. Let's see . . . law school graduation was less than a month ago and you have already passed the bar exam."

"Sounds like you have been talking to my dad."

"Guilty. You called him with the news and he called me. We are both proud of you."

"I can't take all the credit, Uncle Harold. Not every law student has a Supreme Court Justice for a mentor and occasional tutor."

"Well," Sanders responded in a warm and thoughtful manner, "your dad and I go back a long way. Mark, you have finally failed to live up, or should I say down, to the dilatory behavior of Peck's bad boy. I think it's time we retired that nickname, even if it was always in good fun. I know your dad urged you to go to law school, but I could tell you were developing a passion for the law early on."

Mark gave an affirmative nod and replied, "I guess I just got hooked. My biggest surprise was getting accepted to law school in the first place." In a suspicious and inquisitive manner, he continued, "I don't suppose you know anything about that."

The question fell on a smile and deaf ears as the Justice motioned toward a soft chair and offered Mark a seat. "Son, I'm glad I was able to get in touch with you before you pack your bags and head back to Charleston. I've got about 45 minutes before I'm due in court. But that should give us enough time to chat about a situation that may interest you."

Sanders unfolded a road map of South Carolina and spread it out on a large coffee table in a formal sitting area. "Mark, pull your chair up to the table and look at this map with me."

"What are we looking for, Uncle Harold?" Mark replied as he leaned forward in his chair to examine the map.

"Have you ever heard of the Claiborne Plantation?"

"I've heard of it; somewhere in the Low Country North of Charleston. That's about all I know."

Sanders pulled a pen from the breast pocket of his shirt and drew a jagged circle around an area on the map. "It's comprised of several large pieces of land located between Georgetown to the north and McClellanville to the south."

Mark let out a low whistle. "That's a lot of real estate, Uncle Harold."

"Over 15,000 acres to be exact."

"I'm curious. You said it might interest me. In what way?" Mark asked as he diverted his attention from the map and looked at Sanders.

The Justice looked at his watch as he leaned back in his chair and removed his reading glasses. The fact that he deftly evaded the question wasn't lost on Mark. "The last owner of this land was a man by the name of Thomas Claiborne. He died in 1924 and left all of the land and some other business interests and assets in an irrevocable trust. The beneficiary of the trust is his great granddaughter, a woman by the name of Naomi Richards. She was 11 years old at the time of his death. According to the terms of the will, when Mrs. Richards, Naomi, dies, everything in the entire trust will be given or deeded to Thomas Claiborne's closest living relative."

Another but louder and longer whistle from Mark. "Looks like somebody is about to hit the big one. . . . And that would be?"

"That's the rub. There are two people claiming to be Claiborne's closest living relative after Mrs. Richards passes. One is a businessman by the name of Donald Claiborne, who lives in Georgetown and the other is a young lady by the name of Rachel Devening. She teaches biology at the local junior college and she is Naomi's great or great, great granddaughter. I'm not certain about the total number of generations since Thomas. I have trouble trying to sort out relationships in family trees. She's about your age, mid to late twenties. She also lives in Georgetown and, along with teaching she looks after her grandmother Naomi." Harold looked again at his watch. "Mark, if everything I've been told over the years is true, Rachel will be the sole legitimate heir to this estate. She is one generation closer in relationship to old Thomas than Donald Claiborne. The problem is, he can prove his relationship and she can't. This is all a matter of public record and for years everyone has assumed that he would be the eventual heir until Rachel started stirring things up."

"At least he's got the right last name," Mark said.

"And I'm sure that's part of the problem," Harold replied wistfully. "It would sound logical to most people that a Claiborne would be the rightful heir to the Claiborne estate."

The two men sat looking at each other across the table.

"With a suspicious smile on his face, Mark said, "Let me guess Uncle Harold, is this where I come in?"

With an expression of resolve, the older man replied, "It is. Mark, Rachel is a marvelous young woman and she needs help. She is really up against it. I tried to help her about a year before I was appointed to the Supreme Court. I looked at the situation from every possible angle, but like others who have tried to help, I kept running into the same stone wall. Time is now Rachel's greatest enemy. I believe Naomi is 92 years old. She is not in the best of health and if Rachel can't prove her relationship to old man Claiborne before she dies, it's all over."

"What can I possibly do to help?"

"I'm not sure you can help. I'm not sure anyone can. But here's what I have in mind. I know Joe is anxious for you to join him in the law firm but when I spoke with him recently on the telephone he said he would like you to have some time off before jumping into the business. I talked with him at some length about the Claiborne matter and we both think you ought to take a crack at it."

"Uncle Harold, almost any attorney is more qualified than me to represent her."

"I'm not sure she needs an attorney, at least not yet."

"Mark exhaled in a minor display of defeat and replied, "All right, I have absolutely no idea what I'm getting involved with but, count me in."

"Terrific," Sanders exclaimed as he rose from his chair. "You carried a double major at the Citadel in history and economics in undergraduate school and lord only knows this entire matter is awash with history and economics. Son, the potential value of this estate is probably measured in hundreds of millions. With a prize that big you know the lawyers will come out of the woodwork just itching to get in on the action. I think you have the perfect qualifications. You have a great analytical mind and you are a great listener. Someone needs to step in who can look at the entire matter with a new perspective. You are just the ticket." Sanders wrote Rachel's name and telephone number on a small piece of note paper and handed it to Mark. "Give me until noon tomorrow to call her and tell her about you. Then give her a call, make arrangements to meet, and see what you can do."

"Uncle Harold, how do you know this young lady? How did you become involved in this, to begin with?

"Good Question. Rachel is . . ." After a short thoughtful pause, he continued, "Let's just say she is a friend of the family. Oh, here are some words you may come to dread as the years in your law career go by. This work is Pro Bono. The trust watches expenses carefully and would not approve attorney's fees; especially for someone whose principal goal is to upset a lot of apple carts. Your dad knows all about it and he tells me you will be working on the law firm's payroll."

"How long do you expect this to take?"

"I would say as long as you and Rachel feel like you're making good progress. If you reach the point that you have exhausted your efforts or Naomi passes away, fold your tent and join the world of work in the legal arena. I'm sure you will keep your dad fully apprised of your progress and, in the end, he will decide if and when it's time to pull the plug."

"Uncle Harold, I'll make it a point to send you a weekly email to let you know how it is going."

"I'm sure you would, but I'm afraid that won't be possible. This is a very sensitive issue and going to become more so in the weeks and, perhaps, months to come. There is a lot at stake and even the State of South Carolina has a serious interest in the outcome. As a Supreme Court Justice I have to be extremely careful about any personal or professional interests beyond the court. I don't believe anything about my involvement to date or our meeting today is in violation of any judicial ethical standards but it all has to stop here."

"I understand," Mark replied while extending his right hand for a parting handshake.

As he approached the office door he was stopped by Sander's voice.

"Mark, this may turn out to be one of the greatest scavenger hunts or just an enormous waste of time. At least you will have a great looking client."

"Uncle Harold?"

"In my day I think the term we used was *knockout*. I believe the term mostly used today is *hot*." Justice Sanders looked once again at his watch and with a slight grin said, "Time for court."

. . . .

At a quarter past 12 noon the following day, Mark placed a call from his cell phone in his car on his way back to Charleston. The telephone connected on the second ring. "Hello, this is Rachel."

"Miss Devening, this is Mark Bradley."

Rachel enthusiastically replied, "Mr. Bradley, I've been expecting your call. Justice Sanders called me late yesterday afternoon and told me all about your meeting."

"Please call me Mark. I'm sure he told you I just graduated from law school and I have no professional legal experience. But he didn't seem to think that would be a problem, at least for now."

"Not at all Mark. In fact, what I need is a problem solver. The Justice told me quite a lot about you and I'm anxious to get started."

"At least, for the time being, I'm at your service. I suppose the first thing is to arrange a meeting. I'm available as soon as it's convenient for you."

"I have classes on Tuesdays and Thursdays, so I'll be tied up all day tomorrow. But starting with the day after, I'll be free until next Tuesday."

"Then Friday it is. How about I drive up to Georgetown Friday morning and we can meet someplace where we can talk?"

"Mark, I'm sorry if I sound mysterious, and I'm certainly in no danger, but this trust matter has taken center stage among the locals and I feel like I'm being watched wherever I go. I would much rather drive down to Charleston, at least for our first meeting."

"I perfectly understand. My parents live in Charleston but they have owned a beach house on the Isle of Palms for years. It's where I will be staying for the foreseeable future. Why don't you come here, let's say around noon? We can have lunch on the island and have as much of the afternoon as you wish to get started."

Rachel agreed and Mark gave her directions to the beach house.

"Well, Miss Devening, I'm looking forward to meeting you. Oh, dress casually, it's a beach."

"Will do and, Mark, please call me Rachel."

Chapter Two

Mark began his run on the beach shortly after first light. At 6 feet and nearly 200 pounds he was 10 pounds over his football playing weight at the Citadel. He was determined to shed at least 15 pounds and the 2 inches he had gained around the waist from the sedentary lifestyle of a law student. He jogged several miles to the north end of the island and began to pick up the pace for the return trip. He was preoccupied with his meeting with Rachel and filled with a nagging curiosity about the whole affair. "Just a few more hours to go," he thought as he turned from the beach to the steps leading up to the walkway that spanned the sand dunes and led to the second floor porch.

As he emerged from the shower he managed to grab his cell phone on its third ring.

Having scanned the caller ID as he raised the phone he answered, "Hey Dad, what's going on?"

"Good morning Son, your mother and I are going to Savannah this afternoon to spend the night and Saturday with some old friends. I think you remember the Murphys. Probably play some golf, or maybe get in some offshore fishing."

"Sounds great. Have a good time."

"I'm sure we will, but before we leave your mother wanted to stop by the beach house to see if everything is in order and if there is anything you might need."

"Dad, I can't think of a thing. There's no point in crossing the bridge to come out to the island before you leave. Why don't you plan on stopping by after you get back?"

"My sentiments exactly," Mark's father replied with a chuckle. But these are my marching orders. We'll be there around eleven o'clock if that's all right with you."

"I'll look forward to seeing you.

Mark's thoughts were on his visitor as he dressed in pressed cotton khaki slacks, a light blue Polo shirt, and boat shoes with no socks. "Casual enough for the beach," he thought. "And formal enough for a client," he hoped.

. . . .

When Mark's parents stepped through the front door he shook his dad's hand and gave his mother a hug. As he stepped back he said to her, "Hmm, let's see, you've been to the spa, the hair is a little shorter and maybe one or two shades lighter. Mom, if you don't stop looking younger, people will think you're my older sister instead of my mother."

While trying to suppress a grin, Vivian Bradley retorted in a feigned scolding manner. "You seem to forget, I've spent my entire life around lawyers and I know a damned lie when I hear one." The grin turned into a broad smile and the forced stern voice turned into a soft South Carolina drawl. "But I taught you well. You're a true Southern gentleman and remember, flattery will get you everywhere. Now, surely the two of you have things to talk about. Why don't y'all have a Coke on the sun porch? I'm going to look through the cupboards and make a list of supplies to pick up for you when we get back from Savannah. I'm also going to move some of our clothes into the front guest room so you can have the master bedroom." When the two men didn't respond immediately, she waved her hands like she was shooing chickens and ordered, "Now scoot."

As the two men settled into deck chairs with cokes in hand, Mark's father said, "Tell me about your meeting with Harold."

"Dad, I'd give ten to one odds that Uncle Harold has already told you everything about our meeting."

"You'd win that bet," he replied with a grin. "We talked about it at some length."

"When I asked him about Rachel and how he had come to know her, he simply said that she is a friend of the family. What can you tell me about her?"

"Soon you will know everything there is to know, but Harold and I both think it's best if it all comes from Rachel. I guess we are hoping that by starting at the beginning and working your way through the entire matter without secondhand information from us, you might run across something that has been missed. It's thin any way you look at it but we don't know what else to do. By the way, have you arranged a meeting with her?"

"I have. As a matter of fact, she should be here in 20 or 30 minutes. I offered to meet her in Georgetown but she said she would be more comfortable coming to Charleston for our first meeting. We're going to have lunch and spend the afternoon working on my education. Dad, one thing bothers me. This seems to be an open ended commitment. It may only last a week or two but it could go on for months. I don't want to be a financial burden to the firm."

"I appreciate that. We'll just play it by ear and see how it goes. Frankly, I'm doing it as a favor to Harold. We have exchanged more than one favor over the years."

"I'm missing something."

Noting the confused look on his son's face he said. "Let me tell you a few things about Harold Sanders."

"You know we were in law school at the same time. It was customary for students to gather in small study groups in the law library and a few other places on campus. But Harold usually studied by himself. He certainly wasn't the first black to attend law school at USC but these were the early 70s, and let's just say, his presence was simply tolerated. I ran into him in the law library. We were the only ones to show up. I guess they were all getting an early start for the weekend. Harold and I talked about a paper we had to write on the subject of fiduciary responsibility. We talked about it for several hours. That evening, walking back to my apartment, I realized I had been treated to several hours of intellectual discussion with probably the smartest man I had ever known. He was then and he still is. I often wondered if I would have made it through law school without him. It damn sure wouldn't have been easy.

I remember the first time your grandfather met Harold. I had invited him to come to Charleston to spend a weekend. We arrived in town mid-morning and Dad wanted us to meet him at his law office and then go on to the yacht club for lunch. Said he wanted to show off the two smartest law students at USC to a lot of his old friends. On the way to the office, I told Harold that I had told my father everything about him and that he was anxious to meet him. When we walked into the office my dad looked at Harold and froze. For a moment he was speechless. I guess it was one of those, Guess Who's Coming to Dinner Moments. Harold looked at me and said, 'I guess there was one thing about me you didn't tell him.' We all sat for a moment without saying anything. Finally, your grandfather looked at Harold and said, 'If I had ever been treated as rudely as I've treated you, I would have turned and walked out. But you obviously have more class than that and I can't think of anyone I would rather have lunch with at the yacht club than you.' They became fast friends and remained so until the day your grandfather died."

Joe Bradley continued. "Harold ran out of money before the beginning of our final semester and faced the prospect of dropping out. Dad went to the Dean of the Law School and told him that Harold was the first recipient of a scholarship started by his firm and instructed him to send Harold's tuition bill to him. Harold protested but gave in when Dad told him if he didn't accept the money, it would go to the next person in line. Dad handed Harold a personal check for his rent and living expenses for the semester. I remember Harold shaking his head and saying, 'I'm not going to talk you out of this, am I?' With that, Harold took out a piece of paper and made out a promissory note for the entire amount and handed it to Dad and said, 'If you will consider it a loan, we've got a deal.' It took him several years but Harold paid back every penny.

Finally, about eleven years ago I was called before a review board of the Bar Association to answer charges that I had violated the lawyer client relationship by divulging certain proprietary information about a client. I was certain I hadn't crossed the line but I also knew the judge who was reviewing the case and was afraid I might be disbarred. Even if I had prevailed in the disbarment proceedings it would have nearly ruined my legal career. The reviewing judge wound up dismissing the case with prejudice. This all took place about two years after Harold had been appointed Superior Court Judge.

As I rose to leave the hearing room the Judge looked at me and said for my ears only, 'Don't ever underestimate the power of friends.' Harold would never own up to it but I know he saved my ass."

With a look of firm resolve, Mark's dad stated, "We will see this through to the end."

As Mark thoughtfully considered the things his dad had told him another thought about Harold entered his mind. "Dad, didn't you once tell me that Uncle Harold's first wife died shortly after you both finished law school?"

"That's right," he replied. "He was a broken man."

Mrs. Bradley opened the screen door to the sun porch. "Mark, a car just pulled into the driveway. It looks like you have company."

Mark looked at his father. "That must be her."

"We'll finish this story another time. Better go greet your guest."

Mark walked down the front steps to the ground level parking pad and arrived at her car just as she closed the door and turned toward the house unexpectedly facing Mark less than 5 feet away. She was stunning and he had to react quickly to avoid being caught staring. "Rachel, I'm Mark Bradley," he said while extending his hand.

She appeared a little flustered but quickly regrouped and returned the gesture by taking his hand. "I'm Rachel Devening, and delighted to meet you."

For an instant, he thought she looked familiar, but a quick brain scan of faces and places turned up empty.

The chemistry between them was instant and compelling. After 3 or 4 seconds of shaking her hand, Mark collected his composure and replied as he gestured toward the front stairs, "Let's go on in. There are some folks I'd like you to meet."

As they entered the beach house, Mark's parents turned to greet them from their position in the great room. "Rachel, I would like you to m . . ."

Before Mark could complete the introduction, Rachel stepped forward with her hand extended. "Mr. Bradley, what a wonderful surprise."

"Likewise my dear," Joe exclaimed. "It's been much too long." Turning to his wife he said, "Vivian, you remember Rachel Devening, the young lady we met for dinner with Harold Sanders. Must be 5 or 6 years ago."

"How could I forget; I thought you were lovely then but just look at you now. I hope you can come to see us sometime soon. We'll get away from these stuffy old lawyers and have a girl's day out."

"I can't think of anything I would enjoy more, Mrs. Bradley."

Noting Rachel's obvious pleasure and relaxed manner in his parent's company, Mark said, "Dad, Rachel, and I were planning on having lunch at the Oyster Bar restaurant before getting started. Why don't you and Mom join us?"

"We'd love to but we have to get on the road to Savannah. Certainly, another time."

Mark accompanied his parents to their car and stopped his dad with a hand on his shoulder before he could open the door. With a hint of exasperation in his voice, he said, "I guess I didn't realize you knew her."

Joe Bradley looked at his son apologetically and replied, "I'm sorry for the omission, but this won't be the only surprise. There are more ahead. Enjoy your lunch and . . . good luck."

Chapter Three

Mark drove down Palm Boulevard to the local seafood restaurant overlooking the Intracoastal Waterway. Rachel was radiant in an orange and red floral print sun dress with spaghetti straps and open toed beach sandals. As they walked across the parking lot three men came out and about stumbled into each other when they saw her. One of them stepped back and opened the door.

Rachel responded with a smile and a polite "thank you," as she walked in.

"My pleasure," came the reply.

Just as they were seated, Mark commented, "I don't mean to embarrass you, but I'll bet that happens a lot."

"You mean the men in the parking lot? I suppose it does but I just try to take it as a compliment."

After placing their order, Mark said, "I recall Uncle Harold telling me that both you and your grandmother, Naomi Richards, live in Georgetown."

"Uncle Harold," she questioned with an inquisitive look?

Caught off-guard, Mark replied, "Well of course he isn't my real uncle. He's black and I'm whi . . ." He adjusted himself in his chair wishing he could retrieve his comments and continued. "That just didn't come out right. Let me start over. Harold Sanders is my father's closest friend and I have called him my uncle for as long as I can remember. He is one of the finest men I have ever known."

"I agree," Rachel replied with a smile and addressed the original question. "Actually, Naomi is my great grandmother and we both live in Georgetown. We both live in the same home on Front Street. Naomi occupies most of the house and I live in a separate apartment on the side. We both lived in the mansion house at Claiborne Plantation until I started teaching a few years ago and she began to need more frequent care. We both hated to leave the house. She lived there for almost 90 years."

"It seems when I get one question answered, at least two or three more pop up. Have you always lived at Claiborne?"

Before she could answer the food arrived.

She looked directly at Mark across the table and with a barely discernable wink said, "Why don't we table that question and make it first on the docket after lunch."

Mark looked at his quarter pound burger with a large order of fries and a Coke next to Rachel's scoop of tuna salad on lettuce with sliced tomatoes and ice water. The need to lose 15 pounds and 2 inches at the waist seemed more urgent than ever and this was not the way to do it.

Conversation during lunch revealed more about Mark's first client. She had a Master's Degree in biology, graduated from the College of Charleston, and had an engaging personality. "On top of all this," Mark thought, "she is so damned easy to look at."

When the waitress refilled her water glass, Rachel responded with, "Merci."

"French?" Mark asked.

With a look of embarrassment, she responded," I wasn't trying to be a showoff. It just slipped out. One of our ancestors was a French Nobleman and for many generations most of the children in our family learned French along with English."

As they pulled out of the parking lot, Mark noticed two men sitting in a dark green sedan parked facing the direction he would be going. He couldn't see their faces but they didn't strike him as typical beachgoers.

Inside the Bradley beach house, Mark offered Rachel a chair at the eating area table.

"You asked how long I have been at Claiborne."

"I did," he replied.

"I went to live with Grandma Richards when I was 12. My parents were killed in a plane crash."

Mark noted tears beginning to well in her eyes and he focused his total attention on her as she continued.

"We lived in a suburb outside the beltway around Washington DC and my parents both worked for the Federal Government. My dad was a mid-level manager with the Department of Agriculture and my mother worked for the IRS in the enforcement Division. They had planned a trip to Barbados for their 16th wedding anniversary. The three of us flew to Charleston and my folks drove me up to Claiborne to stay with Naomi while they were gone." After a long pause she said, slightly choking, "I never saw them again."

"Rachel, "I'm sorry sounds kind of hollow but it's all I can think to say. We can stop today if you would like."

She replied while wiping her eyes with a tissue, "No, I'm fine."

"How about some iced tea?"

Mark left and returned a moment later with two glasses of tea and some sweetener.

Mark resumed his questions. "Naomi would have been well up in years when you were twelve. I'm surprised you remained with her instead of a younger relative."

Rachel's eyes brightened. "She was 76 at the time but smart as a tack and full of life. My mother had a sister, my Aunt Jane. But she had passed away years before. Naomi was my closest living relative and going to live with her just seemed the natural thing to do." With increased emphasis, she continued, "She means more to me than anything else in the world. Mark, the wealth of the estate is not that important to me." As she spoke, anger began to rise in her voice. "But I would give anything for some measure of retribution for her sake. They have treated her like dirt almost her entire life."

"They . . . meaning . . ."

"The trust managers," she interrupted.

Mark paused to mull over her claims and anger. Finally, he said, "I'm definitely going to want to hear more about this. But for the moment, let's talk about another matter." He pulled a document from a folder lying on the table alongside a yellow legal pad and handed it to her.

"Rachel, this is an attorney/client agreement. Even though you may not have an immediate need for an attorney, I think this is in your best interest. If, at some point, this whole matter winds up in court, anything you have told me or anything I have learned in my capacity as your attorney would be considered privileged information between an attorney and his client. In short, I couldn't testify against you. The agreement also states that my work on your behalf is pro bono. There is also a cancelation clause at the end. All you have to do to end our relationship is sign the cancellation notice and send me a copy by registered mail."

"Sounds good to me," Rachel replied approvingly as she retrieved a pen from her purse to sign the paper. "Mark, Harold Sanders and your dad, and now you. I'm not sure I deserve all this, but I hope you know how grateful I am."

After she signed the document, Mark reached for the yellow pad and looked at her across the table, and said, "Why don't we start at the beginning?"

Rachel suddenly became almost convulsed with laughter. "I'm sorry Mark," she said as she reached across the small table and placed her hand on his forearm. "You don't know how many times I've heard that - - - and that tablet. I've got boxes of files and at least a dozen 3 ring binders filled to capacity. How about if I try to give you an overview of the whole story and then we can begin the process of filling in the details whenever you're ready?"

Mark shoved the tablet aside and with an agreeable smile said, "If we aren't going to be taking notes right away, why don't we move to the soft lounge chairs on the back sun deck."

With their chairs side by side about an arm's length apart they had a commanding view of the ocean.

"This is such a beautiful place. I love the blue sky and the ocean," Rachel said as she took her seat. "It's restful and almost mesmerizing."

"I agree," he said. "I've been coming here every chance I get for as long as I can remember,"

"Rachel," Mark queried, "From what little I know, it seems that the two major factors are the trust and who is going to get it. You could start with some explanation of the trust and its value or you could begin with explaining why you can't prove your relationship to Thomas Claiborne. Oh, and a little more about your contestant for the trust. I believe his name is Donald Claiborne."

Sensing a definite step forward, she replied, "Why don't we talk about the land in the trust and save the family tree discussion until we can meet at the mansion house on the plantation."

"Sounds like a plan," he responded as he opened the road map he had brought to the deck. "Uncle Harold gave me this map and made a rough outline of the plantation. Here is a fine line marker if you would like to make any changes. He said it totals about 15,000 acres."

"Actually, it's nearly 20,000 acres," she responded as she took the marker and began making a more detailed drawing. "It includes a large section about eight miles south of Georgetown that is separated from the mainland by the Intracoastal Waterway. The remainder of the property is higher ground that runs parallel to Highway 17 and has provided most of the income of the trust for years."

"Income?" Mark asked.

"Mostly from logging pines trees and produce farming. There are large parcels that are leased to vegetable growers as well as some roadside businesses on the highway that are operating from buildings leased from the trust.

The hot September sun was directly overhead and Mark, noting her evenly tanned complexion, still wondered if she was comfortable. "It will probably be another hour or two before we have any shade. Are you ok in the sun?"

"I love sitting in the sun. I don't burn easily but I probably should have remembered to bring some sunscreen."

"I'm sure we have some," Mark quickly replied and headed into the house. Two minutes later he returned to the deck carrying the sunscreen. "SPF 50," he said as he handed her the bottle.

"Perfect," she replied. She pulled the skirt of her dress halfway up her thighs to keep it away from the oily sunscreen. As she leaned over to apply the lotion to her legs the bra top on her sundress dropped just enough to reveal quite a lot more of her breasts than the dress designer probably had intended. Mark was afraid she would catch him looking if he suddenly looked away. When she straightened up, she applied lotion to her arms and chest and the small exposed portion of her breasts. When she finished she looked up and handed the bottle to Mark. With a beguiling smile, she asked, "Would you mind putting a little on my shoulders and my back?"

He didn't mind a bit!

Chapter Four

Mark and Rachel continued to discuss the land portion of the trust for some time. Finally, Mark said, "I can't say that I know much about land values or income from logging and leasing operations, but this whole area doesn't appear to meet Uncle Harold's assessment. I think he used the term, hundreds of millions."

"It's right here," Rachel replied pointing to the barrier island separated from the mainland by the Intracoastal Waterway. "Almost eighteen uninterrupted miles of pristine, white sand beach. It's the longest stretch of undeveloped privately owned beach on the entire East Coast."

Mark sat staring at the map and shaking his head in amazement. "Bingo, . . . this is the brass ring. It's what this whole thing is about!"

"The math is simple. Eighteen miles is over 80,000 feet. Divide that by the width of a building lot, say 75 to 80 feet, and you've got almost 1,200 lots. At two million a pop you've got over two billion dollars. That doesn't take into account all of the lots on the Intracoastal as well the interior lots on the mainland."

"Why haven't the trust managers already developed it?" Mark asked, still in awe.

Again, Rachel pointed to a spot on the map. "A bridge and the road to get there."

"Bridge?"

"To develop the island you would have to build a tall four lane bridge across the Intracoastal Waterway, not to mention the rest of the infrastructure. Current estimates of the bridge alone are over 300 million."

"What's so complicated about using the land as collateral, borrow the money and repay the loan from the proceeds of the lot sales?

"Not complicated at all," Rachel agreed. "Just one small problem. According to the terms of Thomas's will, none of the land can be sold during the life of the trust."

"And," Mark interjected, "No bank is going to loan money with nothing but leasehold interests to back it up."

"Now you've got the picture," Rachel exclaimed.

"I certainly do, I most certainly do."

. . . .

Mark looked up from the map and said, "This is a lot to digest. The Friday night beach crowd won't start showing up for a few more hours. How would you like to take a walk on the beach?"

"Really," Rachel replied. "I was hoping we could. When you said you were living on the Isle of Palms I decided to bring along some shorts and a shirt, just in case. I'll get them out of the car and change, . . . if that's ok?"

"You can use the guest room to change. It's the second door on the right as you come in. I'll do the same and meet you back on the deck."

Mark exchanged his slacks for shorts and waited on the deck while she changed and opened the door for her when he saw her coming through the house. She was wearing slightly flared red walking shorts and a white sleeveless blouse with pointed collars, a la Katherine Hepburn. With dark auburn, mid-length wavy hair, hazel eyes, and red lipstick that matched her shorts, her beauty was simply beyond Mark's ability to comprehend.

"What do you think?" she asked as she stepped onto the deck.

"Beautiful, just beautiful," Mark replied with the only words he could manage to get out of his mouth."

"Thank you. It's kind of retro. I'm glad you like it."

"It?"

"The outfit. I'm glad you like it."

"Oh . . . sure, the outfit. It's very nice."

As they started down the beach near the water's edge Mark asked her to tell him more about the development potential on the island.

"I would guess you're talking about five star hotels, championship golf courses, marinas that can handle ocean going yachts, upscale shops and restaurants, and exclusive gated communities. The development would likely spread beyond the trust property."

"Rachel," Mark said as he stopped and turned to face her. If your claim of being Thomas Claiborne's closest living relative can be proven, you will become one of the wealthiest people in the country. I know I'm jumping the gun a little bit, but what would you do with that kind of money?"

"Me, nothing. If the trust becomes mine, much of the land will go to the State of South Carolina. If the estate passes to Don Claiborne, he will develop every inch of the property and squeeze every dime out of it."

"Rachel, pardon the expression, I don't mean to sound like a smart ass but the last I checked, developing land and making a profit is perfectly legal."

"I know, but it's the wrong use for this land. It's a biological treasure. There are so many species of fish and birds and mammals and reptiles, not to mention the plant life. Much of the prime development property has never been disturbed by man. It's a repository of eco systems that can be traced back thousands of years, probably millions. Besides, Naomi wants to see it remain in its natural state forever. Thomas Claiborne was a good steward of the land and we believe it's what he would want."

When they turned and began retracing their steps back to the Bradley beach house, Mark summed up the situation. "If Claiborne inherits the trust he will turn the property into a modern commercial version of Atlantis and if it goes to you, you will give it all away."

"Not entirely, she replied. I would like to keep the mansion house and several hundred acres around it and I would keep all the land near Highway 17 that has been logged and farmed for years. The state of South Carolina would probably turn a portion of the beach and the surrounding area into a state park and designate the remainder as a wildlife preserve and marine research area."

"Sounds like you have been talking to the South Carolina Parks Department."

"I have. Harold Sanders arranged a meeting for me with the Director of the State Department of Parks and Recreation, John Righthouse. That was about five years ago. In fact," she recalled, "Your dad went to the meeting with me."

"With a chuckle, Mark replied, "I'm not surprised. John was one of my dad's classmates at the Citadel."

"I guess I'm confused. I thought you went to the Citadel."

"I did. And so did my father and my grandfather and . . . Rachel, The Bradley's have been going to the Citadel since before the War Between the States. Once you wear the ring you become part of a circle that has never been broken. Righthouse would try to help because of my father if for no other reason. But, let me guess. South Carolina wants the property."

"They want it so bad, they can taste it. It would instantly become the crown jewel of South Carolina and the integrity of the natural state of the land would be forever protected."

"One thing for sure," Mark exclaimed, If this ever goes to court, the State of South Carolina could be a powerful ally."

"Your dad assured me they would," she responded with a sheepish look on her face.

"Sounds like we're back to the same old problem, proving your relationship to Thomas. When can we talk about that?"

"I think that's next," she responded. "But I would like to combine that conversation with a visit to the mansion house on Claiborne Plantation."

"I'm all yours." Mark eagerly replied. "The sooner the better."

"Would 10 o'clock in the morning be too soon?"

"Not at all," Mark replied as they reached the steps to the walkway over the sand dunes. "Just give me directions."

When they reached the deck, Rachel pulled her chair around directly facing Mark's as he took his seat. She sat with her hands clasped and elbows resting on the arms of the chair as she spoke looking directly into his eyes. "I can't tell you what a wonderful experience this afternoon with you has been. If I sound forward . . . well, so be it. You have been like a breath of fresh air. Uncle Harold . . . excuse me, Harold Sanders said you would be a good listener and you have been so patient with me."

"Catching, isn't it," Mark noted with a smile.

"Catching?" she responded with a puzzled look.

"Calling Harold Sanders Uncle."

After a slight hesitation, she said with a laugh, "I guess I picked that up from you . . . I know there are a lot of questions you are anxious to have answered and I promise, . . . let me put it like this; Paul Harvey, the old radio newscaster was my dad's favorite and he especially got a kick out of Harvey's line, 'and now, the rest of the story.' Tomorrow won't tell all of the rest of the story, but most of it."

"Fair enough," Mark replied with a warm smile as he reached out and took her hand."

Mark opened the car door for Rachel as she was preparing to leave. She turned, standing directly in front of him and said, "Uncle Harold told me a lot about you but he failed to mention how nice looking you are." She placed her hand on his shoulder and gave him a quick kiss on the cheek.

"I'd like to know what I did to deserve that so I can make sure to do it again," he responded as his face began to turn slightly red while he placed his hand on the cheek that her lips had touched.

"My dad was a red headed Irishman from a little logging town in Alberta, Canada. He always told me that a quick kiss on the cheek is due reward for someone who has been especially, kind. It's an old Irish custom."

Mark watched her car head south on Palm Avenue while wondering, "How in the hell am I supposed to keep my mind on my client's business when I can't keep my mind off my client?"

During his four years at the Citadel, when Mark's parents were out of town he seldom missed an opportunity to turn the beach house into party central. Citadel cadets, College of Charleston girls and enough booze to float the Yorktown were the order of the day. Next to amassing enough demerits during his freshman year to set the modern record for penalty tours, girls had always been his greatest failing. Yet, there was something different about Rachel. She had a brilliant mind, a strong sense of purpose, a fetching personality and was drop dead gorgeous. "Moreover," Mark thought to himself, "she was alluring; the kind of person who makes you feel good just being near."

As she drove North on Highway 17, Rachel Devening was in a near state of bliss. She had never met a perfect man but, in her eyes, Mark Bradley came closer than any man she had ever met. When he had taken her hand on the deck a tingling sensation ran down her spine and through her legs. "Damn," she thought to herself, "I had forgotten what it was like to feel this way." She was only a few minutes away from the beach house but was already looking forward to their meeting at the mansion house the next morning. With a smile on her face, she wondered how he would react to the "rest of the story."

Chapter Five

Autumn in the Low Country of South Carolina brings near perfect weather with an abundance of sunshine, moderate temperatures and fall foliage and hibiscus in full bloom. Traffic on Highway 17 was light and Mark had set the cruise control slightly below the speed limit in an effort to arrive at Claiborne at precisely the appointed time, 10:00 AM.

About 8 miles south of Georgetown he turned right, heading east, on a small road posted with a small white sign with black English block letters that read, Claiborne Plantation. Although it was a private road, it remained asphalt for nearly three miles until it turned to hard packed sand just before turning south and arriving at a large security entry gate. The gate was open as Rachel had promised. About a hundred yards ahead and on the other side of the road he could make out a small one story house through a grove of pine trees and several outbuildings. He thought little of it and proceeded through the gate and drove slowly down the quarter mile lane to the mansion house. The lane was bordered on each side by hundred year old live oak trees that overlapped and formed a covered entry.

Mark's eyes grew larger with amazement the closer he got to the mansion which sat in a large clearing at the end of the lane. The Georgian style house was a full two stories tall with large dormers cut into the roof revealing the presence of a third floor, all set on a five foot high foundation of bricks laid with symmetrical arched openings. On the front of the house was a large two story portico with a front facing gabled roof supported by massive round columns.

The lane led directly into a large perfectly round drive in front of the mansion which surrounded a large pool with a white marble sculpture of the Greek Goddess, Athena. Mark circled around to his left arriving at the entrance stairs to the porch on the driver's side. At the top of the porch stood Rachel Devening. She was wearing a sleeveless white blouse and a short flared kaki skirt. "Not a mini skirt," Mark thought; but short enough to reveal the long tanned legs he had spent the previous afternoon admiring at the beach house."

"Good morning Mr. Bradley, welcome to Claiborne Plantation," Rachel exclaimed with an accentuated southern dialect as Mark emerged from his car.

"Spoken as a true Southern bell Miss Devening," Mark proclaimed with a grin as he approached the wide welcoming exterior staircase. "If they were casting Gone With the Wind, you'd be a lock for Scarlett."

Rachel met him half way down the steps with her hand extended. "Thanks for coming Mark. It's a beautiful morning. I hope you had a pleasant drive."

"I did," he replied with a smile as he took her hand. "But I have to admit, I just wasn't prepared for all of this. I'm not sure what I was expecting but this place, the live oak tree lined entrance and this grand old home. It looks like something you would see in a movie."

"Actually," she replied, the grounds and the exterior of the house were used in two films. One was a black and white movie from the 1930s and the other was in color in the early fifties."

For a moment Mark stood next to her admiring the front entrance grounds. Finally he turned and said. "I'm ready for the tour if you are."

She gently squeezed his hand as she turned to lead him to the front door. "The house was built during the 1780s and had been here nearly 70 years by the time Thomas Claiborne arrived from England in 1854 to take over the plantation."

The front entrance lead directly into a massive two story high room with a wide curved staircase leading up to a balcony on the second floor. "For years this room has been called the ballroom. It's large enough to hold a ball or any other large gathering of people."

On the left side of first floor was the dining room separated from the ballroom by wide sliding doors. The rear of the dining room was open to a room in the back of the house that was used as a pantry and for final preparation of food to be served in the dining room. "Until the kitchen was moved inside when electricity was brought into the house, the actual cooking was done in a separate building behind the mansion," Rachel commented as they slowly moved through the rooms. "Most cooking was done over an open fire drafted by a chimney. The process was simply too hot to be done in the main house and there was the ever present danger of fire."

In the center of the rear of the house was a large reasonably modern and well equipped kitchen. In addition, Rachel pointed out a second set of stairs that led to the second and third floor bedrooms. Following a hallway, they arrived back in the ballroom.

Rachel led Mark to a suite of rooms on the right side of the house separated from the ballroom with sliding doors that matched the doors to the dining room. The first room was designated the library. There were built in book shelves, several writing desks and a Queen Anne sofa and two matching chairs. All of the walls were paneled in English walnut and the union of the tall walls and ceiling were adorned with dark oak hand carved corbels. A large brick fireplace was the focal point of the room located in the center of the interior wall. "The Claibornes were all well-educated. Mark, mostly in the finest schools and universities in England, and their books were among their most important possessions."

"Are any of the books from the original collections?" Mark asked.

"Only a few. Most of them were moved to the Claiborne house in Georgetown and later to a special collections room at the public library where they could receive proper care. The summer heat and intense humidity takes a serious toll on books or any kind of paper."

Beyond the library, moving toward the rear of the house was Thomas Claiborne's office. "This is the only room in the house that has remained virtually unchanged. Naomi's parents who were her executors until she was 25 years old kept this room off limits to anyone other than the closest family members. Although she was only eleven years old when he died, she revered the old man and has kept the office exactly like it was the day he died."

Beyond the office was the master bedroom and bathroom. "This area used to be a large open air porch covered by the second floor bedrooms. From the porch Thomas could see boats landing at the dock on the lagoon before all the vegetation and trees matured and obscured the view. Around 1900 the stairs to the second floor master bedroom became difficult for the old man and the porch was enclosed and remodeled as his bedroom and bath."

The tour continued to the upper floor bedrooms with Rachel holding the back of her skirt close as she lead the way up the stairs. "This area has been redone several times as the number of people living here changed over the years." She opened the first door to the right beyond the balcony landing at the top of the stairs. "This was Thomas's bedroom until he moved to the first floor and it was my room from the time I was twelve until about two years ago when Naomi and I moved to the house in town," she said with a bit of nostalgia. The grandeur of the room was inescapable. The ceilings were at least nine feet high. The front two windows overlooked the front approach to the house and the reflecting pool. Through the two windows Mark could catch glimpses of the lagoon through the trees. "Rachel, you must have felt like a princess in this big house with this incredible bedroom."

"I don't want much for myself from the trust, but maybe you can begin to understand why I want this house and some surrounding land. It needs to be in the hands of someone who cares and appreciates the history it represents."

"Would you move back here if you inherit the trust?" Mark asked.

With a slight laugh Rachel responded, "No way. It's much too big for one person or even a family. I'm hoping either the State or a private foundation winds up with it and restores it to its original state."

"Why not at least apply to have it placed on the National Historic Register? Even if you lose the trust the new owners would play hell trying to tear it down or alter it significantly."

She instantly retorted with venom in her voice. "I've tried that but the trust managers, the bank, won't sign the application. They don't want anything to hinder them when they begin to unleash the grand development plan."

"That would be Donald Claiborne," Mark observed.

"Precisely, the ass hole of the Western World," she responded as she started for the stairs leading down to the main floor.

As they walked back into the kitchen, Rachel turned and looked at Mark. "I'm sorry for blowing off steam but the whole mess just . . . just . . ."

"Just pisses you off?" Mark interrupted.

She stood, stone faced for a moment, and then began to laugh. "That's right, it just pisses me off."

As her laughter subsided she reached into the refrigerator. "I remembered you like iced tea. I brought some with me and I thought we might have a glass in the back garden."

The garden was a finely manicured English design with curved holly hedges surrounding a small sitting area on a stone patio sheltered from the sun by a white pergola. They sat in ornamental garden chairs facing each other with a small table in between. For several minutes there were no words spoken as each struggled to find just the right words to describe what they both realized were rapidly growing feelings for each other.

To Rachel's relief, Mark finally began to speak. "I think you described our time together yesterday afternoon as a wonderful experience and I just wanted you to know I feel the same. I had a hard time sleeping last night thinking about seeing you again this morning and I finally gave in and got up about an hour early."

"Mark, that's so sweet. I . . ."

She was suddenly startled by a man's voice as he approached the garden from the front of the house.

"Rachel, I don't mean to intrude, but I was just making my rounds and I thought I heard someone in the garden. Besides, I thought you might need some help with the locks and bars."

"Think nothing of it Stan," Rachel responded as she caught her breath and rose from her chair. This is Mark Bradley, a friend from Charleston. Mark this is Stan Watson. He and his wife have been caretakers at Claiborne for many years and they live in a house not far from the front entrance."

"I'm glad to meet you Mr. Watson," Mark expressed as he shook Stan's hand and recalled the small house he had seen partially hidden by pine trees from the front entrance.

"I think I can handle the bars with Mr. Bradley's help but, perhaps you would like to join us for some iced tea Stan?"

"Thanks, Rachel but I've been out mowing and I've got to get cleaned up to take Claire grocery shopping. I'll bet that woman hasn't missed Saturday afternoon grocery shopping for the 45 years we've been married."

Mark was trying to sort out the meaning of locks and bars as Stan disappeared around the house. Rachel commented, "The Watsons have worked at Claiborne since they were first married. Stan is the one who keeps these grounds immaculate and Claire has always helped

Naomi clean and cook and take care of the house. Even to this day Claire stops in town to see grandmother almost every day and drives her wherever she needs to go."

"Locks and bars?" Mark asked with a puzzled look.

"It's not as mysterious and onerous as it sounds," Rachel replied with a chuckle. We'll get to them in just a few minutes."

"Everything in due time," Mark thought, wondering how long it would take to finally get up to speed on the entire matter.

Mark finished his iced tea and spoke as he looked across the garden. "The more I see and the more I learn, the more I understand why this all means so much to you." Turning back to look directly at Rachel he asked, "Now, are we ready to talk about your relationship to Thomas Claiborne.?"

"That's where we are," Rachel replied as she rose from her garden chair and picked up Mark's glass. "I'll refill our glasses and be right back."

Mark watched her go up the stairs on the back porch and felt tinges of that unexplainable feeling of butterflies in his stomach and unfulfilled desire.

From the kitchen window, Rachel could see Mark sitting under the pergola. "Having tea with a handsome man in an English garden on a beautiful Saturday morning is about as good as it gets," she thought as she refilled the glasses.

Chapter Six

Rachel set the glasses on the garden table and brushed her hand across his shoulder as she turned to take her seat.

"Thomas Claiborne," she stated, was simply the newest in a long line of Claiborne to take over the family business. The first Claibornes arrived on the South Carolina Coast in the early 1700s. They were drawn by the vast potential for rice production along the fresh water tidal creeks and rivers here in the low country. They were already well established in sugar plantations in Barbados and saw South Carolina as a perfect fit for their system of crop production with slave labor. It took them some years to cut the cypress trees and build dikes around the river islands to flood the fields for rice, but once they did the money from the sale of rice came pouring in."

"I remember from a history class that it took more labor to build the dikes around the plantation fields than it took to build the great pyramids of Egypt," Mark interjected.

"By the mid-1700s they were firmly established and had acquired additional land and seven or eight more plantations up the Waccamaw River and several more to the South on the Santee River. This was the home plantation and its central location on the lagoon made it possible to travel to all of the individual plantations by boat."

"The Claiborne men were always educated in the best schools in England and one after another came to Claiborne to take their turn at managing a growing financial empire. Thomas came here in 1854 at the age of 23. After two years of intense field education . . . , I guess today it would be called on the job training, his parents returned to England. Shortly before leaving England, Thomas was married to a young woman by the name of Katherine. I'm told it was an arranged marriage. She followed him to South Carolina a short while later and was about four months pregnant when she arrived."

As Rachel spoke, she used garden shears to cut and gather a bouquet of red Dahlias from the garden. "Mark, this is really where the story begins. Grandfather Thomas and Katherine are buried in the family cemetery. Come with me and we'll take these flowers."

They followed a narrow stone lined path through heavy vegetation and old trees for what seemed to Mark to be about a city block. As they walked, Rachel continued the story. "Sadly, the baby was stillborn and Thomas immediately set out to prepare a final resting place. He built a mausoleum near the back of the cemetery. Naomi told me she thought he was paranoid about not being buried underground because of the high water table."

The path ended in a clearing at the cemetery. They walked slowly past old grave markers to the door of the mausoleum. "They had two more children in quick succession and, ironically, as her first child had died in birth, Katherine died giving birth to their third child. Katherine and Thomas and their firstborn son, Charles, are entombed here.

The mausoleum was built from solid limestone blocks with a dark gray slate roof and a wide, door carved from heavy cypress logs. Carved into a limestone block above the door were classic old style letters that prominently displayed the name, Claiborne. Across the door were two wide iron bars resting in iron flanges mounted into the limestone door frame. Each of the bars was secured by a large Master padlock.

Rachel pointed to the door and said with a subtle grin on her face, "Locks and bars. The original lock gave out years ago and the door has been blocked by these bars for as long as I can remember."

"Stan wondered if you needed help with these bars," Mark stated with some trepidation. Are you planning on going in?"

"We are," Rachel replied as she removed the padlocks. "If you can lift the iron bars from their mounts and set them to the side on the ground we can open the door."

Mark did as instructed and Rachel strained to pull the door open by a large brass handle. Looking at Mark's hesitant expression, she said, "This isn't morbid curiosity, Mark. I've been in here a number of times. Since the first body was interred here, someone from the family has always inspected the tomb to make sure no leaks have developed in the roof and walls. Naomi told me Thomas used to come here to inspect and pay his respects at least once a month as long as he lived. It was due to be inspected and I thought today would be a good time. I'm not sure you can learn anything from looking at some caskets but I promised Harold I would show and tell you everything possible. After you," she politely directed, pointing to the open door.

As they stepped into the dark chamber, Mark judged the mausoleum to be about nine or ten feet wide, perhaps nine feet high, and twelve feet from front to back. Just inside the door were three limestone casket shelves on each side. Caskets had been placed opposite each other on the two top shelves. On the right side rested a casket on the middle shelf and the other three shelves were empty. The interior of the tomb was surreal and made Mark feel as though he had stepped into an ancient and grisly dark world. On the back wall was a small altar with a marble statue of Christ on the Cross mounted on the wall. At the altar was a kneeler just wide enough for two people.

On the side of the altar was a vase filled with dried stems and flowers. Rachel emptied the vase and filled it with some of the red Dahlias she had brought from the garden. When she finished arranging the flowers she retrieved a small penlight from a pocket in her skirt and began passing the light over the ceiling and walls looking for leaks. "I think Thomas tried to build this place for eternity," she approvingly remarked as she concluded her inspection.

Mark noted the century and decades old undisturbed layers of dust on the caskets and limestone shelves. On each wall, several inches below the ceiling, were narrow strips of stained leaded glass that transformed the sunlight into thin beams of multicolored light that eerily pierced the darkness. When Rachel's light struck the sides of the caskets it revealed a patina layer with a greenish hue. "These caskets look like copper," Mark said.

"They are," she replied. The caskets were made from cypress wood, just like the framing and wood siding on the house. It's nearly impervious to water and high humidity. The wooden coffins were then lined with copper sheeting and all of the seams were sealed with lead. I'm told there is a layer of lead between the edges of the caskets and the tops that form an air tight seal when the top is closed."

She pointed her light to the top casket on the right wall and said, "This is Thomas Claiborne. He was the last to be placed in the tomb in 1924. Switching her light to the opposite wall, she continued, "And this is Katherine whose body was placed here in 1856. The coffin here on the second shelf is their first son, Charles, and he was the first to be placed here."

Mark squinted as he stepped back into the sunlight and was only too happy to place the bars back in position to be secured by Rachel with the padlocks. "Thomas was about my age when his wife died leaving a newborn child and another about a year old," Mark observed. "How could he have cared for the children by himself as well as managed an agricultural empire?"

"There were always slave women with milk who came into the house throughout the day and night to breastfeed the children," Rachel replied. "Thomas also brought a young slave girl into the mansion house as a full time nurse and nanny."

Holding about half of the fresh cut flowers, Rachel said, "We have one more stop to make." She took his hand as they left the cemetery and held it tightly as they returned to the house. As they proceeded, Mark confessed, "I have a hard time keeping track of the generations. Was Thomas your great, great, great grandfather or . . ."

She replied with an understanding smile, "The boxes of files and binders I told you about yesterday contain a complete and detailed family tree beginning with Thomas. I was sure you would want to look through them, so I've gathered them all up at Naomi's house to send with you. As far as trying to describe someone with the correct number of 'greats' in their title; if it is someone in direct lineage beyond my parents, I simply refer to them as grandfather or grandmother.

They passed through the garden and down an old wagon path for nearly a quarter of a mile. Along the way, she pointed out ruins and remnants of old buildings. "In Thomas's time, Claiborne was like a small town. There were barns and stables, a blacksmith shop, a cooperage for making barrels and a cooking and canning building where slave women put up preserves of vegetables and fruit for the winter months." There were long rows of crumbling rock foundations that had once supported small buildings. "Slave quarters," she said in a quieter and sad voice. "Before the Civil War, all of Claiborne's plantations combined had nearly a thousand slaves. There were normally 60 to 80 slaves here on the home plantation." After a pause, Rachel spoke in a manner that sounded as though her comment was something that needed to be said. "Thomas was a good man. To be sure, he was a slave owner and there can never be an excuse for that. At the same time; however, he never mistreated them like some of the other plantation owners. He saw to it that they were properly clothed and well fed.

When a steer was slaughtered for the family to eat beef, the slaves ate beef. Sunday was always a day of rest and one of these old foundations was for a church. Even though it was against the law in South Carolina to teach slaves how to read and write, he saw to it that they were taught well, including arithmetic."

Claiborne Plantation 1855

Thomas Claiborne arrived at his father's plantation near Georgetown, South Carolina 1n 1854.

His parents would remain for two years before returning to England. In the interim, Thomas would gradually take control of the Claiborne enterprises which included seven rice plantations located in the tidal areas of the Waccamaw and Santee Rivers while being tutored in rice growing and slave management by his father.

The Claiborne plantations held nearly a thousand slaves. Most were second generation Claiborne chattel, since the importation of slaves into the United States had become illegal in 1808. Thomas was only 2 years old when slavery was abolished in England in 1833. Even so, he had been exposed to the continued inhumane and ruthless treatment of free blacks doled out by overseers who regarded regular punishment and physical abuse as the only reliable method of motivating the black Africans whom many considered to be dim witted.

As expected, Thomas quickly became an expert in all the phases of rice production, including planting, harvesting, milling as well as shipping and trading. Slavery was the one issue with which he would never feel comfortable. Industrialization in England lessened the demand for slave produced products as new and more efficient methods began to gain favor. The management of slaves was often a subject of conversation between father and Son. Thomas's argument was always the same.

Seated on the rear porch of the mansion house overlooking the docks on the lagoon while enjoying cigars after a Sunday dinner, Thomas raised the issue once again. "Father, if we are going to increase production and overall profits, we have to improve efficiency. And since there are no new machines or farming methods at our disposal, we have to improve the efficiency of our slave based labor."

"Granted," replied his father. "But I know of no way to drive them any harder."

"Precisely; we need to stop driving them and improve their lives so they can realize at least some of the fruits of their labor; better food, no whippings, and fair treatment. We have to improve our mutual ability to communicate. Most of them speak a Creole combination of English and their native tongues and idioms gathered over the years from only God knows where. I've been here over a year and I still have great difficulty understanding most of them and making myself understood."

"That's the overseers' job. They understand slave talk. Besides, what alternatives are there?"

"We set up small schools on the plantations during the winter months. We teach them better spoken English and, while we're at it, how to read and write and do simple arithmetic."

"What you propose is against the law. Educated slaves are more likely to rebel and turn on us. I fear, instead of a more content labor force, you will wind up with no labor force at all."

With his frustration at a peak, Thomas declared, "For as long as I can remember you have been preparing me for this job. Now, either you will let me do it or Katherine and I will be on the next ship to England."

The old man who was in failing health and longed to return to the life of Nobility in Britain knew he was outmatched, and relented. "Slavery is ending around the world. One day it will end in South Carolina. If your methods are the only way to improve our situation; so be it." Thomas could hear the sound of defeat in his father's voice. "Son, you will have my full support," he said as he extinguished his cigar and turned to go back into the house.

As the growing season was nearing an end, Thomas traveled by small river steamer to the outlying plantations to inspect their readiness for harvest. Accompanied by the steamer Captain, he made his way along a brush lined lane from a plantation dock to the central area where tools and equipment, and working livestock were kept. Suddenly, from a distance, they heard a man screaming and ran in the direction of the sound. As the lane emerged into the large clearing, they could see a tragic and all too familiar scene. With a forced gathering of slaves assembled to watch, the overseer was whipping a male slave with a leather cat-o'nine tails. He was stripped to the waist and tied to a whipping post. Thomas stopped to catch his breath and yelled to the overseer, "Mr. Anderson, put that whip down and untie him."

Anderson turned to see Thomas Claiborne. "Mr. Claiborne," he exhorted, "this boy's a slacker. Complainin about not feeling well, just to get outta work. Your father's gonna be none too happy when the harvest isn't in on time. But we got a cure for that."

"Mr. Anderson, I'm going to be none too happy if you don't untie that man."

In a condescending manner, Anderson replied, "Your dad has always left these matters in my hands. When I'm finished here we can go out and inspect the rice fields." With that, the overseer raised the whip to return to his business.

Thomas grabbed a hoe that was leaning against a shed and swung the heavy oak handle sideways striking Anderson across the back of his thighs. The overseer yelped and instantly dropped to his knees. Thomas put his foot on his back and pushed him face forward to the ground. "Untie that man," Thomas ordered, "and put this one in his place." When the surrounding slaves had done as directed, Thomas picked up the whip and said, "I've never used one of these. Let's see how it works." Thomas ripped Anderson's shirt from his back and brought the nine tails down on his back as hard as he could swing. The screaming continued as Thomas lay on five lashes. Anderson dropped back to the ground when Thomas cut the ties with his knife. "If you are ever caught on Claiborne property, Mr. Anderson, you will be shot on site."

Thomas Claiborne was a force to be reckoned with and the word spread quickly.

. . . .

As they continued walking Mark seemed to be deep in thought. "I can almost hear the wheels turning in your brain," Rachel said.

"Unless Thomas remarried and. . ."

"He never did," Rachel quickly interjected.

"Then it would seem that you and Donald Claiborne descended from one or both of Thomas's children; they were . . ."

"Elizabeth and Robert," she replied in anticipation.

"A person's first reaction would simply be to trace the family tree down through the generations to see which of the two of you is the closest blood descendent of Thomas. But of course" he conceded, "if it were that easy, this whole problem wouldn't exist and I wouldn't be here."

Holding his arm with both hands, she replied. "I wish the whole problem didn't exist but I'm sure glad you're here."

"I am too," he responded as he placed his hand on hers and they continued on into a thick stand of old loblolly pine trees.

"Another cemetery," he remarked as they ventured into a large open area surrounded by pines.

"This is the old slave cemetery, Mark." She walked past several rows of flat limestone markers and bent at her knees to place the flowers at the head of a stone.

"I thought it was really sweet of you to take flowers to your grandparent's tomb, but who are these for?"

As Rachel brushed the fallen pine needles from the marker, letters appeared that suddenly revealed the name, Rachel. She looked up at Mark and with a soft and loving voice, she said, "They're for my grandmother. I was named for her. Thomas was my Grandparent four times removed, but not Katherine. The young slave girl I mentioned who Thomas brought into the house to care for the children . . . ; she was my grandmother."

Mark seemed frozen in astonishment. He tried to hold back the words that escaped from his mouth. "But you're whi. . ."

"White," she replied. "Am I?"

Chapter Seven

Mark reached down and placed his hand under Rachel's forearm to assist her as she stood up. Mark pointed out, "There's no last name on the grave marker."

"She didn't have one. Most of them didn't," Rachel replied in a sad and thoughtful manner.

He stood quietly looking at the grave marker for several minutes while *the rest of the story* began to unfold in his mind. "She didn't have a last name, or a birth certificate," he surmised. "She and Thomas were not married, and their child . . ."

"Her name was Mary," Rachel interjected.

"And their child; Mary, like her mother, had no last name or birth certificate.

"Mary took the Claiborne name," Rachel replied, "but of course, it wasn't unusual for a slave, or in this case the child of a slave, to take the landowner's last name."

"In short," he continued, "Donald Claiborne is a direct seventh generation descendant of Thomas and Katherine and he has all the documentation necessary to prove it." With a firm expression, he looked directly at Rachel. "You're a direct sixth generation descendant of Thomas and Rachel and missing just one piece of paper to prove it; a signed birth certificate showing Rachel and Thomas as Mary's parents. Uncle Harold said when he tried to help you; he kept running into the same stone wall. I guess this is what he was talking about."

As they started back, Mark took her hand and held it until they were back at the house. He exclaimed with a cautious note of confidence, "At least now I know what we have to work with." After a quick glance at his watch he said, "How would you like to drive into town for some lunch? My treat."

"Lunch sounds great, but if you will settle for a cob salad with sliced grilled chicken, it's in the frig. I fixed it this morning and brought it with me."

"Sounds good to me," Mark replied.

In the kitchen, Rachel removed two plates covered in foil from the refrigerator and placed them on opposite sides of the large formal dining room table at the end near the front window. Next to the plates she placed napkins, silverware, and water glasses along with a pitcher of ice water. "Just one more thing," she said. She made one last trip to the kitchen and returned with a chilled bottle of white Moscato wine and two glasses. She handed Mark the bottle along with an opener. "If you will do the honors, lunch is served."

After his first bite, Mark said, "The lady can cook."

Rachel remarked with a smile, "Thank you."

"In fact," he stated, "the chicken salad is terrific, second only to the company."

With a slight flush on her cheeks, she replied with a smile, "Ditto."

"If it's all right with you," he asked, "would you mind if we picked up where we left off at the cemetery?"

"Not at all," she quickly replied.

"Thomas was about my age and suddenly found himself with three children in the house, the first two from Katherine and the newborn, Mary, the daughter of a White plantation owner and a black slave girl."

"She was a mulatto," Rachel stated. "They were also known as Creoles." Rachel continued in a terse but subdued tone, "Slave women were chattel and their white masters were legally free to do with them as they pleased, including sex."

"What happened to the three children?"

"They all continued to live at Claiborne through the rest of the 1850s with Rachel responsible for the children's daily care and Thomas running Claiborne and the other plantations. At a later time, Robert would have been sent back to England for schooling at a University but with the threat of Civil war, Thomas decided to send both he and Elizabeth back early to his parents and they left just before the bombardment of Fort Sumter."

"And Mary?"

"Mary and her mother remained at Claiborne until the war began to turn against the South. Grandma Richards told me that Thomas became concerned for Rachel's and Mary's safety because they were mulattoes and managed to send them to France. Interestingly, mulattoes were often well accepted among white society in Charleston and Georgetown. Some of them had been given their freedom and others were often allowed to come and go the same as free whites. For the most part, whites, blacks, and mulattoes coexisted in a reasonably well ordered society with each group subject to different constraints and rules of conduct."

"I'm familiar with that," Mark offered, "but the war changed everything."

"I guess the white upper class realized that if the South were to lose the war that slavery would be abolished. Perhaps they were afraid of uprisings or reprisals from the suddenly free black majority. At any rate, they drew a line in the sand and said white people will stand together on one side of the line and black people, including anyone with any amount of black blood, will be on the other side. Mulattoes were immediately shunned from white society and they often were not well accepted among the blacks."

"Why France?" Mark asked.

"Thomas had incredible wealth from the rice plantations and he banked most of his money in France. France had abolished slavery in 1795 and he felt that Rachel and Mary would be better accepted in France than in England so he took them out of Charleston Harbor on a blockade runner."

Mark finished his last sip of wine and as he placed the empty glass on the table said, "I know you've told this story more than once. I hope you don't mind going through it all again for my sake."

"Mark, you're so easy to talk to," she replied, "and you don't jump to conclusions. I'd be surprised if you're not suffering from information overload."

Mark laughed and replied, "We have covered a lot of ground but I know there's a lot more to go and I'm anxious to continue." With a short pause and a curious look he asked, "What's next on the agenda?"

"I think it's time you met Grandma Richards. She's looking forward to meeting you."

"Just say when and I'll be there."

"I was hoping after church tomorrow at her house in Georgetown. She asked me to invite you to Sunday dinner. We get out of church at eleven and we'll eat at noon if that works for you."

"Perfect," he replied.

They walked together through the ballroom and out the front entrance onto the portico. "Speaking of Naomi," Rachel remembered, "I've got to take her to her hair appointment in town and I'll have to be going soon."

Mark turned to her. "I told you this morning in the garden how I felt about being with you yesterday on the beach." Taking her hand and stepping closer he said, "It just keeps getting better."

Rachel put her hand on his shoulder and leaned in to kiss him on the cheek. As she did, her hair lightly brushed across his face sending a minor shockwave through his body. He gently turned her head to his and as they drew closer their lips slightly parted. The kiss was everything he knew it would be. It was the reason he couldn't sleep. It was all he could think about standing on the deck of the beach house in the early hours of the morning looking out at the sea. After just a slight break for air, they began kissing again with their arms wrapped around each other. Mark lowered his hand below her waist and pulled her close. She stepped back against a porch column pulling him with her.

After a few moments, Rachel leaned her head back and said after drawing in a long breath, "If I'd known this was going to happen we could have skipped lunch."

"Why don't you call Mrs. Watson and ask her to take your grandmother to her hair appointment," Mark slowly responded while brushing his lips over her ear.

"Groceries," she retorted.

Suddenly, snapped back into futile reality, Mark sighed, "She hasn't missed Saturday afternoon grocery shopping in 45 years." Searching to shift to a more positive note, he said, "Well, at least we have come to the end of the surprises." Getting no response, he stated firmly, "The surprises are over . . . right?"

Slightly breaking eye contact with him, she responded with a sly twist in her tone, "Maybe just another one or two."

Mark looked up and simply rolled his eyes. "Alright, one more surprise ought to be worth one more kiss; then I'll be on my way."

They gently broke their embrace and Mark spoke softly, "What's the surprise?"

"It'll keep," she said.

Mark started down the portico stairs, and as he reached the drive, he turned and asked, "What should I wear?"

"We will be dressed in our church clothes and Sunday is kind of a formal day for Naomi. A suit would be nice."

"A suit it is."

As he reached his car door he looked back at Rachel leaning against a portico column. "Mr. Bradley," she called out in her resurrected Southern dialect, "It was such a pleasure having you at Claiborne Plantation. Please do come again."

"Once again, spoken like a true Southern bell, Miss Devening. The pleasure was all mine."

As she watched his car heading down the lane toward the front gate she breathed deeply and thought, "This is happening so fast. I've got to slow it down." She wondered if she could. She wondered if she wanted to. After quickly recovering from the shock of discovering that her great, great, great, great grandmother was a black slave girl, he had continued to pursue the problem at hand apparently without any personal reservations. She hadn't expected him to be put off by it. But, "even in this day and age," she realized, "there were those who would be."

When he reached the gate, Mark noticed a car coming out of the driveway from the Watson's house across the road. "The Watsons going grocery shopping," he noted with a touch of chagrin. A sudden flashback entered and left his mind before he could identify its meaning. He wondered how anything could stick in his brain that was filled to the brim with Rachel Devening.

With his car on cruise control heading South on Highway 17 he thought about Rachel's heritage.

In two days he had stuck his foot in his mouth twice. Once, while lamely trying to explain why Harold Sanders couldn't be his real uncle and then at the cemetery when Rachel had revealed that her ancestral grandmother was black. "Thank God," he thought to himself he hadn't complimented her for her great tan.

Chapter Eight

Following another restless night, Mark was back on the deck of the beach house with a cup of black coffee searching the sky for the first rays of the sun to appear in the east sending shimmering gold streaks across the unusually placid Atlantic Ocean.   For the third time in as many days he would be meeting with Rachel Devening to learn everything he could that might lead to a solution to her problem; any form of legal declaration that would establish Thomas as Mary's father and connect all the dots that would lead directly to Rachel.

"Surely," he thought, "someone has already realized that a DNA sample taken from Thomas's remains should clear up the matter once and for all." As anxious as he was to find a quick and easy answer, he was determined to follow the time honored advice of coaches who admonished his players to stick to the fundamentals and let the game come to them. His father and Uncle Harold had been down this same road and he wondered how anyone might think he could possibly see something they hadn't. And, of course, the entire matter was complicated by the fact that it was becoming difficult to put his growing feelings for his client aside long enough to maintain an objective point of view. "How in the hell do I separate the way I feel about her and the job at hand?" he asked himself. The answer was immediately forthcoming; "You don't stupid, deal with it."

He laid down on a chaise lounge on the deck and found some of the sleep he had missed. A patio umbrella blocked the emerging sun and he slept until he was awakened by the constant ringing of the doorbell. He tried to shake the sleep as he walked through the house to find his mother waiting at the front door. "Mom," he said as he opened the door in his robe. "I slept late. Come on in and I'll fix some coffee."

"Your father had to usher at the early service so I thought I'd drop by to see how things are going."

"If you mean the Devening case, it's kind of like studying for a final. I've crammed my brain full of information about the Claibornes and I'm going back again today."

"On Sunday?"

"I'm going to have Sunday dinner with Rachel and her great grandmother."

"Just two days on the job and you have already been invited to dinner. Sounds to me like things are going just fine."

Mark handed his mother a cup of coffee with cream and joined her at the kitchen table.

After small talk about his dinner invitation and a second round of coffee, Vivian spoke about Rachel. "I don't think I've ever met a nicer young woman and she is simply beautiful."

"Really," Mark replied, while trying to suppress a grin, "I've been so absorbed in her case, I hadn't really noticed."

"Right," she laughed. "Just like you didn't notice your eyeballs fall out of their sockets when she walked into this house on Friday."

"Was I that obvious?"

"Well, let's say you managed to not make a fool out of yourself. And, besides, women enjoy admiring glances." As an afterthought, she asked, "What are you going to wear?"

"Rachel said they would be wearing dresses to church and she suggested a suit. I guess some tan slacks and my light blue sport coat will be ok."

"Mark, labor day is past," she said as she headed for the master bedroom to look through his closet. "Here," she proudly exclaimed as she removed a suit bag from the rod. "The suit we bought you at Berlins men's store last month when you finished law school. It's perfect. Lightweight charcoal gray wool with just a hint of dark blue." She found a navy blue and cream diagonally striped tie. "Here," she said handing him the tie. "A white dress shirt and black dress shoes and you'll be set."

"What does Labor Day have to do with it?"

"Men," she retorted. "You and your father may not know much about dress and etiquette but you can bet the ladies do."

. . . . .

Front Street in Georgetown was deserted as Rachel stepped onto the sidewalk and began a morning run that would take her up and down the streets in the historic section of the quiet village that 150 years earlier had been the largest rice shipping port in the world. She couldn't help thinking of Thomas Claiborne and the role he had played in the development of Georgetown and the economic structure of the Low Country following the devastation caused by the Civil War. She was certain he would approve of her plans for the Claiborne land but equally afraid that the lack of a birth certificate for Thomas's daughter, Mary, would turn her hopes into a bad dream.

The morning sun was reflecting in the harbor and in the east facing windows of the antebellum mansions along the way. She checked her watch as she ran making sure she hit her checkpoints on time. For the remainder of her run she was lost in a single thought . . . Mark Bradley. She knew they meant well, but hoped his father and Harold hadn't set him up for a fall. "Mark's Uncle Harold," she thought, as a broad smile spread over her face.

Thirty minutes before the 10 o'clock service, Rachel checked her dress in front of the full length mirror in her bedroom. It was a dark reddish brown fitted dress with a full skirt just above her knees and a scooped V neck top that displayed a considerable portion of the top of her breasts. She stepped out of her small apartment on the side of the house onto the wrap around porch and proceeded to the front door. She gave three quick knocks and let herself in. "Grandmother," she called.

"I'm in the kitchen with Claire," the old woman called back.

"What are the two of you cooking up?" she asked as she walked into the kitchen and plucked several pretzels from a bowl on the counter.

"Beef Bordelaise," Claire responded as she was deveining shrimp at the sink for the appetizer. "Naomi told me Joe Bradley's son is coming to dinner so I thought I'd fix something special. You know, they say the way to a man's heart is through his stomach."

"I've always thought that was overrated," Naomi muttered as she lifted a bottle of Bordeaux from the wine rack and turned to set it on the counter. As she turned she was looking directly at Rachel. "Claire, will you look at this."

"Oh my, Rachel your dress is beautiful," Claire responded.

"Now that's the way to a man's heart," Naomi exclaimed.

Rachel protested, "I'm not looking for a way to his heart. Mark Bradley is my attorney and he is trying to help us. Besides, there is nothing wrong with making a good impression."

"You'll certainly make a good impression in that dress," Naomi responded.

"Grandmother, the top is cut pretty low. Are you sure it's all right for church?"

"Naomi studied the dress for a moment, and then replied, "I think I've got just the thing." She went down the hall toward her bedroom and came back with a cream colored lady's hankie trimmed with a wide border of lace. She folded it twice and inserted the end in the V of Rachel's cleavage and folded the lace border over the top of the dress. Standing back to admire her handy work, she exclaimed, "Perfect! You could bow to the Pope and not worry."

As the ladies were leaving for church, 60 miles away Vivian Bradley was preparing to leave to meet her husband for the late service at the Episcopal Church in downtown Charleston. "I wish I could stay long enough to see you all dressed for dinner. I know how handsome you'll look. After a pause, she said, "Don't you have some kind of hair dressing that will keep your hair in place when it's combed?"

"I just put a little water on the comb but it doesn't stay in place very long," her son replied.

"Let me share a little secret. Wet your hair with hair spray and comb it just the way you want it to look. When it dries, run a comb through it once more. It'll look totally natural and stay in place all day."

Mark stood, slightly bewildered, looking at his mother and wondered to himself, "Hair spray and Labor Day. What next."

As she opened the front door she turned back to her son, "Don't forget, we're having the annual cookout tonight. You should have plenty of time to stop and change on your way back from Georgetown."

Chapter Nine

When Naomi and Rachel returned to the house Claire told them that all the food had been prepared except the filets and the bordelaise sauce. "I'll start them about a quarter till twelve," she said. "That should have them ready by the time you finish the shrimp cocktails and salad."

"What would I have ever done all these years without you, Claire? You know you are welcome to join us."

"I appreciate that Naomi, but the grandkids are coming over this afternoon and I've got another meal to fix."

"Claire, is there anything I can help you with?" Rachel asked.

"No dear, I wouldn't want you to get anything on that pretty dress."

"Speaking of which," Naomi remarked, "I think we can dispense with this."

With that, she reached to Rachel and snatched the lace hankie from the bodice of Rachel's dress.

"Grandmother," Rachel spurted. "Why did you do that?"

"It was just the right touch for church, but now we have a different occasion."

While trying to suppress a laugh, Rachel replied, "Grandmother, you're bad, just plain bad . . . But I like the way you think."

. . . .

Mark parked on the street in front of the classic two story American Colonial home on a corner lot on Front Street just before noon. As he began to open his door, it instantly shut at the hands of a uniformed traffic cop. "Read the sign mister," he growled as he pointed to the street sign that read No Parking on Sunday between 10: AM and 2: PM. "Church traffic makes this block too congested for parking,"

"I'm sorry officer, I didn't see the sign."

"Just move it," he snarled as he walked away.

'Must be having a bad day," Mark thought as he turned the corner and pulled up to the curb on the side street. He positioned himself at the front door, rang the doorbell, and promised himself he wouldn't let his eyeballs fall out of their sockets. Rachel opened the door and there went the eyeballs. "What the hell," he thought. "If there's a law against staring, arrest me."

Rachel blushed as she watched him try to unlock his focus from her dress and said, "Mark, you're right on time. Please come in." As he stepped through the doorway, Rachel whispered, "Nice suit."

He followed Rachel into the parlor where Naomi was sitting in a maple colonial split back chair with Claire standing next to her.

Mark, I'd like you to meet my great grandmother, Mrs. Naomi Richards and Mrs. Claire Watson. You met Claire's husband, Stan, at the mansion house yesterday."

"Mrs. Richards, you don't know how much I've been looking forward to meeting you. And Mrs. Watson, I'm certainly pleased to meet you as well."

"It's my pleasure, Mr. Bradley," Claire responded. "I'm sure you all have things to talk about and I've got to get back to the kitchen to finish dinner."

Naomi spoke in a clear and warm tone. "Rachel, why don't you and Mr. Bradley take seats and join me while we wait for Claire to call us to dinner."

Rachel and Mark sat next to each other on a settee across from Naomi. He was prepared for the fact that she would be of mixed race; in this case, third generation Creole. At 92 she was still an attractive woman; slender, with few wrinkles, and snow white wavy hair set off against her brown skin. After a moment to relax, Naomi said, "Even after all these years Sonny still calls me every week; every Saturday morning at ten o'clock. We spoke for quite a while yesterday and he had nothing but good things to say about you."

"Sonny?" Mark questioned.

"I'm sorry; I guess I'm the only one who calls him Sonny instead of Harold. Jane met Sonny when they were freshmen in college and the first time she brought him home for a weekend the two of them were sitting on the same sofa as you and Rachel, and I remember pointing my finger and reminding him that Jane was my granddaughter and he had better be on his best behavior. I was smiling when I said it but he knew I meant it. It embarrassed Jane half to death."

"Mrs. Richards, I first talked with Uncle Harold, excuse me, Justice Sanders, about your situation earlier this week. I asked him how he had come to know you and Rachel, but he was due in court and didn't have time to explain. I'm afraid I'm a little in the dark."

"Mark, Jane and Margaret were born at Claiborne and spent much of their lives there. Their parents both died young, like Rachel's, and I finished raising them. After she met Sonny, she never dated another man and married him the day after graduation and just before he started law school."

"I beg your pardon, Margaret?"

"Margaret was Rachel's mother. She and Jane were sisters."

Mark seemed momentarily stunned. He turned to Rachel and said slowly, "If Jane was your Aunt then Harold Sanders is your . . ."

"Uncle," Rachel completed his thought.

Naomi rose from her chair. "Please excuse me for a moment; I'm going to check on Claire."

After she left the room, Mark again turned to Rachel. "Don't I feel like a complete idiot? Here, all this time I've been calling him Uncle Harold and he's not. But he is your Uncle."

"Mark, at first I thought you knew and, well, we had so many things to discuss, I guess I just let it go. Besides, he was my uncle by marriage, not blood. And for that matter, uncle is often a term of endearment, like all the children who grew up captivated by the stories of their own Uncle Remus. I hope you're not upset with me."

Her hand placed gently on his knee as she spoke quelled any feelings of frustration from, once again, being the last to know, and his demeanor softened as the realization that he couldn't be upset with her began to sink in.

"I believe the proper term is, dinner is served," announced Naomi as she stepped back into the parlor."

At the dining room table, two places were set for Rachel and Mark on one side of the table and one place for Naomi on the other; with banded china plates, silver flatware, crystal glasse,s and finger bowls half filled with water and a slice of lemon.

"Claire has prepared some of our favorite dishes, Mark. I hope you enjoy them."

"I can hardly wait, Mrs. Richards. The aromas coming out of the kitchen are mouthwatering."

Claire brought in three plates with cooked shrimp in a red sauce.

"This is the Claiborne version of shrimp creole," Naomi explained. "Instead of hot sauce we use freshly ground horseradish to spice it up." As an afterthought, she cautioned, "You might want to start with a small bite. It's as hot as a poker."

His first bite wasn't small enough and he followed it with a large gulp of water and tried to catch his breath while replying, "It's delicious Mrs. . . . Richards, but . . . you're right, it's . . . hot."

The shrimp creole was followed by a parsnip remoulade salad and the main dish was Beef Bordelaise with asparagus sautéed in garlic and butter. When the beef arrived Naomi asked Mark if he would pour the wine that was sitting in the middle of the table. "It's French Bordeaux," Naomi offered. "Perfect with beef."

"I'd be delighted." Getting into the spirit of the elegant occasion, Mark stood, retrieved the open bottle, and proceeded to serve the ladies in a standing position from their left sides."

"Mark, please give your father my regards. He is such a gentleman and so congenial. He tried so hard but was simply never able to overcome the lack of a birth certificate for grandmother Mary."

"I'll pass it along this evening. My folks are having their annual society cookout; attendance required." After a pause Mark commented, "Rachel was just beginning to get into your family history. We reached the point where Thomas sent his first two children, Elizabeth and Robert, to England and near the end of the war took Rachel and their daughter, Mary, to France. I'd love to hear more."

"And I'd love to tell you. But first, let's finish dinner and dessert and then we'll move onto the garden porch."

Following a French dessert of Tarte Tatin, they moved to soft chairs on a screened porch on the back of the house overlooking a small garden and Georgetown Harbor. Once again, Mark and Rachel found themselves drawn to a day sofa, sitting together, and giving little thought to the fact that their hands had come together. After a few moments Mrs. Watson came onto the porch and spoke to Naomi, "I'll finish up the dishes before I go."

"Claire, I forgot you told me you had to get home to get ready for your grandkids. What are you still doing here?"

"Oh . . . My son called me a little earlier and said they had to cancel. I hope everyone enjoyed dinner."

Mark stood up and said, "Mrs. Watson, it was probably the finest meal I've ever had."

She smiled and replied, "That's very kind of you, Mr. Bradley." As she left the porch she unexplainably left the door open.

"As soon as the war began, Mark," Naomi began, "mulattoes and creoles were turned away from white society where some of them had come to enjoy a better style of life than the house and field slaves. Thomas was concerned about Rachel and Mary's safety, especially when it began to appear that the South was losing, so he took the two of them to France."

"I believe Rachel told me that he got them out of Charleston on a blockade runner."

"It was in the middle of the night," Naomi replied. "He took them to live with a business associate who lived on the French coast. At first, they lived in the guest house but, less than a year later, Thomas returned and bought a house for them in the same town. For about the next 15 year,s he sailed to England in the early summer to spend time with Elizabeth and Robert, and then on to France to live with Rachel and Mary until autumn when he would have to return to South Carolina to tend to business. They lived near a monastery and mother and daughter were both taught together by the nuns. They learned French at the monastery and Thomas saw to it that they had schooling in English. To this day, we are still a two language family." After a reflective pause, she completed her thoughts, "Not much family these days. Rachel and I are the only ones left."

"Rachel told me she had some file boxes and binders filled with a lot of information about your family history. I'm anxious to begin looking through it."

"It's all in the closet by the front door, "Rachel responded. I'll help you load it in your car when you leave."

"I'm not sure what you're looking for Mark, but hopefully you may find something in all those files that might help. I often have a hard time sleeping at night and on and off over the past several years I've spent time late at night sorting out those papers. You will be the first person besides me who has seen them all."

"Mrs. Richards, I'm somewhat familiar with mulatto and creole history in this state. Over the years there were a number of mixed race children born to slave women who had simply been taken from the slave quarters by plantation owners and white overseers and other well-to-do white men for . . ., uh," he hesitated.

"For sex, Mark," Rachel tersely remarked. "Purely to satisfy their sexual desires."

"Even though some of the children rose to a higher class in society, they were still just property. And their mothers were generally sent back to work with the other slaves until they were needed again."

"I think about it almost every day," Naomi said. Christ teaches forgiveness, but I confess it's hard."

"This relationship between Thomas and Rachel; didn't seem to fit the typical pattern," Mark observed.

Naomi smiled and Mark could see that her spirits had instantly been lifted. "Why Mr. Bradley," Naomi counseled, with her attention focused on the two of them sitting close together, "I'm surprised that you seemed to have overlooked the obvious. They were in love."

Rachel suddenly felt a twinge run through her body and she lightly squeezed Mark's hand.

"Yes sir, they were in love. I do believe Thomas worshipped the ground she walked on and he was just plain crazy about his daughter, Mary."

Mark noticed the old woman appeared to be tiring. "Mrs. Richards, your stories are fascinating. "I hope I can come back soon to hear more."

"Mark, we are grateful for what you and your father and Harold are trying to do. You are welcome any time. Mornings are always better for me; in fact, tomorrow would be fine."

"I'm going to start sorting out all these boxes and files in the morning and I have an appointment with my dad in the afternoon, but I'm open the rest of the week. How about Tuesday?"

"I have classes all day on Tuesday, Grandmother," Rachel interjected.

"That's all right sweetheart. I guess that means I'll have this handsome young man all to myself. Would 10 o'clock Tuesday morning work for you?"

"I'll be on your front porch at ten sharp," Mark replied.

"Now, if the two of you don't mind I'm going to excuse myself for my afternoon nap. I'm sure the two of you can get along just fine without me," she said with just the hint of a smile and a twinkle in her eye.

After Naomi left the porch, Mark turned and took the chair she had been using and looked directly at Rachel. "We know there was no official record of Mary's birth, but perhaps there are other sources of information, like letters or other documents, even pictures. Anything that would help us demonstrate the likelihood of Thomas being her father."

"You have been so patient and understanding," Rachel said. "But you must be tired of traveling down roads that your dad and Uncle Harold have already been down. Let me tell you something about your dad's involvement that may save you some embarrassment when you see him tomorrow."

Mark moved back to the sofa with her and sat at the end eager to hear what she had to say.

"Your dad interviewed grandmother with a court reporter present to record the proceedings. He asked her everything he could imagine that would help build a convincing case that would establish Thomas as Mary's father. He put her testimony in the form of an affidavit and submitted it to the court along with some of the pictures and letters you will find in the files you are taking. He petitioned the court to direct the county to issue a birth certificate for Mary showing Thomas as the father and Rachel, her mother."

"And?" Mark quickly asked.

"Hearsay," Rachel replied in disgust. "The petition was denied."

"When I see Dad tomorrow, I'm sure he'll tell me all about it. There's just one more thing. I'm sure I'm not the first one to suggest a DNA sample from you and Thomas Claiborne's remains."

Rachel smiled and asked, "When did you think of that?"

"It crossed my mind when I first talked to Uncle Harold in his office, but the thought really blossomed when we went into the tomb and I saw the condition of the coffins."

"That puts you a step ahead of Harold and your dad. Neither one of them thought about it until I brought it to their attention."

"Well, score one for me. Now, the big question; why hasn't it been done?"

"Two good reasons." She quickly responded. First, there are strict laws in this state about disinterment and, unless it's needed as evidence in a criminal case, only the closest living relative can authorize it. Secondly, a DNA test wouldn't prove a thing."

"It wouldn't?"

"Let me give you a short lesson about DNA. Every male passes on his DNA characteristics through the Y chromosome to his sons, and it continues down the lineage until the line of direct male descendants is broken. Thomas and Rachel's direct descendants were mostly women. DNA results wouldn't prove a thing. Ironically, a DNA comparison between Thomas and Donald Claiborne would make a perfect match since the line of direct male descendants beginning with Robert, Thomas's son, has remained unbroken through the years, right down to Donald."

"And that brings us back to Donald Claiborne," Mark sighed. "He can prove his relationship and you can't." Mark looked at his watch and said, "We probably better get the file boxes loaded. I've got to stop at the beach house and change before going on to my parent's house for the cookout."

Mark backed his car up the driveway close to the side porch steps and opened the trunk. As he went back into the house Claire Watson came out of the kitchen and said, "I've finished cleaning everything in the kitchen and I'll be glad to help you with these boxes before I leave."

"That's not necessary, Claire; you've done more than your share today," Rachel replied.

When Mark and Rachel finished loading the boxes they returned to the vestibule inside the front door.

"Mark, if you're free on Wednesday, there is something else I'd like to show you."

Putting his hands on her waist, he replied, "I'd like to see anything you want to show me."

"I've been to your beach. Now I'd like to show you ours; the beach on the island that Claiborne wants to develop and destroy. I guess it isn't really necessary, but It means so much to me and I know when you see it you'll understand why."

"It's a date. What time?" he asked.

"Be here at eleven and I'll fix a picnic basket. We'll have the whole beach to ourselves and we can spend the afternoon exploring."

He pulled her close and gently ran his hand through her hair. "I'd like to explore more than the beach," he said softly as he kissed the side of her neck.

"I think that can be arranged," she replied just before their lips touched. Mark held her close and he could feel the soft form of her body through the thin dress material. "Nothing better to cap off a French meal than a goodbye French kiss at the door."

When their embrace ended and he stepped back to create a little space between them, she took his hand in both of hers and placed it on her breast. Mark searched for something to say but for a moment words failed him. Finally, he uttered an emotional surrender. "Rachel, that's not fair."

Keeping his hand on her breast, she rose up on her toes and kissed him. "It wasn't intended to be fair," she replied. "It's intended to show you how I feel every time you touch me or even look at me."

He pulled her back and took her mouth with his lips and tongue while cupping her bottom with his hand. He dropped his hand down under her dress and felt the backs of her thighs all the way up until he could feel her through the sheer material of her underwear. She could feel his growing excitement pushed against her and pushed back. She gasped quickly for breath and said, "My apartment, the porch to the side of the house."

"God I want you," he said. "You can't begin to imagine how much." He glanced at his watch and with a pained expression lamented, "Two cases of bad timing in two days. If I'm late for my mother's society cookout you'll probably see my name in the obituary column. I'll barely make it if I leave now."

"Now that's really not fair," she protested in a breathy voice.

He stepped back and kissed her briefly one last time and responded with a beaming smile on his face, "It wasn't intended to be fair."

. . . .

Ten minutes after Mark left for Charleston, Rachel's phone rang.

Without bothering to identify himself, Mark asked, "Did you say we would have the whole beach to ourselves?"

"It's posted private land and you can only get there by boat. We'll be the only ones there."

On the way to Charleston, Mark was consumed in thoughts of Thomas and Rachel.

Claiborne Plantation 1850

Following Katherine's death giving birth to their second child, women house slaves stepped in to care for both children. There were usually nursing mothers who could be called upon to provide for an infant and this situation was no different. Although their immediate needs were being met, Thomas hoped to find an unattached female to reside in the house on a permanent basis who could fill the void left by their mother as much as possible.

The manager of one of the Claiborne plantations North of Georgetown felt that he had just the young woman for the position. He was certain that she could not only tend to the children but in time, learn to manage the entire household. In short order, Rachel was transported on the river steamer to the dock at the Claiborne mansion. She gulped when she looked up from the bay to see the great white house. Carrying all of her belongings in a small cloth sack, she walked up the lane to the rear porch where she was taken in by the house slaves. Thomas first saw her when he returned to the house that evening. She was a pleasant looking girl, he thought; a mulatto. She seemed a little shy at first but was not afraid to speak. Her Creole language was more English than most and she quickly began learning the children's routines. "Time will tell," he thought to himself.

Rachel adapted quickly and within a week had taken almost total control of the children. She seemed to have a firm but loving disposition and she was with them from morning to night. The oldest, Elizabeth, who was two years old, was clearly taken with her. As the months went by, Thomas slowly turned over more of the household affairs to her.

Thomas proceeded with his determination to provide rudimentary schooling for the slaves. He set aside several hours each evening to personally tutor Rachel in spoken English, reading, writing, and later on, basic arithmetic. He was amazed at how quickly she learned and found her often getting ahead of him. He was growing fond of her and she was always on his mind.

One day while the children were napping and Rachel was cleaning and dusting on the second floor, she opened the closet door in Robert's room where some of Katherine's clothes had been stored after her death. She carefully lifted a simple but expertly stitched linen dress from the closet and held it to her body, trying to imagine what it would be like to wear such fine clothing. Thomas had entered the back door and removed his muddy boots before walking *through the house. He ascended the stairs quietly trying not to wake the children. As he neared Robert's room, he caught a reflection of Rachel in a dressing mirror positioned just inside the door. He watched her lovingly run her fingers through the folds of the dress and finally return it to the closet before quickly retracing his steps, unseen, to the first floor.*

That evening, following their tutoring session, Thomas handed her a small package wrapped in a cotton shawl. Inside was the dress. It was the first time he had seen her cry.

Chapter Ten

Mark pulled into the garage at the beach house and tapped the switch to close the overhead door on his way into the house. He carefully hung up his dress clothes and changed into walking shorts, boat shoes, and a polo shirt. These annual fall cookouts for family and close friends had a way of lasting well into the night so he quickly threw a change of clothes and his razor and toothbrush into a small bag since he would probably wind up a few beers beyond his limit and decide to spend the night. He had planned to unload Rachel's boxes and files before leaving but was running a little late and decided they would be safe in the trunk until the next day.

Traditionally, the social season in Charleston begins in mid to late September; a time that coincided with harvesting crops on the rice plantations in the Low Country from the early 1700s until the plantations fell on hard times at the end of the Civil War. After the harvest, the plantation owners would move to their stylish homes in Charleston and remain until planting time in the spring. It was a time when social life was in full swing.

Although the rice plantations have long since been abandoned and the reason for the beginning of autumn marking the beginning of the social season has been lost to all but a few traditionalists, there begins, at this time, a stream of activities and functions throughout the social hierarchy that lasts through the winter months.

Vivian Bradley's fall society cookout was an annual event that family and close friends attended, and for which many people hoped for an invitation, if for no other reason than that it would be covered by the Charleston Post & Courier. For some people, climbing the social ladder was their favorite sport, but Mark Bradley had never been caught up in its spurious and unseemly side. To be certain, in the eyes of many, he had led a privileged life, but the lessons of goal orientation, responsibility, diligence and honest endeavors had always come before the rewards of social status. As he crossed the Cooper River on the Arthur Ravenel Bridge on his way to his parent's home in the Charleston neighborhood known as South of Broad, he couldn't help thinking about the secure and lofty social structure the Bradley family had known for many generations compared to the social turmoil experienced by the second Thomas Claiborne family throughout the years. Theirs was a story rooted in the hell and degradation of human enslavement; one in which the matriarch of the family, like so many of her peers, suffered the indignity of having no identity other than the one word name on her grave marker, Rachel.

Vivian was positioned near the front door to greet guests when her son walked in. With a quick kiss on his cheek and a glance at her watch, she said with a feigned scowl, "You escaped your mother's wrath for being late by only three minutes."

"Mom, you know I would never be late to one of your parties. By the way," he softly spoke as he passed by her on his way into the large living room filled with guests, "the suit was a hit."

For much of the evening Mark went about his assignment of mingling with guests, refreshing drinks and adding youthful vitality to a mostly middle aged group including several wives of prominent Charlestonians whose discreet but thinly veiled advances he managed to curtail with expert finesse.

Late in the evening, Mark's dad pulled him aside and said, "I haven't had a chance to talk to you all night. I'm taking the day off tomorrow but I'd like to meet you at the office around 2 o'clock and have you catch me up on your work on the Claiborne Trust matter."

"2 o'clock will be fine," Mark replied. "If it's ok with you I'm going to slip out of here in a few minutes and walk down to the marina and spend the night on the Sea Breeze."

"You don't have to ask. I'd like to get out of here myself." As he started to head toward a gathering of guests he turned, and said, "She's hooked up to shore power so you won't need to start the engines but, in case you do, make sure to run the blower in the engine compartment for several minutes. I just had the tanks topped off and there may be some gas fumes."

After a short walk from the Bradley home to the City Marina, Mark stepped on board the Sea Breeze, a 38 foot yacht. The Bradley's had been boat owners as long as anyone could remember and theirs was a classic ocean going vessel Mark's father had maintained like new for years.

Mark pulled back the covers in the Captain's Berth and opened the side hull windows to let fresh air flow through the cabin. In the galley, he pulled out a bottle of Maker's Mark Bourbon and poured about three fingers over ice into a rocks glass. On the stern deck he sat in a reclining deck chair and, with his feet propped up on the gunnel, looked across the harbor reflecting the night stars and tried to process all he had experienced and learned about Rachel Devening and her family. Mostly, he thought about Rachel, the fetching Creole whom, he willfully conceded, had captured a large part of his heart and he realized that the Claiborne Trust case was quickly becoming a very personal matter.

. . . .

The following morning Mark pulled his car into the garage at the beach house and headed for the kitchen to fix scrambled eggs and bacon before unloading the boxes of files and binders from the trunk and beginning what promised to be a long process of sorting through all the material to firm up his knowledge of the history of the Thomas and Rachel family in hopes of finding that one gem of information that might help him break the stalemate.

He noticed the door to the entry closet was ajar and as he reached to close it he noticed that the clothes hanging in the closet had all been shoved to one side. He was certain he had not left the closet in disarray. He walked through the house and found all of the closets in the same condition. Someone had been in the house looking for something. He called 911 and reported a break in.

When the police arrived he showed them through the house and then retreated to the great room to be available for questions as the two officers conducted a more thorough inspection. One of the officers called Mark to the lower level where he had discovered the door on the beach side had been jimmied open with probably a crow bar or tire iron. Apparently, nothing in the house had been stolen and someone had been looking for something that would likely be stored in a closet or other storage area. They said they would file the incident and left him a card with their number to call if he found anything else unusual or thought of anything that would be of help to them.

Still puzzled by the break-in, he went to the garage and opened the trunk to begin unloading Rachel's file boxes and binders. He had planned to put them in the guest room closet. For a moment he stared at the cargo in his trunk, and then slammed the lid shut while mouthing, "son-of-a-bitch."

Mark met his father at the law office at the appointed time of two o'clock. He set aside news of the break in as they settled into a long discussion about events of the previous three days.

"I'm curious about one thing," he said to his dad, "Naomi and her descendants had to have been a threat to the Claiborne's from the day Thomas's will was read. It had to be common knowledge throughout the Low Country that Naomi's ancestral grandmother, Mary, was Thomas and Rachel's child."

"Hell yes, everyone knew Mary was Thomas's daughter. Everyone in that area has always known it," Joe replied.

"It may sound cruel but, with so much at stake, why didn't one of the Claiborne's just kill Naomi a long time ago and, for that matter, all of her living descendants? It would have ended their problem forever and, besides, in the first half of the last century, finding a bunch of black folks murdered probably wouldn't have made the front page news."

"Cruel to be certain, but true," Joe replied. He leaned back in his swivel chair and declared with a grin like a Cheshire cat, "Old Thomas Claiborne was one smart rascal. He put a provision in his will that would haunt the Claiborne's for years. He was easily one of the wealthiest men along the entire coast of South Carolina. When the rice business began to fail he was already involved in turpentine production, logging, communication lines, and transportation along with the bank he started sometime after the civil war. On top of that, he was respected and admired by just about everyone. Hell, he'd probably done favors and helped just about everyone in the Georgetown and Charleston areas over the years."

"He brought Rachel and Mary home after 15 or so years in France. As you well know, life for blacks in the South following Reconstruction was pure hell and in many cases just downright dangerous. Thomas knew his and Rachel's descendants would be safe as long as he was alive. But he also surely knew that the minute he died, their lives wouldn't be worth two cents. So, he placed Naomi's inheritance in the trust and made the Claiborne Bank the Trust manager. This made them responsible for her financial well-being which really had to piss them off since they were always black haters. Then he put the icing on the cake. He stipulated that if Naomi or her parents were murdered or died of any causes that could not be proven to be normal causes or by verifiable accident, the entire estate would be immediately liquidated with the State of South Carolina receiving the outer island with the beach and all the other land sold to the highest bidder with all of the proceeds going to the remaining members of Naomi's family. Then, to make damn sure they'd get the money, he made the State of South Carolina the executor of the will."

After a pause to reflect on Thomas Claiborne's wile and cunning, he summed up the entire matter, "Can you imagine how much the Claibornes have hated Naomi all these years, yet their most important function has been to keep her safe and alive."

"What about Rachel's safety? After her parents died in the plane crash, and with her Aunt Jane already dead, she became, not only the sole target, but the bull's eye."

"That's long been a concern for Harold and me," Mark's father responded with concern. "When she went to live with Mrs. Richards, I guess the Claibornes figured they didn't have much to fear from a twelve year old. But, about the time you entered the Citadel, she went to her Uncle Harold to see if anything could be done to prove her interest in the trust. Harold pulled a few strings and got her a one semester internship with some kind of a science or biology lab in New York. The plan was to keep her out of town and out of harm's way while I filed the petition to have a birth certificate issued for Mary showing Thomas Claiborne as her father. But the petition was denied. I'm sure the Claibornes assumed the threat had passed and all they had to do was wait until Naomi drew her last breath. Donald Claiborne must be aware that you have been nosing around. But I don't think anything will come of it as long as he and the rest of the Claiborne family are confident that no new evidence has turned up."

"I'm afraid it's started, Dad," Mark pronounced with foreboding, and went on to tell him about the break in at the beach house.

"It had to be the personal family papers they were after," his dad alluded. "Where are they now?"

"Everything is still in the trunk of my car."

"Well, let's get them in the office and in the vault. I'd say you better keep everything here and you can use the large office in the back for any desk and computer work you need to do. This whole office complex has redundant security systems and their papers and anything else you are working on should be perfectly safe."

Chapter Eleven

Mark was beginning to think his car could drive itself on his trip North on Highway 17 on Tuesday morning to keep his appointment with Naomi Richards. He was anxious to spend more time with her but wished Rachel would be there. He saw her car in the parking lot at the community college just off the highway as he neared Georgetown. "At least," he thought, "he would have the whole day with her tomorrow; on a private beach to boot."

Claire Watson greeted Mark at the front door and escorted him to the porch at the back of the house overlooking the harbor. Naomi stood to greet him and extended her hand.

"Mrs. Richards," Mark exclaimed, "Please keep your seat. You don't have to stand for me."

"Actually, Mr. Bradley, I was standing for me," she said with a smile. These old bones get stiff if I sit too long. Have a seat young man and some of Claire's homemade iced tea."

"Mrs. Richards, I'm sure when I have a chance to look through the family history, the entire lineage from Thomas Claiborne down to Rachel will become clear but right now I'm having some difficulty keeping it all straight."

"I thought you might so I wrote down a brief version of our family tree. Only the child in each generation who is part of the direct line between Thomas and Rachel is shown." Ironically, they are all girls." With a laugh, she continued, "There were plenty of boys in our family Mr. Bradley but the direct line between Thomas and Rachel is all women."

She drew a circle around Mary's name. "We have written birth records for everyone except Mary. Everyone has always known she was Thomas and Rachel's daughter, but I guess we just can't prove it."

Family Tree from Thomas Claiborne to Rachel Devening

Thomas Claiborne and Rachel -no last name – they were never married.
Daughter, Mary Claiborne, born 1857 (She was given the plantation owner's surname by custom) There is no known birth record for her

Alexandre Charbonnet and Mary Claiborne
Daughter, Jean Charbonnet, born in 1877

John Connet and Jean Charbonnet
Daughter, Naomi Connet, born in 1913

George Richards and Naomi Connet
Daughter, Mildred Richards, born in 1933

Harold Jefferson and Mildred Richards
Daughters, Jane and Margaret Richards
Margaret born in 1952

John Devening and Margaret Richards
Daughter, Rachel Devening, born in 1977

After some small talk, Mark turned to the business at hand. "Mrs. Richards, I have to confess. With no hope of a birth certificate for Mary and no hope of DNA testing, I have no more idea than my dad or Uncle Harold which way to turn. I guess I'm hoping that the more we dig into your family history we might get lucky."

"If I gain nothing more than the pleasure of your company, I will be well satisfied," the old woman replied in a genuinely warm tone.

"You mentioned that Rachel and Mary remained in France for about 15 years. Tell me about their return."

"The first to return was Robert Claiborne from England. When he finished at the university, Thomas brought him back to help with the business. Along with all of his other business ventures, he had just started the bank. Robert wasn't much for outdoor work but he really took to the banking business. I guess this would have been in the mid to late 1870s."

"Robert, I'm told, was a big help in running the bank and managing the finances of the other Claiborne business interests, but Thomas needed someone who could help manage the logging and turpentine business and the construction of roads and rail spur lines as well as the rest of the Claiborne interests."

"Who did he find?"

"My grandfather," she replied with pride. When rice production was at its peak in the years before the war, Thomas had enough rice to avoid the buying and shipping co-ops and shipped his rice directly to a buyer in France by the name of Maurice Charbonnet. It was his guest house where Rachel and Mary lived for their first year. When Mary was in her early twenties she married Miesure Charbonnet's nephew, Alexandre. He was educated and ambitious and Thomas believed he was just the man he was looking for." With a wistful smile, she recalled a time many years ago. "When I was just a child, I can recall old Thomas telling me he gave my grandfather six months to learn English before bringing him to South Carolina. He said my grandmother Mary about drove him nuts but she managed to cram enough English in him to satisfy Thomas and six months later Rachel, Mary, and Alexandre boarded a steamer for Charleston."

"How did it all work out?" Mark asked with his curiosity peaked.

"That's when all the trouble started," Naomi replied with a subtle hint of bitterness.

"What kind of trouble."

"Robert hated black people with a passion. Reconstruction was over and strict segregation was becoming the law of the land. When Thomas told Robert about his plans, he was irate; but I guess he managed to suppress his feelings until they arrived. Thomas and Robert were having a discussion in the study in the mansion house and it got out of control. My grandmother told me they began shouting at each other and she heard Robert tell his father to keep that half black bastard daughter of his on the plantation and away from town."

"What did Thomas do?"

"He beat the living hell out of him and damned near killed him. My grandmother told me she ran into the study and pulled her father off him. Thomas told Robert he owed his life to this half black bastard woman and if he ever said another bad word about her he'd finish the job. Robert was living in Georgetown and never again sat foot on Claiborne Plantation."

"How did they manage to conduct business together after that?"

"I guess they realized they needed each other," she answered with a sigh of resolve. "The Claibornes stayed in town and the black folks and Creoles who lived on the plantation avoided town like the plague. It was at that time that Thomas built this house. He used it as an office when he was in town and for some social occasions that required his presence. He lived two lives; one in Georgetown near his white family and business interests and the other on the plantation with Rachel and their descendants. After all these years nothing has really changed. Old hatred runs deep, Mr. Bradley, especially when racial prejudice is involved and a fortune is at stake."

Chapter Twelve

As Mark pulled onto the front circular drive at the Claiborne mansion, Rachel was attaching a canvas enclosure on an old dented, and rusty Jeep.

"Just leave your car in the drive and throw your things in the back and we'll head for the beach," Rachel said as Mark opened his car door. They were both wearing jeans and long sleeve shirts as Rachel had suggested for walking through tall sea grass to get to the beach."

Both of their shirts were white and Mark suggested, "We look like a matched set."

She suspected there was nothing implied by his comment, but she liked the sound of it.

"That's something different," Mark observed as she walked over to meet him.

A little confused, she asked, "What's different."

"The jeans. This is the first time I've seen you wearing pants."

"I guess it is," she agreed. "Which do you prefer?"

"There ought to be a law against the way you look in those jeans, but I think I prefer dresses."

"I'll make you a deal," she responded with glee. If you will take me to dinner this evening, I'll wear a dress." As an afterthought, she added, "One I know you will like."

"You're on," he replied with a grin as he put his arms around her for a kiss. "I brought a change of clothes and a sports coat just in case."

"Beach first, then fooling around," she said while pulling away and denying him a second kiss. With a sparkle in her eyes she added a single word, ". . . maybe."

"This old Jeep's been around here as long as I can remember." She wheeled around the circle and headed for the main gate. It's perfect for driving through the plantation low country." She turned east toward the coast on the hard packed sand road. "I put the canvas on in case it rains. The sun is shining right now but there is some heavy rain coming in from the west and I hope it doesn't spoil our picnic on the beach."

The old road was bordered on both sides by sea and saw grass as tall as the jeep. After about three miles, the road dipped slightly down and ended at an old wooden dock at the side of the Intracoastal Waterway. "That's our ride to the beach," Rachel said as she got out of the Jeep and pointed to an old center console boat sitting on a lift covered with corrosion and salt spray."

With a chuckle, Mark said, "Looks like the lift and the boat have been around as long as the Jeep."

"They're all old, but I guess they're like the Energizer Bunny; they just keep on ticking." Rachel unlocked the winch and lowered the small boat into the water with the large winch wheel. After stowing the picnic basket and their bags with beach wear in the boat, Rachel slipped behind the wheel on a hard bench seat and remarked, "It's never failed us yet." As she turned the key in the ignition switch, the old Mercury grumbled to life and they set out for another rustic old dock at the barrier island on the other side of the waterway.

While Rachel tied up the boat, Mark retrieved the picnic basket and the beachwear bags. "Right this way," she directed as she started along a narrow sand trail encroached by seagrass. After slugging through the sand and grass for about ten minutes, they arrived at a small clearing on top of a large sand dune. Suddenly, for as far as their eyes could see, stretched the clear blue water of the Atlantic Ocean. "What do you think?" Rachel asked when the coast came into view.

For a moment Mark stood speechless as he surveyed the incredible landscape. The beach was wide with nearly white sand and disappeared into the horizon in both directions. "I've never seen a beach that seemed to go on forever."

"It's a naturalist's dream. No signs of ever any human habitation and just an occasional fisherman."

"It's also a developer's dream," Mark lamented.

They set the bags on the beach far enough from the rising tide to be safe and started walking. It was 75 degrees with no wind and brilliant sunshine that made the silica in the sand sparkle like diamonds; a lovers' paradise.

Along the way, Rachel gave Mark a detailed description of the vegetation and marine life. She was in her element and could barely contain her excitement as she referred to the wonder of the undisturbed biological and botanical treasure chest that seemed to come to life through her vision. "I want to show you something," she said as she started toward the dunes at the back of the beach. She began walking carefully through the tall grass. "Follow in my footsteps and try not to disturb any of the vegetation." She stopped on the back side of the dune and gestured with a slow sweeping movement of her arm and hand. "Look at this bed of seagrass. It's a little shorter with broader leaves than all the rest. I've sent several samples to the Botany department at USC. There are literally hundreds of species but, so far, we haven't been able to identify this one. I may have discovered an unknown variety. They might accept research on this species for the subject of my dissertation if I decide to go on for a Ph.D Seagrassbeds are some of the most productive ecosystems on earth and a find like this has to be protected. I've been slowly transplanting a few sprigs to a more protected marsh near the plantation house in case this part of the beach was to take a direct hurricane hit and wipe out this patch." She turned to see a somewhat confused but understanding smile on Mark's face. "I'm so sorry," she gushed. "I've been rattling on nonstop but, it's so important."

"I know it is," he replied with sincere interest.

They paused for a moment and Mark turned to her as he spoke. "I've always understood the money . . . ; the value of this land for development. In a capitalist system, we worship the pioneers and the entrepreneurs who have the courage and where-for-all to build monuments for mankind. This I have always understood. But the magnitude of this place and the treasures it holds are simply beyond comprehension. Your dream . . . , to keep it just the way it is . . . the way it has always been. Now I understand."

They stood together nearly overwhelmed by the grandeur. "You're a special man, Mark Bradley," Rachel said holding his arm as they looked across the surf to the endless sea. "I hoped; no, I knew . . . I knew you would feel the same way I feel."

"We can't let this get away, sweetheart," Mark said in a determined and purposeful manner. Following a long embrace, they headed back up to the beach for their picnic.

"Sweetheart," she thought to herself. It was the first time he had used such a direct term of endearment when talking to her.

When they arrived back at their bags, Rachel pulled out several large beach towels and handed them to Mark. "Why don't you spread these out and I'll get our lunch out of the basket."

"This time I made a shrimp salad," she said as she set two Tupperware containers on the towels. I picked the shrimp up at the fish market this morning. They're huge and I couldn't resist." She set out two containers of salad dressing. "A light vinaigrette and ranch and," she added with a slightly sassy tone, "a bottle of Moscato. Just like the one we had for lunch the first day you came to the plantation."

"Where in the world did you learn to cook," Mark exclaimed, chasing his words with another forkful.

She laughed at his enthusiasm for the food. "How quickly you forget; my father might have been Irish, but the rest of me is pure French Creole. In our family, learning to cook is not only a rite of passage but an expectation."

When their meal was over they sat together looking over the sun drenched blue ocean while finishing the Moscato. Behind them, and unnoticed, the sky was nearly black with the forecasted thunderstorms beginning to roll in from the west.

Their lighthearted banter began to take a serious turn as Mark told her about the break-in at the beach house. "I'm concerned for your safety. All the files in those boxes may not reveal anything that will help us prove that you are a direct descendant of Thomas Claiborne, but the people who tried to steal them don't know that."

"How can you be sure they were looking for the file boxes?" she responded.

"I can't be absolutely certain, just ninety nine percent," he angrily remarked. "The thing that disturbs me most is how anyone knew I had the files. There were four of us at the house when we loaded them into my trunk. I didn't tell anyone and if we can eliminate you and your great grandmother; that leaves Mrs. Watson."

"Mark, you really don't believe Mrs. Watson was involved. She has been just like family for as long as I can remember. Besides, any number of people could have seen us loading those boxes in your car."

"I know," he responded apologetically, "but when Naomi mentioned that Claire had to leave to fix dinner for her grandchildren she said they had called and had to cancel. The funny part about that; I never heard her phone ring and that all happened after Naomi told us about the file boxes she had prepared to send with me. Mrs. Watson even offered to help carry them out to the car. I'm sorry for having a suspicious mind," he said, "but I just don't think we can be too careful."

Rachel ran her hand through his hair on the side of his head. "I think, . . . I hope you're wrong but I'm grateful for your concern." She moved her hand to the back of his head and pulled him to her lips. They laid back on the beach towels and began the kissing and exploring for which they both had been aching since their first meeting at the beach house. Mark began moving his hand up the inside of her thigh and Rachel, doing nothing to discourage him, took their kissing to the next level by lightly tracing the inside of his lips with her tongue while firmly pressing her body against him. She gently rolled him over on his back and straddled him just below his waist and began to unbutton his shirt. She leaned over and whispered in his ear, "I always thought I was a little bashful until I met you. I'm beginning to think you've turned me into a wild woman."

"We seem to have a lot in common," he said with a grin as he reached up to unbutton hers. With her shirt unbuttoned, he moved his hands across her bare skin to her back and began to unfasten her bra. "I'm a little clumsy," he said sheepishly.

"Let me give you a hand," she responded as she reached behind her back and adroitly undid the hook while at the same time shedding her shirt and bra. She quickly finished his buttons, pulled his shirt open, and laid with her breasts on his chest as they resumed the deep French kissing. Just as Mark rolled her on her side and reached for the button and zipper on her jeans, a huge bolt of lightning cracked followed by rolling peals of deafening thunder.

They both flinched. "Damn, I thought we were goners," Rachel shouted in Marks's ear. "Grab the stuff. We've got to get out of here."

Rachel rose up and slipped into her shirt while Mark stuffed the towels into the beach bag. "Here," he said as he handed her the bra which had been gathered up in a towel.

"Just put it in the bag. I'll put it on later," she said hurriedly as she finished putting their lunch trash in a plastic bag. Lightning began in the western sky, one strike after another. The black foreboding storm clouds had moved in directly overhead bringing strong winds and the temperature felt like it had instantly dropped twenty degrees.

Chapter Thirteen

With everything in hand, they began to run toward the path that would take them through the dunes and across the island to the boat. "Hold up," Rachel said, slightly winded when they were about a hundred feet from the boat. "She stood straight up with her hands on her hips drawing a long deep breath. "I've got to pee," she exclaimed. "Go ahead and throw all of these things in the boat. I'll be right behind you." As Mark turned and began to move toward the dock, she yelled," Reach over and start the engine so it can be warming up."

As soon as he reached the boat he followed her instructions and stowed the beach bags in the bow. He had to get in the boat to reach the ignition switch which was on the center console. The motor started on the third attempt and he instantly turned and put his foot on the side of the boat to step onto the dock, and when he raised his foot from the gunnel, the little boat began rocking back and forth. He started running back toward Rachel and saw her come out from behind some tall bushes on the path. As he neared her she dropped down on one knee to retie the lace on her sneaker. He took her arm as she started to stand. "Everything's ready to go," he said as they started plowing back through the soft sand.

They had only made about ten feet when, suddenly, they heard a "swoosh" sound come from the boat followed in two seconds by a bright fireball and a violent explosion. They stood stunned but quickly turned and dropped to the sand from the intense heat. As Rachel was falling to the ground she felt the sharp pain of being struck by a piece of flying fiberglass. For a few seconds, they could hear debris falling, and then it was over. When they arrived at the dock a small portion of the bow was nose up in the water and still secured to the dock with the landing rope. The rest of the boat had been shattered by the explosion and the motor had landed on the bank of the waterway about forty feet upstream.

For a moment they stood on the dock looking at the destruction in total shock. "It had to be a gas explosion," Mark resolutely observed. The wind began blowing harder and rain drops began to fall. Mark noticed the garbage bag Rachel had set on the dock. He grabbed the bag and emptied it on shore. "Sorry to be a litterbug but we can use this." He stepped back on the dock and spoke as he reached down to slip off his shoes. "Take off your pants and roll them up and put them in the bag.

"Excuse me?" she questioned.

As he stood up and unzipped his jeans, he responded smilingly. "We're going to have to swim. You can either swim without them or drown with them. Without them is probably the better choice."

She went from fearing the gravity of their predicament to yielding to the humor in his approach and relented. "What the heck, you about had them off back on the beach anyway."

They both stripped down to their underwear and Mark rolled the clothes tight and put them in the bag along with their shoes. "How about the shirt," she asked.

"You could swim in the shirt but it would be nice to put on something dry on the other side." Off came the shirt.

Mark pulled the laces from their shoes and tied them together. He tied one end of his small makeshift cord to the garbage bag holding their clothes and the other end around his left ankle. "Are you ready?"

"As ready as I'll ever be."

"You do swim, don't you?"

Looking at the thousand feet of waterway in front of them, she replied with trepidation, "I don't think I've ever swam that far at one time in my life."

"Don't worry, I'll stay right with you, and if you get tired, just take hold of my arm." Holding hands, the underwear clad swimmers jumped together into the water and began their swim after adjusting to the shock of the cold water. The water temperature was in the 68 degree range and the air temperature had fallen to nearly forty. Even though the Intracoastal Waterway was protected by land on both sides, they were swimming directly into the strong westerly wind. The water was rough and the rain was coming down in torrents as they clawed their way toward the distant shore. Three or four times Rachel grabbed his arm and held on while she caught her breath. When they were within one hundred feet of land, she gulped down a mouthful of seawater and began to gag. When she was able to resume nearly normal breathing, Mark turned her over on her back, and with his arm around her chest said with exhaustive effort, "Just lay back and relax. The rest of the way is on me."

After holding onto Rachel and swimming with one hand with the clothes bag tethered to his ankle, Mark was nearing the point of total exhaustion when they finally reached land. Together, they crawled onto the shore and for a moment laid face down in the sandy gumbo clay in the pouring rain. Mark pushed himself up to his knees and helped Rachel to her feet. Without shoes, they had to move gingerly across the rocky sand to the Jeep. He helped her into the passenger seat and shielded his face from the rain with his arm as he moved around to the passenger side door. He threw the garbage bags with their clothes into the back seat and quickly started the engine. "I'll turn on the heat as soon as it warms up."

"The heater doesn't work," she responded in a weak monotone voice.

Mark retrieved the bag, ripped it open and handed Rachel his shirt. "Dry off with this." He dumped the rest of their clothes out between the seats and said, "Get that wet underwear off and pull your jeans on."

With panties and Jockey shorts on the floorboard, they both struggled into their jeans. Mark helped her into her shirt and reached down to slip her sneakers on her feet. She began uncontrollable shivering and Mark drove back to the plantation house as fast as he could safely navigate the rain drenched sand road. When they arrived, he helped her into his car and reached in the back seat and pulled the sports coat he had intended to wear to dinner that evening out of the garment bag and draped it around her shoulders.

A driver in a car parked on a side street about a block from Naomi's house in Georgetown watched a man and a woman brave the rain and blowing wind and run for cover to the front porch.

"Son-of-a-bitch," he said out loud to himself as he jerked the gear lever into drive and pulled away.

Chapter Fourteen

Inside the apartment, Rachel was still shivering as Mark sat her on the sofa and wrapped her with a blanket he found in the linen closet. "We've got to get you warm and I think I've got just the ticket." He went into her bathroom and turned the shower on as warm as he thought she could stand and closed the door behind him to allow the steam to build up. He walked with her to the bathroom and opened the door. "Just drop your clothes on the floor and I'll have towels for you when you're ready to get out."

Her shivering stopped when she stepped under the faucet but the hot water seemed to drain what little energy she had left. When she pulled the curtain back to get out she saw several large towels sitting on the stool and her terrycloth robe hanging on a wall hook. She wrapped a towel around her hair and decided to forego the aggravation of using the hair dryer.

"Feel better?" Mark asked as he rose from his chair when she came into the small living room.

"I think I'll live," she answered with a weak smile. "I'm just so tired."

He put his arms around her and when he laid his hand on her back she winced, "Ouch, that's sore"

"Let me see," he replied while pulling the robe down from her back. "This is part of your problem. You have a large abrasion, about the size of my hand."

"I remember getting hit with something just as we turned away from the explosion."

"It's not serious he said as he gently applied some Vaseline to the sore while she sat on the side of her bed. But, along with the shock of the explosion and the long swim in hypothermic conditions, your body just can't take any more. You need a long sleep." He pulled the covers over her as she slipped under the sheet with her robe still on.

As he started to close her bedroom door behind him, she spoke quietly. "Would you mind calling me about nine in the morning to make sure I'm up? I've got class at eleven."

He walked back to her bed and gently kissed her on the cheek. "Sure thing," he responded.

He locked her front door and stepped back out onto the side porch of the house. The sky was still dark but the rain had slowed to a drizzle. He thought for a moment and decided he should tell Naomi about the boat accident.

Naomi opened her front door and gladly welcomed him in. "I'll bet this rain really put a damper on your day at the Beach with Rachel," she exclaimed as they walked into the parlor.

"You could say that," he said laughingly. "Actually, the rain wasn't the only problem."

Mark very carefully told Naomi about the boat accident and assured her that Rachel would be just fine after a good night's sleep. "I guess these things just happen. But at least no one was seriously hurt."

Naomi's cheeks seemed to turn pale and with a look of horror on her face, she responded, "These things just don't happen. I don't believe for a moment it was an accident."

Mark was stunned. "Mrs. Richards, I'm sure it was just a matter of some gas fumes that accumulated in the bilge well and exploded when I started the engine. It was probably my fault for not opening the cover before I turned the key on."

"It's Rachel, Mark. They mean to kill her just like they killed my granddaughters, Jane and Margaret."

"They what?" Mark retorted with alarm.

"If Rachel is able to prove her ancestry, the Claibornes will lose a huge fortune. If she dies before I do, their fortune is safe. The same was true of her mother and Aunt Jane. Their passings were both ruled accidental death just as Rachel's would have been if she had been sitting in that boat when it exploded." Then she added, "As well as yours."

Mark listened with sincere interest as she continued. "Over the years the trust provided enough income to provide college educations for several generations of children in our family and I was only too happy to provide the money for Sonny, excuse me, Harold, to go to law school. I know the Claibornes cheated me out of a lot of money from the trust over the years, but I couldn't prove it. I guess I figured as much as they hated me and black folks in general; as long as I had enough money to take care of family, I wouldn't make a fuss.

Not long after Harold started law school, Jack Claiborne, Don's father, who was the Trust manager at the time, told me the profits from the farming and logging operations had fallen way off and the money I received was barely enough to put food on the table, let alone pay for law school". Naomi leaned back in her chair and took several deep breaths before continuing.

"When I told Harold and Jane, they were furious. Not because of the loss of money for law school but because they knew Claiborne was a liar and a cheat. Mark, they were both highly intelligent and well educated. They had been around farming and logging production for years and they could see what was being produced and they knew the markets for produce and timber had not declined.

Harold went to see Mr. Claiborne. He would never tell me much about their discussion but I knew it wasn't pleasant. He mentioned something about fiduciary responsibility and malfeasance. Harold must have put the fear of God in him because my normal payments resumed not long after." As an afterthought, she mentioned, "Later on, when I was able to start helping Harold and Jane again, he mentioned something about being able to repay a loan from your grandfather."

"I'm sure your relations with Claiborne were anything but cordial, Mrs. Richards. But what did that have to do with Jane's death? In fact, I guess I never heard how she died."

"They said she drowned, but I've always known that was a lie. Jack Claiborne was a black hater. It was a well-known fact that as a younger man he was a member of the local chapter of the KKK. Can you imagine how he must have felt being verbally dressed down by a black man; especially one as smart as Harold Sanders. Then there was always the matter of the trust and the will. Jane was the older of my two granddaughters and Claiborne had to know that if I died before Jane he would likely have to face her, with Harold's assistance, in a huge battle over the estate."

"They said she drowned," Mark patiently guided her.

"They found her on the beach near a rocky jetty just north of the end of the path that you and Rachel took today. She loved the beach and often went there to collect shells and sharks' teeth. They said she must have walked out on the jetty and then slipped and hit her head on the rocks and fell into the water and drowned."

"It sounds plausible, Mrs. Richards."

With her voice growing stronger and more determined, she quickly responded. "Jane would never have walked on that jetty. She couldn't swim and was deathly afraid of water. She was all right in a boat or walking on the beach but she was warned about walking on the jetty from the time she was a small child. I've been there with her many times. She wouldn't go near it under any circumstances. I'm certain someone hit her on the head with a rock and threw her in the water."

Mark sat for a moment trying to assimilate this information that was new to him. Finally, he looked at Naomi and asked, "What about Rachel's mother, Margaret? It's my understanding that she and Rachel's father died in a plane crash. I know that they brought Rachel to stay with you and continued their trip to Barbados from Charleston. I assumed their plane crashed at some point along the way or during landing."

"There was no problem with their flight to Barbados, Mark. They decided to visit a nearby island and chartered a small plane. The plane exploded and went into the ocean shortly after takeoff. Their bodies were never recovered and there was never any official explanation for the crash. I don't think it was mechanical problems that caused that plane to explode. I think it was human interference."

Mark thoughtfully responded. "The two people who were a direct threat to the Claiborne's inheritance were both killed, and today the final threat to their estate almost met the same fate; death by accident. It might all be coincidental, but too much to ignore."

As they walked to the door, Mark assured her, "I'll have to sleep on this for a day or so and discuss it with my father but I promise to get back to you."

"I know you will do your best," she replied while wiping a small tear from her eye.

Chapter Fifteen

That night Mark laid awake for several hours going over and over all of the events that had transpired that day as well as the short time he had known Rachel. It was messy and growing more complicated, and dangerous. He set the alarm for 8:50 as a reminder to call her at 9 o'clock.

"How are you feeling," he asked when she picked up the phone.

"Actually pretty good," she responded cheerfully. "That's probably the best night's sleep I've ever had. At least it was the longest."

He told her about talking to Naomi about the boat accident but didn't go beyond that. He assumed Rachel was aware of her great grandmother's suspicions but didn't want to bring it up, just then. They talked until Rachel had to finish getting ready for class. "Listen," Mark concluded, "You will have four days before your classes next Tuesday. Why don't you pack a bag and stay with me at the beach house for a few days?"

He didn't have to wait long for an answer. "With what sounded like a sigh of relief, she said, "I'd love to. I could sure stand to get out of here for a while and I'd love to spend time with you. I'll call Mrs. Watson and make sure she can look after Naomi." In no more time than it took him to walk to the kitchen and drink a glass of orange juice, she called back. "Mrs. Watson said she would be glad to stay with her as long as I'm gone. I should be in your driveway by 7 o'clock if the offer still stands."

"Mark could tell she was excited. He was too. "I'll be sitting on the front steps waiting for you."

. . . .

Later that morning Mark pulled into a run-down marina on a backwater lagoon from the Ashley River. There were boats of all manner everywhere: sitting on trailers, tied to the dock, and sitting on lifts. It was a haphazard collection of watercraft with no semblance of order. As soon as he got out of his car he spotted the person he had come to see walking out of the overhead door opening in a large rusty corrugated steel building, an old friend and football teammate from high school, Chad Ainsworth. "Chad," Mark yelled to his friend.

Chad approached Mark with a smile and immediately reproached him. "Well, to what do I owe the long overdue presence of the honorable Mr. Bradley; battalion commander at the Citadel, the heartthrob of half the young ladies at the College of Charleston, and the scion, son, and heir to the Bradley legal machine. I saw your picture in the social section of the newspaper at your mother's annual society cookout. Looks like the lonely housewives South of Broad have new meat on the table."

As they met and shook hands, Mark replied. "You know, I think the thing I enjoy most about you is your affable and pleasing manner. Actually, I had a little time on my hands and decided to do a little slumming and just couldn't think of a better place than right here."

"Well, if slumming is on your mind you have come to the right place. Come on in the office and we'll have a cold one; beer or coke, your choice."

Mark followed Chad past the steel building from which there emanated a myriad of sounds one might expect from a repair facility to an old camper trailer with a sign on the door that read Ainsworth Marine."

Chad pulled a couple of beers from a small refrigerator and held them out to Mark. Mark took one and Chad popped one open for himself. "Now, what really brings you here?" Chad asked

Mark told him about the boat accident. "Doesn't surprise me; people get killed every year from gas fume explosions in boats," Chad acknowledged as he took a swig of beer.

"It might have been attempted murder," Mark replied. "I got out of the boat after I started it and it was at least a minute or so before it exploded. If it was intentional, someone assumed we would be in the boat and underway when it blew."

"Damn, Mark," Chad replied, "are you serious? You really think someone was trying to kill you?"

"That's what I'm beginning to think."

Chad sat for a moment with a studious scowl on his face and finally said, "Alright, tell me everything about it and don't leave anything out. Let's begin with the type of boat we're talking about."

Mark went through the entire event in great detail and was frequently interrupted with questions from Chad.

"There's an old center console boat out in the yard. Let's go take a look and see if it's the same boat or at least similar."

Mark agreed that the boat on a trailer in the yard was essentially the same or, at least a lot like the one that had exploded.

Chad walked with Mark to the parking lot. "Could someone have rigged that boat to explode, and if so, how did they do it? That's the question. It may take me a few days to figure it out. I'll give you a call."

When Mark was within three blocks of the Ashley River Bridge, his phone rang. "If you've got enough time, turn around and come back. I'll tell you how it was probably done."

Mark smiled as he returned Chad's serve, "What took you so long?" The screen on his phone displayed the words Call Ended. Mark managed a U turn and headed back to the marina.

Chad and Mark walked out to the old boat. On the way, Chad said, "You told me that when you were on the beach the boat was completely out of sight."

"For at least two hours," Mark replied.

"This is boat sabotage 101," Chad proclaimed when they reached the boat. "This one has an open bilge and fuel compartment but the compartment on your boat was covered with a hinged lid; perfect for making a bomb." They climbed into the boat and Chad continued as he reached into the bilge area. "The first thing I would do is dump several containers of water in the bilge to make sure the pump would activate. Then I would set this adjustable stop right at the water level so the slightest rocking from wave action, or in your case, causing the boat to rock by stepping on the side to get out would cause the water to slosh around and turn on the pump." Chad pulled two wires slightly away from the pump. "Like any switch, it has two wires; one in and one out." He retrieved a razor utility knife from his pocket and stripped small sections of plastic insulation from the two wires and twisted the two bare sections together. "Now, the boat rocks, the water pushes up the float and activates the switch that starts the pump. It won't take long for the two wires to get blazing hot; enough to ignite gas fumes."

"How do you make sure there will be gas fumes to ignite?"

"That's the easy part," Chad remarked as he pulled a short piece of fuel hose from his jeans pocket. He used the razor blade to cut a small slit in the hose. "When the motor is not running there is no pressure on the line and the gas won't leak out. But when you start the motor, the suction from the fuel pump puts pressure on the line and gasoline will spray out of the cut. You started the engine, the cut hose began to spray fuel into the covered bilge and when you stepped on the side of the boat to get out, the rocking motion of the boat caused the pump switch to activate and, well, you know the rest of it. I'm just surprised you had enough time to get far enough away from the boat before it exploded."

"I was running. I wanted to get back to Rachel to help her through the soft sand before the rain started. I guess if she had been with me at the boat we would both be toast."

Mark noticed a long boat on a trailer completely covered with a tarp. "What's under wraps, Chad?" Mark inquired while peeking under the tarp.

"Give me a hand and I'll show you." Together they peeled back the cover to reveal the most beautiful boat Mark had ever seen. The primary color was yellow trimmed in a psychedelic array of all the primary colors and more. Painted along the front of the boat was the name, Southern Screamer. "It's a cigarette racing boat. It was repossessed by the bank and I got it for a song."

"A song?" Mark questioned.

"Yea, I got it for $150,000. Put about thirty thousand in it and figure it'll bring around $220,000 to $230,000. It's a Top Gun with a pair of Mercury Racing HP525EFI engines with 1.5:1 Bravo One drives and 2-inch "shorty" Sport Master gear cases. Got a fella coming down next month from Maine to look at it."

"Chad, I didn't understand a thing you said but it looks like it's flying, sitting still."

"It's scary fast. I've had it up to 90 in calm seas but I know it will top out over a hundred."

On the way back to Mark's car he said, "I really appreciate the help, even if it wasn't what I wanted to hear. By the way," he continued, "why don't you clean up this dump? You're probably the best go-to boatman on the coast with more customers than you can possibly handle. Hell, Chad I'll bet there's not a handful of attorneys in Charleston who make as much money as you do."

Chad laughed and slapped his friend on the back. "If I cleaned it up and made it look successful, they'd think I was over charging them."

"Mark grinned and stated, "Point taken Mr. Ainsworth, point taken."

Chapter Sixteen

After crossing the Ashley River, Mark made a turn to the right and headed for his father's law office.

"Mr. Bradley, your son stopped by to see if you were free," the receptionist said as she quietly stuck her head into the conference room where he was meeting with several of the firm's attorneys.

"Great timing," he replied. Tell him to wait in my office. I'll be free in about ten minutes and we'll have lunch.

"If you think the break in at the beach house was serious business, wait until you hear the rest of it," Mark said after the waitress finished taking their order."

Mark spoke through lunch and when he was finished, opined, "You look like I felt, shell-shocked."

As they entered the office foyer, Joe Bradley asked the receptionist to see if she could get Frank Zeller on the line. In his office, Joe sat in a soft chair in the client's seating area. "Frank is the agent in charge of the regional FBI office here in Charleston. The incident occurred on the Intracoastal Waterway which is patrolled by the Coast Guard and maintained with federal funds. I suspect the FBI and, perhaps, other federal agencies will have jurisdiction. Frank should be able to help or, at the very least, best advise us." For several minutes Joe could only sit enveloped in thought with a concerned look on his face. Finally, he looked at his son and spoke with great trepidation. "Mark, this is serious business. If what Chad Ainsworth said is true, someone might have tried to kill you and Rachel. She's Harold's niece and, Lord knows, I would do anything to help her but we might have to rethink our involvement in this whole matter. No estate or amount of money is worth getting someone killed."

With almost a sense of resignation, Mark replied, "I'm no hero, Dad. There are a lot of heroes out in Confederate Cemetery and they all shared one thing in common. Being heroes got them killed. I don't want someone coming after me, and I damn sure don't want someone going after Rachel."

Frank Zeller's call came through and after a short explanation of the situation, Joe hung up the phone and said, "He's coming over. His office is just a few blocks down the street."

For several moments they sat quietly absorbed by the brutal reality of the situation. Mark ended the silence. "Tell you what, Dad; Rachel is coming down this evening to stay with me through the weekend. Let's see what Frank has to say and let it ride a few days. I went ahead and ordered the security system, as you suggested, after the break-in at the beach house. It includes surveillance cameras inside and out and some exterior motion detectors. I'm sure we will be just fine and then we can address the matter with clear minds the first of the week."

Joe nodded in agreement and said, "I've got to call Harold Sanders. He needs to know what's going on."

The following afternoon the crew of a small salvage barge began retrieving debris from the explosion as a Coast Guard boat vessel stood by. The process was supervised by a small group of marine forensic experts.

On his way home, Mark was mindful of Frank's advice to avoid discussing the matter with anyone except Rachel until the forensics report was in. He hoped it wouldn't take more than a few days. He knew if the explosion was determined to be the result of an intentional act, Rachel's life would be in imminent danger. The only saving grace would be whether or not the guilty party would be able to cook up another attempt that would look like an accident, which seemed to be an emerging pattern. He hoped he would be able to convince her to stay with him until she had to return to work on the following Tuesday. By then they would have to begin making decisions.

Mark spent the rest of the afternoon cleaning house. Rachel's apartment was spotless and he didn't want her to think he was lacking in domestic talents. He was, but he was determined to hide the evidence.

A little after five, Mark's phone rang and his father's number was on the caller's ID. "When I told your mother that Rachel would be spending a few days with you, she reminded me about her promise of a girl's day out. I think she wants to take her out for lunch and a little shopping on Saturday. Later in the evening, we can all go out to dinner. And then, if the two of you would like, you can go to church with us and we'll have Sunday brunch at the Yacht Club. I know it sounds like a lot, but talk it over with Rachel and let us know what you both would like to do. No pressure, Son; whatever the two of you decide will be fine with us.

"Right," Mark thought after ending the call, "no pressure." Actually, his parent's interest in Rachel pleased him. If his mother had a little matchmaking in mind, who was he to object?.

Chapter Seventeen

As promised, Mark was sitting on the steps of the beach house when Rachel pulled in the drive. He opened her door and she hugged him and held on. "I've never been happier to be somewhere with someone than I am here with you. I thought my last class would never end and there were at least five students waiting with questions about next week's test."

"It's starting to get chilly. I've put some logs in the fire pit on the back deck. How about we cozy up to the fire with a glass of wine and watch the last rays of the sun on the ocean."

It's the best offer I've had today," she said before turning her lips to his for a kiss.

Mark got her suitcase out of the back seat and Rachel retrieved a hangar bag from the rear side hook. After depositing her things in the master bedroom, Marked handed her a woolen shawl his mother used for cool evenings. "Is Merlot all right with you?" he asked as they walked into the kitchen.

"Merlot is perfect. A glass of red wine by the fire with good company is hard to beat."

"Mark had already started the fire and he positioned a love seat with soft cushions in front of the fire pit and facing the ocean. This is just what I needed," she said as they pulled the seat close enough to the fire to feel the heat.

She took a sip of wine and suddenly began laughing while holding her hand to her mouth to keep it from spraying from her mouth.

"Whoa," Mark said while handing her a napkin. What is that all about?"

"I don't know why it crossed my mind," she answered trying to contain her laugh. I hope my bra burned up in the fire. Can you imagine what someone might think if they saw that bra laying out on the bank amid all that wreckage?"

"Well, at least yesterday's adventure will give you a great story to tell your grandchildren."

"It would," she agreed, but I'd have to leave out parts of it."

"And what parts would that be?"

"You know darn well what parts, smart aleck," she retorted as she lightly jabbed his side with her elbow.

"Besides," she said as her voice turned soft, "Those are special personal memories I'll cherish for the rest of my life."

"I forgot the hors d'oeuvres," Mark exclaimed as he stood. I've got some cold shrimp and crab on ice in the kitchen with some Creole style cocktail sauce."

While Mark was fetching the food, Rachel pulled a wrinkled piece of paper from the pocket of her slacks and slid it under her leg where it would be easy to retrieve if she decided she needed it.

After her first piece of shrimp, Rachel said, "Naomi said she told you about her suspicions concerning my parents and Aunt Jane."

Without a noticeable reaction, Mark replied, "She did, and I thought it would be best to discuss it with you in person."

"She's right, you know. The thought of three potential heirs to one of the largest fortunes in history dying by accidental death is almost too much for coincidence. If you hadn't come back for me on the island, you would have been killed. I'm frightened Mark, for both of us."

"I'd be surprised if you weren't. I wasn't going to bring this up until tomorrow but there are some things I learned today you need to know." Rachel listened in horror as he related his conversations with Chad Ainsworth, his father, and Frank Zeller. He also told her about the increased security measures that had been installed in the house. "We should be safe here," he concluded.

"My God Mark, this thing is getting out of hand."

"The cat's out of the bag, Honey, and I've got a feeling it's just the beginning."

"Mark, "I'm so sorry I ever got you involved in all of this, she said on the verge of tears."

"You can't blame yourself for anything . . . ."

Before he could continue she handed him the folded paper. "What's this?" he asked.

"I can't undo anything that's been done," she replied, "but I wasn't the only one who nearly got killed. At least this will get you out of this mess."

It was a copy of their attorney/client agreement and Rachel had signed the cancellation clause.

For a moment Mark sat looking at the black empty ocean deep in thought.

With a smile she hadn't expected, he said, "Looks like I've been fired. Probably just as well because between us, there is already a serious legal conflict of interest."

Confused, she said, "I don't understand. What conflict of interest?"

"Well," he conceded, "It turns out that the Attorney has fallen in love with his client, and when the boat exploded it got real personal."

Rachel's jaw dropped in disbelief and she seemed frozen in place unable to form words. ". . . I, I mean . . ."

"You look more in shock than you did when the boat exploded."

She moved closer to him and said, "Kiss me and tell me again. I just want to make sure I heard you right."

He put his arms around her and kissed her, first gently and then with passion. He spoke softly with genuine sincerity. "I love you. I have from the first time I met you."

She looked in his eyes and said, "I love you too."

For nearly ten minutes they sat embraced, without talking, trying to understand the cascading emotions exploding in their minds.

Rachel leaned away from him and said, "Things just got a whole lot more complicated. How do we manage a love affair and fend off someone trying to kill us at the same time?"

"Fair question. Hopefully, the forensic team Frank Zeller is sending with the salvage crew will be able to confirm or reject Chad's theory. If they can determine it was not an accident, we'll have to circle the wagons and come up with a plan. Between the two of us, my father, Frank Zeller, and I would bet, Harold Sanders, we will have a formidable team. Now," he said, with emphasis, "How about we get out of the crime solving business for the night and get back to working on this love affair."

Without a second thought, she stood up and said, "Let's go inside." She went into the master bedroom with a promise, "I'll be out in a minute."

The final light of day was gone and Mark had earlier dimmed the lights in the house. When she appeared she was wearing a long sleeved white shirt like the one she had worn to the beach. Her slacks were gone and the shirt tail hung down just below her bottom. She took him by the hand and in the bedroom turned his back to the bed and gently shoved him to a sitting position. "Now, except for the blue jeans, I think this is about where we were on the beach before we were interrupted by a cruel force of nature. The rest is up to you."

Mark slid over on the bed and Rachel straddled him as she had done on the beach. Slowly, they began to unbutton each other's shirts. When he finished her buttons, she said, reaching behind her back, "I know you're a little clumsy. The bra and shirt fell to the floor. He reached up with his hands and cupped her full breasts. I think you've wanted to do that since the first day when I caught you looking down my dress as I leaned over to put sunscreen on my legs. "

"Guilty as charged, your honor," he confessed. I guess I wouldn't make a very good voyeur."

"You can look at any part of me any time you want. Just keep working on that bra snap and you will get the hang of it in no time. Meanwhile," she whispered as she lowered herself with her breasts on his chest, "I think we are safe from thunder and rain but there might be some lighting."

They were in love. They were together and all the stars were perfectly aligned.

Claiborne Plantation - 1852

The 1850s was Thomas Claiborne's opportunity to put his personal stamp on the family's agricultural and growing financial empire. He continued to expand the land holdings and the production of rice was setting new records every year. On land that couldn't be flooded for rice production, he planted indigo and produce, and he continued to expand the lumber and turpentine business. His talent for animal husbandry was demonstrated in herds of cattle developed through selective breeding and a large stable of race horses he hoped might one day challenge the best England had to offer. His acumen as a planter and businessman and leader of men soon became well known and he was being courted by the political factions from Columbia to Charleston.

Talk of secession was spreading through the State and culminated with an ordinance adopted by the legislature in 1852 to declare the right of South Carolina to secede from the Federal Union. He tried to be a voice of reason in a sea of discontent but the pro slavery and states' rights factions continued to intensify their efforts heading for an eventual showdown with the Federal Government. There were several outcomes of which Thomas was certain. If the political powers in South Carolina were ever successful in their pursuit of independence through secession from the Union and a Northerner and anti-slavery President occupied the white house; there would almost certainly be war. Even if many other Southern States would join with South Carolina, it would be a war the South could not win unless either England or France would join in the Southern cause and declare war on the Union.

One way or another, he believed slavery was operating on borrowed time and its abolition would destroy the slave plantation system of agriculture throughout the South. He began banking his share of the profits from the Claiborne plantations in France and hoped he would be ready if the clouds of war ever started raining bullets and bombs.

His greatest concern was for his children, Elizabeth and Robert, and as time went on, the woman who cared for them, Rachel. By her second year at Claiborne house, she had matured into a beautiful young woman, and her striking features were not lost on Thomas. The evening tutoring sessions, created in the spirit of learning, satisfied their growing mutual desire to be together. This alluring Creole woman was reading her way through Thomas's library and weaving her way into his heart.

One evening as Thomas was finishing work by lantern light in his study, Rachel paused in the doorway and said, "Good night Master Claiborne, I'm going to bed."

"Good night, Rachel," He replied.

As she turned to leave, Thomas quickly rose from his chair and gently took her arm, and said, "Please don't call me master anymore. Call me Thomas."

She smiled and replied gratefully, "I'll call you Thomas when we are together, but I can't when we aren't alone. What would the others think? They would be jealous and it would hurt their feelings."

He reluctantly conceded. "For the time being, but it won't be forever." They stood for a moment in silence facing each other. He put his arms around her and kissed her softly on the cheek. Pulling her to him until their bodies were touching, he moved his face from her cheek and kissed her on the lips. She neither yielded nor resisted.

Embarrassed and stepping back, he said, "I'm sorry Rachel. That was improper, but it's something I've wanted to do for a long time." In a manner of polite retreat, he concluded, "Good night. I'll douse the lanterns on my way to bed."

Without a word, Rachel walked out of the study, through the library, and proceeded up the stairs. She was in a state of ecstasy. Everything for which she had long hoped and dreamed seemed to be coming true. She had been taken by men before, but it had been as property rights and love had never been involved. She left his presence quietly because even if she could manage to find the words for a proper response, in her jumbled brain, she was too stunned to speak.

In his nightshirt, he pulled back the blankets on the bed ,and as he extinguished the lantern he was startled by her voice. "Thomas," she softly spoke as he turned. "It wasn't improper. I've long dreamed of you kissing me." He could see her silhouette in the doorway framed by the light from the moon shining through the windows. She stepped close and placed his hands on her waist. "I wouldn't object if you would like to do it again."

He pulled her close and began feeling the smooth curves of her body through the thin material of her nightgown as he kissed her repeatedly with more passion than he could remember. "My God, Rachel, I've wanted you for so long," he whispered as he searched for words and breath at the same time.

She calmly moved back a step. "You must know, Thomas, I'm not a virgin. I've been with men. I tried to avoid them, but the overseers at my old plantation took me at their will. I tried to resist once but all I got for my trouble was beaten and raped."

"Thomas put his finger to her lips. "It's all right. That will never happen to you here."

With her voice breaking, she said while looking into his eyes, "I hoped one day it could be my choice."

"Is it now?" he asked.

She spoke with conviction, "Yes."

He began trying to untie the bows that held her gown together from the waist up. Having little success, he said, "I guess I'm a little clumsy."

"Let me help you," she said with a smile. "They're like shoestrings. Just pull the cut end of a ribbon and it's done," she said as her fingers nimbly went down from her neck to her waist leaving the bows untied.

The gown fell to the floor when he pushed the top from her shoulders. He took her in his arms and kissed and caressed her. They made love late into the night as the moon rose in the Eastern sky and again just before the sun began to signal the dawning of a new day.

Thomas came down the stairs that morning carrying a satchel and wearing fine traveling clothes; dark brown breeches with white leggings and a ruffled white shirt and a day coat that matched his pants.

"Lawdy, Miss Rachel," one of the house maids exclaimed when he walked into the dining room for breakfast. "Just look at Master Claiborne all dressed up fancy for his trip to Charleston."

Rachel stepped in from the kitchen and replied with proper decorum, "You do look most presentable, Master Claiborne."

When the house maid left the room, Rachel leaned down from behind his chair and whispered in his ear, "You are the most handsome man in all of South Carolina."

Once each quarter he spent three or four days in Charleston, meeting with bankers, business associates, and on this occasion, potential investors in a railroad he was planning to build northwest from Georgetown upstate to connect with the main North/South line.

As a surprise, Rachel had fixed lunch for Thomas to enjoy on board the side-wheel steamer to Charleston. She intentionally waited until he left through the back door on his way to the docks and the riverboat that would take him to the steamer landing on the coast.

Acting surprised, Rachel proclaimed loud enough for all in the house to hear, "My word, Master Claiborne has gone off without his lunch." She grabbed the lunch box wrapped in cloth and headed down the path calling his name. Her timing was perfect as she reached him in a growth of trees where they were hidden from the sight of the house and the docks. "I made lunch for you," she said as she reached him. Thomas briefly looked at the packaged lunch before wrapping her in his arms and kissing her.

"We can't be long. Someone is sure to notice," she said.

"There's something I meant to tell you last night," he said with genuine sincerity.

"And what would that be?" she asked displaying some curiosity.

"I love you. I don't know exactly when it began but I've felt this way for some time. I have no way of knowing what roads we will travel, but know this; you are in my heart and it is filled with love." He gave her a final goodbye kiss and turned to continue down the path to the dock.

For the second time in two days, she had no words. She was in a world she had never known.

Chapter Eighteen

There had been little sleep in the beach house and its occupants had surrendered to the beckoning of the first rays of the sun dancing across the ocean water and beginning to warm the deck.

"We could have slept in," Rachel said with a yawn as she snuggled up next to Mark in her robe.

"We could have stayed in bed, but I don't think we'd have been sleeping," Mark replied with a statement that sounded more like an invitation. Together, they left the porch and went back to the bedroom.

By the time they had showered and eaten breakfast, the sun had turned to gray clouds and a light rain began to fall as promised by the morning weatherman. "If it's going to be an inside day, why don't we start going through some of Naomi's file boxes," Rachel offered. "I'm kind of anxious to see what's in them myself."

"I took them to Dad's office. We can spend the day and have lunch downtown."

"You're on," Rachel instantly agreed.

After several hours of shuffling through papers and making two stacks; one for further review, Mark came across a collection of annual financial reports that started all the way back to the year following Thomas Claiborne's death. Mark remembered Naomi's comment about Jack Claiborne cheating her out of a lot of money .when he was the Trust manager. He shared that thought with Rachel and said, "These reports don't seem to be very detailed. Many of the early ones are just one sheet and none more than two or three."

"It's the only thing she ever got; just one report a year. After Thomas died, I think the family was afraid to question anything. Most of them were glad to have a place to live and enough regular income to make due," Rachel replied.

"My dad's law firm often uses a forensic accountant and financial analyst in cases that involve accounting irregularity and fraud. I don't know what he can make of these, but we'll have him take a look."

Mark opened a manila envelope marked "pictures." "Who are the people in this picture?" he asked, handing it to Rachel.

"Isn't this a beautiful picture?" beaming as she spoke. "The man is Thomas Claiborne. The lady next to him is Rachel and the younger woman is their daughter, Mary. It was taken outside their home near La Rochelle on the coast of France. I would guess Mary was about fifteen or so at the time."

"Thomas was a nice looking man, but the women were simply beautiful." Turning his attention to Rachel, he said, "There is definitely a strong family resemblance."

With an appreciative smile, she replied, "Did someone teach you how to always say the right thing to a woman, or does it come naturally?"

They had lunch down the street in one of Charleston's eateries coveted by the locals.

They ordered coffee after lunch and settled into a conversation about the problem at hand.

"What can you tell me about the investigations into the deaths of your Aunt Jane and your parents?"

She disdainfully replied, "I don't even have to think about that one. The Sheriff's Department stamped Jane's death accidental the minute the autopsy was completed and closed the case. Naomi said that, even though Harold had just completed Law school, he was an emotional wreck and they blocked his every effort to continue the investigation. Back then, a young black lawyer had no chance against the good ole boys."

"You mean the Sheriff's department."

"Mostly, I mean the Claibornes. The sheriff and police chief and just about everyone else in the court house and city hall were puppets for the Claibornes. They were always the first to contribute to local charities and host fundraisers for public works and schools. From all appearances, they seemed to be classic benefactors. But, from what I've heard, through the bank and their investment company they had their hands in just about everyone's pocket."

"Jane died some years ago," Mark contemplated. "When you mentioned the Claibornes, you must have been referring mostly to Donald Claiborne's father."

"Jack Claiborne," she instantly responded. "Behind his shiny veneer, he was mean and ruthless, and," as a closing declaration, "a no good, black hating son-of-a-bitch."

Mark snapped back in his chair and, with a patronizing smile, responded, "Why Miss Devening, you should really try to not suppress your feelings."

"You better be nice to me," she said softly in his ear as she leaned over and touched his cheek with hers, "the next time you have your tongue in my mouth I might bite."

"Ouch," he yelped, "that would hurt. Back to the Claibornes," he directed, while still smiling from their exchange. "What about Donald? Is he as bad as his father?"

"Jack was old school but Donald would impress you as the consummate professional businessman and smooth as silk, but deceptive. When he speaks with you, he tries to make you feel like he is your best friend, and he's good at it. But once you get to know him, you realize he is just trying to use you. He got out of the daily operation of the bank but remained as Chairman of the Board. He also runs the land management and investment company his father started years ago."

"The bank is the manager of the Claiborne trust and I . . ."

She interrupted before he could finish his thought, "To hear Donald tell it, the Trust is strictly in the hands of the trust department and his only responsibility with his investment and land management company is to keep the land portion of the Trust rented and profitable."

"Sounds like you have gotten to know Mr. Claiborne rather well."

"I worked as a file clerk at the bank for two summers after I started college."

"And?" Mark inquired.

With a terse reply, "I finally got tired of him hitting on me and quit."

During the drive back to the beach house, Mark asked her if she had changed her mind about pursuing her fight for the trust in light of the boat explosion and little progress to show after nearly two weeks. "I have to admit, I think I was beginning to weaken, but our conversation at lunch about the Claibornes just got me fired up. I'm in this to the end. You?"

With a grin, he eagerly responded, "You might have fired your attorney, but you're not going to get rid of me."

As they neared the beach house the gentle rain was still falling and prompted a proposal from Mark. "Let's take a change of clothes and go back into town and spend the night on Sea Breeze."

"Sea Breeze? "Is that what I think it is? It's a boat, isn't it.? Are you kidding me? I don't care if I never see another boat, let alone sleep on one."

"It is a boat," he conceded. "Actually it's my parent's yacht, a big one. It has all the comforts of home and a fully stocked liquor cabinet. It's moored at the marina behind a security gate and we won't have to start the engine because it's on shore power. Best of all, it has the most comfortable bed you can imagine. Although, it's a little small, so two people have to sleep close together."

With only a little hesitation, she said, "Sold me, let's go."

On their way to the marina, they picked up a pizza and a bottle of red wine. Dressed in robes they finished the bottle by candlelight, listening to the tiffany of the rain playing on the cabin roof.

Chapter Nineteen

"Are you certain you don't mind if I spend the day with your mother?" Rachel asked as they crossed the bridge over the Cooper River on their way back to the beach house in the early Saturday morning fog.

"Do I mind? No. Will I miss you? Yes. Want to hear something crazy? Sometimes when I'm with you I miss you just thinking about not being with you." He looked at her and said, "I'm not even sure I understand what that means, except, I think it means I've got it bad."

"I hope it's incurable," she replied, placing her hand on his arm.

Mark's mother rang the doorbell at 9 AM as promised. "Good morning, Mrs. Bradley," Rachel said in a cheery voice as she opened the door. Mrs. Bradley gave her a quick hug, and responded, "Sweetheart, please call me Vivian, or better yet, Vie."

"Vie, it is," Rachel responded with a full smile. Mark's mother had earlier suggested that Rachel take the clothes she intended to wear to dinner that evening with them which would save her another round trip to the beach house. The plan was shopping in the morning and early afternoon following lunch and a stop at the beauty parlor in the afternoon and a massage if time allowed. "This way," she explained, "we won't be hurried and Mark can meet us at our house when it's time to go to dinner."

Mark smiled as he watched his mother's car head down the street on its way to the retail environs of Charleston. He brewed a pot of strong black coffee and took a cup to the deck where he leaned back in a beach chair recliner and became lost in the tranquil and mysterious beauty of the ocean. "A chance to think," he thought, and he had plenty to think about.

The deeper he dug into the Claiborne trust, the more he began to understand about Thomas Claiborne. By all accounts, he was a good man, but by whose standards? Rachel had made a point of telling him that Thomas treated his slaves well. Yet, the mere fact of keeping well treated slaves was, in and of itself, a contradiction. The birth of Thomas and Rachel's daughter, Mary, occurred several years after he brought her into the plantation house full time to care for his two children. Did that suggest that Thomas had not taken Rachel sexually, early on, as he had every legal right to do and, as Naomi had revealed, their's had developed into a loving relationship that had stood the test of time?

"Somewhere," he thought to himself, "there has to be some evidence that would prove Thomas was Mary's father and provide the missing link in the family lineage that would establish Rachel's inheritance according to Thomas's will." From what he had learned about Thomas's penchant for thoroughness in business and concern for the wellbeing of the slaves on his plantations and family, it didn't seem likely that he would allow the daughter he loved to face life without a surname and roots.

Mark lowered the back on the deck recliner and stretched out to take in the full measure of the sun. He was preoccupied with Thomas Claiborne and the travail he and Rachel must have endured sustaining their love during such tumultuous times. The social status that many mulattoes had often enjoyed before war clouds began to gather over the South had disappeared. Southern whites were afraid of the possibility of black uprisings and reprisals if the South were to lose the war and, regardless of skin color, mulattoes were grouped with all blacks who were shunned and pushed even deeper into the dregs of society.

Charleston, South Carolina 1864

Late at night a carriage driver pulled up in front of a home in Charleston and began loading luggage brought by a man from the house to the side of the street. Once the luggage was loaded, the man retreated to the house to accompany a woman and a child to the carriage.

From the candlelight coming through the windows, the driver caught a glimpse of the color of their skin, and said, "Mister, I'll take you to the docks but I'm not taking them."

"Good Lord, it's so late, no one is going to see us and, it's so dark, even if they did they wouldn't be able to tell . . ."

The driver interrupted and wasn't interested in listening to reason. "I told you, no blacks are going to ride in this carriage."

At that instant, the man pulled a revolver from inside his coat and shoved the muzzle against the driver's head. "Now," he commanded, "you are going to drive all of us to the docks or you will die. In which case, I will drive. The choice is yours."

The carriage traveled through the streets of the once proud city of Charleston which had been reduced during the war years from a booming city of over 40,000 to less than 10,000.

The southern half of the peninsula withstood a two year long bombardment from the sea and was now uninhabitable due to constant shelling. The only residents staying in the lower section were the residents too poor to find safe shelter and those who pillaged the unoccupied homes. [1]

A man came off the ship to meet them as the carriage pulled up to the gang plank. "Might you be Thomas Claiborne?"

---

[1] The Evacuation of Charleston
And the Last Days of Elizabeth and William Henry Suder by Bill Draper, 2014.

"I am, and to whom do I have the pleasure?"

"I am Captain Sean Hennley. If you will follow me, sir, I'll take you to your cabins and I'll have my men bring your luggage aboard."

In the light of the cabin, Thomas was surprised to see how young was the Captain of this mighty side-wheel steamer. "No disrespect Captain; however, I would have thought the Captain of this vessel would be much older."

"No disrespect taken, Mr. Claiborne. Blockade running is a nasty business. A lot of the Captains are dead and many of the rest would rather sit on land than take unnecessary chances."

"Do you expect any problems getting out of the harbor tonight?"

"There is just one Union frigate outside the harbor standing guard. But there is no moon tonight and she probably won't even see us. Besides, the sea tonight is dead calm with no wind to fill her sails.

After a two day trip to Nassau in the Bahamas and a week at the newly constructed Grand Victoria Hotel, the travelers boarded a fast clipper ship bound for La Rochelle, France. Their stay in Nassau was the first time they had been in public together and, much to his displeasure, Rachel dressed and bore the role of a servant and nanny to her master's daughter to avoid the scrutiny of the blockade runners and freebooters who swarmed the hotel. As had been his custom for many years, Thomas would sit each evening to make his daily diary entry.

"Thomas," Rachel commented at the end of their third day at sea while he was blowing the ink dry in his latest entry, "for as long as we have been together you have never missed a day."

"It serves several purposes," he replied. "It's a business journal and a family journal, but most of all, I think it makes me a better man."

"Strange," she replied with curiosity, "how so?"

"Each day I realize that whatever I say or do might be recorded in my journal and sometimes it gives me pause to consider if I am saying or doing the right thing."

"Did it give you pause when you threatened to kill the carriage driver back in Charleston?"

Looking first at their daughter, Mary, asleep in her sea bunk and then directly at the woman he loved, he responded, "Not in the least, and it's duly recorded."

Thomas stayed in France with Rachel and Mary for several days while the ship was taking on provisions before heading for England, where Thomas intended to spend some time with Elizabeth and Robert before heading back to South Carolina. On the day of departure, they stood at the wharf for an extended farewell. Thomas assured them that they would be in good hands with Monsieur Charbonnet. "This terrible war can't last much longer," he told Rachel. "I'll be back as soon as possible."

"I know you will," Rachel replied, as she began to cry.

It was the first time they had been apart for more than a few days since the day she first came into the Plantation house to care for his children. She prayed for his safe return and longed for the day they could walk proudly down the street side by side without the color of her skin being a social hindrance.

Chapter Twenty

With Rachel out for the day with his mother, Mark decided to continue going through the file boxes at the Bradley Law Office. One thing that seemed conspicuous by its absence was any personal correspondence between Thomas and Rachel during the years she spent in France. Just one letter with a salutation that read, "Dear Rachel and my daughter Mary," or any other reference by Thomas referring to Mary as his or their daughter might convince the Judge to order the county to issue a birth certificate for Mary. But there were no letters to be found.

When he tired of sorting through papers, he decided to take a look at the Claiborne trust property on the county's GIS (Land Survey) system online. In short order, the entire property and all the surrounding land were revealed with all of the established boundaries, public and common easement and pertinent survey notations. The size of the trust property was simply immense and even taking out the barrier island with the beach and all of the marsh lands, there were still more than several thousand acres suitable for crop production. Although Mark knew little to nothing about farming, the very size of the property seemed to belie the amount of income Naomi derived from the property.

As he glanced at the properties surrounding the Claiborne Trust, he noticed that many of the parcels were owned by different corporate entities. "Nothing unusual about companies owning property," he thought. But he noted the preponderance of corporate ownership seemed peculiar.

The telephone ringing broke his concentration. "There was no answer at the beach house and I thought I might find you at the office," his dad said. "I'll come on over if you don't mind hanging around for a while."

"Come ahead," Mark replied, "I'd enjoy the company.

A half hour later Joe Bradley walked into the conference room followed by Harold Sanders.

"Uncle Harold," Mark exclaimed as he rose from the conference tables covered with assorted papers from the file boxes, "What a nice surprise. What brings you down to the Low Country?"

As they took seats at the table, Harold replied, "The court is in recess for the rest of the month and I thought this would be a good opportunity to see how things are going with your investigation." After a brief pause, he continued, "However, the break in at the house on the Isle of Palms and the boat explosion are unsettling, to say the least. I never intended to get you involved in a burglary and attempted murder investigation, especially since you and my niece seem to be the intended victims."

"Mark," Joe said, "Frank Zeller called and said the preliminary forensic report on the explosion is in and asked if he could meet with us. He should be here any minute."

"Gentlemen," Frank began as he took his seat at the table. "The full report won't be finished for several weeks but I wanted you to hear the preliminary results. The fact is, there aren't any. Chad Ainsworth's theory is certainly plausible but, so far, the evidence doesn't support any wrongdoing. However, we can't conclude that this was just an accident. The explosion blew the motor and transom onto the shore and shredded the fuel line. The lab techs found a small cut in the line but the heat from the fire fried the insides of the opening masking any trace evidence that a razor or sharp knife would have left. They are continuing to look at it. The electrical components of the bilge pump along with the wires that Chad said could have been shorted out to make sparks were next to the external fuel tank when it exploded. The full report may reveal some additional information, but I doubt it. Right now, I'd say it's 50/50."

"A fifty percent chance it was an accident, "Mark offered, "and a fifty percent chance it was attempted murder?"

"That's about the size of it."

"I know we all appreciate your fast response to this matter, but it sure doesn't give us much to go on."

"Joe, I pushed this investigation along as a favor to you. This meeting never took place and I never said what I'm going to say."

With a nod from Joe, Frank continued, "We all know there is only one person who has motive. He's the only one who will benefit from Rachel's death and, I hate to say, the size of the fortune at stake would turn more peaceful men into killers." With that said he looked directly at Mark and issued stern advice "Be careful son. This is dangerous territory."

"I agree," Mark said solemnly, "but you said it's 50/50 and it could have been just an accident.

"You're right," Frank said, "but let me ask you; does it make you feel any better knowing there's only a 50 percent chance someone tried to kill you?" The silence in the conference room was deafening.

Frank was stopped on his way out by Mark's question. "Has the press picked up on this?"

"A reporter from the newspaper is due in my office in thirty minutes. He will want to know why the FBI and Coast Guard are involved. Simple enough, it happened in an area under Federal jurisdiction, and unexplained incidents of this magnitude are always investigated.

Finally, he will get around to asking if we suspect foul play. Answer; we never jump to conclusions. I don't think I have to tell you what inferences the readers will make. Gentlemen, have a good day."

. . . .

After thoughtfully studying the matter for several minutes, Harold concluded, "I think it's too risky to go on. I said earlier that no amount of money is worth putting anyone's life in jeopardy. I plan to stay with Naomi over the weekend before going home. I'll tell her about our decision and I know she will agree. Besides, Naomi inherited the house in Georgetown directly from Thomas' will, outside of the trust. It's worth a lot of money and I know it will be left to Rachel in Naomi's will. She has also provided Rachel with a substantial life insurance policy. None of this can compare to the value of the Claiborne Trust, but Rachel will do nicely."

"Harold," Joe replied, "There is a difference between surrender and following a prudent path. I agree the time has come to pull the plug on this effort. Mark, I'm sure you concur?"

Mark was standing and pensively staring through the window at the traffic on the street below when his father posed the question. Without an answer forthcoming, Joe asked again, "Mark, don't you agree?"

Without turning away from the window, he tersely responded, "No, I don't agree." He wheeled around and placed both of his hands firmly on the table. "And I'm quite sure Rachel won't agree. Instead of backing away, we need to hit them with what we've got and keep on digging." Feeling emboldened by his conversation that morning with Rachel and the anger growing within him, he continued. "Dad, I'd like you to file another petition with the court to have a birth certificate issued for Thomas and Mary's daughter, Mary."

"Whoa, young man," Joe petulantly responded. "Even if I wanted to, which I don't, it would just get rejected like the last time."

"No question, "Mark agreed, "But just like the boat explosion, it will make the newspapers. We need to remind folks, as well as Donald Claiborne, that the fight over this estate has not gone away. With the new publicity provided by the newspapers, free of charge, if any harm comes to Rachel or me; even an attempt, Mr. Claiborne would immediately become the only person of interest to law enforcement. They would be on him like a gator looking for lunch and he knows it." He began to laugh. "History repeats itself. It will be in Mr. Claiborne's best interest, or any of his possible accomplices, to keep us safe and out of harm's way. Just like old Thomas Claiborne set up his will to force the bank and the Claiborne descendants into keeping Naomi safe all these years.

"Well, I don't know, I . . ." Joe began to reply before being interrupted,"

"I do," Mark retorted.

He picked up the package from the table with Naomi's annual statements from the bank and placed them in front of his father. "While we are stirring up the shit, we might as well hit them with this while we're at it. These financial statements are brief and don't provide much detail for analysis. After you file the petition, you should send a letter to the trust department at the bank requesting copies of all the records necessary to conduct a thorough audit of the Trust finances as far back as the law allows. I'm sure your forensic accounting firm can provide you with a list of items to ask for."

Forcing himself to at least consider the merit of Mark's plans, he asked, "And what do we expect to find?"

"Probably nothing. Donald is a licensed investment and land manager and the Claiborne Trust is just one of his clients. I can't believe he would risk losing his license for skimming money from the Trust, especially when he appears to be so close to the big prize. Naomi was convinced that old Jack Claiborne cheated her out of money for years until you got involved, Uncle Harold, but there is no evidence to indicate that Donald has been cheating her. If the letter serves only to remind Mr. Claiborne that we are watching him like a hawk, our efforts will be well served. What's your take on it, Uncle Harold?"

"I'm familiar with the subject of fiduciary responsibility and malfeasance," Harold answered with a gleam in his eyes; "However, the rules of conduct in my current position would not permit me to discuss anything regarding this matter. Besides, like Mr. Zeller, I never attended this meeting. The mile wide smile on the Justice's face provided all the response necessary.

"Listen," Mark exclaimed, we all hope we can turn up some type of written evidence attesting to Rachel's relationship with Thomas Claiborne. Other than a birth certificate for Mary, I'm not sure what that would be. Without it, Rachel will miss out on the big prize when Naomi passes. However, if the Claibornes and the bank have been regularly cheating her out of substantial amounts of profit from the trust, at least we can go after them as a backup plan.

"All right Son, it looks like you have won the day, but why don't you file the petition with the court and write the letter to the Trust department. After all, you're her attorney."

"Actually Dad, I'm not," Mark responded with a slightly crafty look on his face and tone in his voice. "She fired me . . . but it was inconsequential. I was about to resign anyway."

"What the hell!" Joe bellowed.

"It turns out there has developed a serious conflict of interest in the attorney/client relationship between myself and Miss Devening."

"And what would that be?" Harold asked, forgetting that he was not at the meeting."

"We're in love, and far beyond the point of impartial judgment and behavior." With a big grin growing on his face, Mark abandoned all of his refined education and upbringing and announced, while shaking his head in a show of disbelief. 'I guess you never think it can happen to you until it does."

Joe and Harold looked at each other in disbelief one minute and understandable acceptance the next.

"Dad, you are still her primary attorney of record, and as long as I am representing the company, I could not be made to testify in a case involving the firm's client. This change will simply require that any legal decisions made in her regard will have to come through you."

Chapter Twenty One

After spending the morning shopping with little to show for their efforts, other than sore feet, the ladies found relief in a booth at the Meeting Street grill where they stopped for lunch. Vivian Bradley declared, "I'd like to have a word with some of the people who designed those awful clothes we've been looking at."

"Not much to look at," Rachel agreed.

"Sweetheart, when you get to be my age, it takes just the right outfit; but you would look great in a gunny sack."

Trying to hide her embarrassment, Rachel replied, "That's kind of you Mrs. Bradley, but I don't think they would let me in the restaurant this evening in a gunny sack."

"In all honesty Rachel, you are such a beautiful young woman and," she continued after a short pause, "I'm sure that fact has not been lost on my Son. I mean, I know he is your attorney but he isn't blind. Damn," she said sounding disgusted with herself, "I know I sound just like a matchmaking, meddlesome mother. Please forgive me."

She reached across the table and placed her hand on Vivian Bradley's hand. "There is nothing to forgive, Mrs. Bradley." Mark's mother's face revealed sheer astonishment as Rachel continued. "Mark is no longer my attorney in this inheritance matter. He was going to resign, but I beat him to the punch and fired him." Rachel continued with "the rest of the story."

As they stood to leave, Vivian put her hand on Rachel's waist and kissed her lightly on the cheek. "I've always known Mark is smart. I guess I never realized just how smart he is. And lucky," she added as a quick afterthought.

The ladies rounded out the afternoon with a massage at a downtown spa and a trip to Vivian's favorite hair salon for a manicure and trim. As much as Vivian wanted to question Rachel endlessly about her relationship with her son, she spoke little of it, not wanting to jinx it.

Mark arrived at the Bradley home by cab at seven and joined his father in the study for a cocktail. "The ladies should be down shortly," Joe said. "Just so you are not caught by surprise, Rachel told your mother about your, uh, relationship."

"Sounds like the cats out of the bag," Mark replied with a smile. "Good, I don't think either one of us is very good at keeping secrets, especially when it's not necessary."

"Mark, I don't know where this is headed, but we both think the world of Rachel and if I say anything else about it I will wind up sticking my foot in my mouth. So", he continued, "we're going to the Cypress room for dinner. They have a small dance floor and a pianist who plays great slow music. .And they keep the lights low enough to eat by candlelight, and . . . I know, the ambiance is romantic and I'm doing exactly what I said I wouldn't."

As the conversation ensued after their order was placed it was obvious that everyone, especially Mark's parents, was treating the subject most on their mind like a gorilla in the room, difficult to evade. Finally, Mark set everyone at ease. "Look, he said in a rational tone, we are in love and that's a good thing. And good things are to be discussed and celebrated, not avoided."

"I'll propose a toast to love," Joe offered with a feeling of relief. All four glasses clinked and the night was on.

After dinner, both couples accepted the invitation to all from the piano player to dance. As they began to move about the floor, Mark said with an approving smile. "That's the same dress you wore for lunch last Sunday at Naomi's house. I love it. You look spectacular."

"I'm sure it's not fashionable to wear the same dress twice in such a short time, but you seemed to like it."

Halfway through the first dance, Mark began to slowly lower his hand down Rachel's back and continued until he thought he had gone slightly beyond the point of propriety. He could feel her curves through the delicate fabric and asked with suspicious curiosity, "Are you wearing any . . . ?"

Before he could finish she reached around and moved his hand back to her waist. "No I'm not," she stated in a succinct whisper. "I forgot to pack clean ones when I left with your mother this morning. And keep your hands where they are supposed to be."

"I'll be a true Southern gentleman for the rest of the evening," he dutifully responded. "You have my word; at least until we get home."

"I'll settle for that," she cheerfully responded.

Mark kept his word, and so did she.

Chapter Twenty Two

Mark slipped quietly out of bed and pulled the bedroom door closed behind him, trying not to disturb Rachel who was still sleeping soundly. He was sitting on the front porch with a freshly made cup of coffee when he saw the paper boy coming up the street. "You got an extra paper?" he asked as the boy walked by the Bradley beach house.

The young man tossed him a rolled up paper. "The Millers down the street are out of town. You can have theirs."

Before Mark could dig in his pocket for some money to reward his generosity, the paper boy turned the corner and disappeared. In the lower right hand corner of the front page read the headline, "FBI investigates boat explosion on the Intracoastal Waterway. "A picture showed the scene of the explosion with the dock half torn away. On page six where the article continued, there were pictures of both he and Rachel. His was a graduation picture from law school his mother had sent to the paper and Rachel's had been gleaned from a recent yearbook at the community college in Georgetown. For the most part, it was a reasonably accurate article and, as Frank had predicted, would leave most any reader with the possibility of foul play.

As the Bradley party was finishing Sunday brunch at the Charleston Yacht Club after church, Mark laid the folded paper he had brought with him from his car and placed it open on the table in front of his dad.

"Got to give Frank credit," his father acknowledged after reading the article. "It pretty much tells the story. I hope you're right, Mark. I hope it keeps the two of you safe."

"We'll see," Mark responded while taking Rachel's hand. "Now it begins."

. . . .

On their way back to the Isle of Palms, Mark summed up the situation. "It's not likely we will ever know more about the boat explosion; whether it was attempted murder or an accident. As far as an audit of the trust finances is concerned, who knows? They might be as clean as the driven snow, or we might find they have been engaged in cooking the books for years. We could wind up filing suit for mismanagement or malfeasance and nail them for a lot of money. Even so," he continued, "that wouldn't get us any closer to the big prize. DNA testing is out. The only way we are going to prove that you are a direct descendant of Thomas Claiborne and legal heir to the estate is to find some rock solid evidence that the court will accept. After a short period of thoughtful silence, he concluded, "And I have no idea what that would be."

"All we can do is to keep looking and hope to get lucky," Rachel lamented. With an uplifted tone, she said, "In the meanwhile, why don't we spend the afternoon at the beach and put all of this business out of our minds for the rest of the day."

"What business are you talking about?"

"You know; the boat and the estate and . . . Oh! You bum. You really get a kick out of getting my goat, don't you? That's all right. You just keep doing it, but keep one thing in mind, paybacks are hell. With a big smile and a smug look of satisfaction, she warned, "And the best part will be, you'll never see it coming."

. . . .

On the pretense of needing to make copies of papers for an 8 o'clock Monday morning meeting in his office, Donald Claiborne pulled out of his driveway. Instead of turning off highway 17 and heading for downtown, he continued south, crossed the bridge over the Sampit River and turned on the old county road that ran along the Waccamaw River and Intracoastal Waterway. The road was not well maintained and was dotted with a few farms and homesteads. Several miles south of town he turned left onto a paved lane bordered by a white estate fence on each side that ended at a surprisingly large house in a clearing on the Marsh.

The person he was looking for was working on a small fishing boat on a trailer parked in the drive. Claiborne slammed his car door and approached the boat. "Luke, he yelled, "what in the hell were you thinking? I told you to keep an eye on them, not kill them."

Luke dropped the wrench he was holding. "Accidents happen. Besides, who said anything about trying to kill someone," he answered with a look of pure hate on his face,"

"The newspaper, you idiot, right on the front page of the Sunday paper. The FBI is investigating. They didn't say they suspect it was anything more than an accident, but they are going to continue to investigate. Now, who do you suppose will be their number one suspect?"

"I'd say that would be you." With that, Luke grabbed Claiborne by the front of his shirt with his greasy hands and shoved him against the boat. "I did your dad's dirty work for years and I'm tired of taking your shit. When old lady Richards dies, a part of that estate you inherit will be mine. Now, that lawyer boy is nosing around, and all you can say is he won't be able to find anything. I've waited around for too many years to take any chances. I'll stay away from them, but if the day comes that Rachel Devening is awarded the trust, I'll kill you before the sun sets. Get the hell out of here."

During his drive back to town, Claiborne realized that Luke Bratton had long since outlived his usefulness. The big question was how to get rid of him.

. . . .

After a long walk on the beach and talking about things that people in love talk about, Mark put a grill on the fire pit for a seafood boil. Into the pot they layered lobster, potatoes, clams, sausage, and corn. A bottle of white wine topped off the feast. When there was nothing left but shells and corn cobs, Mark wrapped a blanket around them to ward off the cool night air. Sometimes, things are simply as good as they can be.

Chapter Twenty Three

Early Monday morning Rachel left for Georgetown and Mark followed a few minutes later. Rachel needed to prepare lesson plans for her classes on Tuesday and Thursday and Mark intended to begin searching through the archives at the local historical society on the off chance that he might run into some document that might make reference to Thomas Claiborne and his daughter, Mary. He knew it was unlikely, but hoped the search might give him inspiration. They planned to meet for lunch at a café with sidewalk tables on Front Street.

"How are the lesson plans coming?" he asked as they were seated.

"Slow. How about your search?"

"Slower," he commented.

"Mark," I reported the loss of our boat to the insurance company. They said it was old and hard to determine a value but they would replace it if I could find something like it."

"Chad Ainsworth has something similar. I saw it when I went to talk to him about the explosion. If anyone can help us, he's the man."

Halfway through lunch, Mark noticed a man get out of late model pickup on the other side of the street and head for a local bar and grill. He was the traffic officer who had made him move his car at Naomi Richard's house.

"Rachel, quick, look at that man across the street. Do you recognize him?"

"Sure, that's Luke Bratton. Why do you ask?"

He told her the story of the parking incident and finished with, "The guy's a real jerk. He treated me like I had committed a felony."

"You've got that part right. He's been around Georgetown for as long as I can remember. He showed up in Georgetown before I was born and hooked up with Jack Claiborne from the beginning. Some folks thought he was related to the Claibornes but it was just a rumor they denied. He's an auxiliary cop. He does traffic control on occasion and other odd jobs for the police Department. He's not stupid. He seems to be well educated and speaks perfect English with a hint of a British accent in a red neck sort of way. Mostly, he works for the Claiborne Management Company in the land rental business and he flies Claiborne's airplane they keep hangared at the airport.

"What does he do for the management company?"

"Nobody really knows but whatever it is he seems to get paid well." She pointed through the small riverside park.to the marina. "That big fishing boat with the two motors tied up at the city dock belongs to Luke. I guess he looks after all of the cropland in the Trust and makes sure that the tenant farmers are meeting their crop production agreements. Stan Watson has been responsible for maintaining the Claiborne mansion and surrounding property for years, but he reports to Luke Bratton."

"I'll bet that's hard for Stan to swallow."

"He can't stand him; like almost everyone else. Jack Claiborne, Donald's father, was domineering. He controlled everything and everyone around him, except Luke Bratton. According to Naomi and the Watsons, old Jack let Bratton do about whatever he wanted; almost as if Luke had some power over him."

"How about his relationship with Donald?"

"Hard to tell. You very seldom see them together. People say that Donald got him the police job to work just enough hours to get health insurance. Other than that, he has always worked for the Claibornes. He's a real creep and he frightens me. His wife finally got tired of his abuse and left him about five years ago."

A moment later, Rachel glanced down the sidewalk and commented, "Speak of the devil, Donald Claiborne is walking this way."

Claiborne recognized Rachel and walked directly toward her. "Rachel," he said in a voice that sounded like the epitome of sincerity, "I read the article in yesterday's paper. My God, I hope you are all right."

"I'm fine," she responded as he stepped aside to clear a path on the sidewalk and placed his hand on her back."

"Ouch," she winced. "Well, almost fine. Nothing like a piece of exploding boat in the back to ruin your day. Donald, I would like you to meet Mark Bradley."

Mark stood and shook hands.

"Are you new to this area Mark, or just visiting?"

"I'm from Charleston," Mark replied.

Claiborne looked at his watch and said, "I've got to be going or I'll be late for the City Council meeting. Nice to have met you Mr. . . . ."

"Bradley," Mark replied, "Mark Bradley."

As Claiborne headed down the street, Rachel leaned toward Mark and spoke softly, "I told you he was a liar. He knows who you are and more about you than you can possibly imagine."

Rachel returned to her lesson plans and Mark spent the rest of the afternoon looking through old records at the Historical Society before returning to the Isle of Palms. There seemed to be no shortage of references to Thomas Claiborne given the fact that he was the biggest rice producer in the biggest rice export area in the world during the years before the war. Yet, he could find no old newspaper articles or other printed accounts of his personal life. "There's always tomorrow," he thought on his drive home,

Chapter Twenty Four

The next morning Mark stopped at the Bradley Law Firm to talk with Phyllis Agan, the attorney who handled most of the firm's real estate cases. He gave her a little background in the Claiborne trust and told her about much of the surrounding land owned by a variety of corporations.

"Let's have a look," she said while bringing up the county GIS mapping system on her computer. "It's certainly not unusual for corporations to own property." However, she conceded that the concentration of corporate ownership surrounding the Claiborne Trust property was unusual.

Mark said, "I can't help thinking they all might be connected in some way but I'm just not experienced enough in real estate law to know how and where to start looking."

Looking at the stack of folders on her desk, she considered the matter and made Mark a proposition. . "Look, my assistant is on vacation this week and I'm about buried. You clerk for me until we get through this pile of folders, and then we will take a closer look at this land ownership situation."

Phyllis had been with the firm for nearly twenty years and was a crackerjack real estate attorney. Mark knew he had a good deal. "I'm yours," he said with a grin, "and lunch is on me."

By 2:PM Phyllis' desk was clean and she brought up the government mapping system on her computer. "Mark, you've been a great help. When you get around to joining the law firm; if you're interested in real estate law, come see me. This part of the firm's business is growing and it looks like you would be a natural. I have a feeling this little project of yours is going to take the rest of the day. I'm sure you have other things to do. I'll call you if I have any questions. Oh, by the way, thanks for lunch," she said with a smile.

Mark spent the rest of the afternoon going through more of Naomi's file boxes. Little by little, Mark was developing a mental picture of the life of Thomas Claiborne from the time he arrived in South Carolina until he died nearly eighty years later. Newspaper articles, old photos, business journals, and personal letters all provided threads that he was beginning to weave into a vision. He was beginning to understand the man.

On his way out of the office at closing time he glanced in Phyllis' office to see her working on his land query. He knew she would work late. She always did.

Phyllis was in the coffee room the next morning when Mark walked in. "There are several more file folders on my desk," she said; "mostly real estate transactions. Why don't you start through them while I finish up your job? I'm going to need most of the morning."

"Sounds like you might be into something," Mark anxiously replied. "Mind giving me a little review?"

With a laugh, she replied, "Not now Mr. Claiborne. But as soon as I'm finished, you will have the whole thing."

"I'll get started on those transactions," Mark said as he started to leave.

"Oh, Mark," Phyllis interjected. "It's all looking very interesting."

Mark was sitting in his father's office engaged in idle conversation when Phyllis came in a little after noon. He jumped up and offered her a seat. "I can't wait to hear what you have turned up."

"You're not getting off that easy," she stated. "This is going to take a while and we're going to discuss it over a very long lunch, which you are buying."

"Just point the way," Mark eagerly responded.

"One other thing," she mentioned sneaking a wink at Mark's father. "I'm going to need to take the rest of the day off. I don't suppose, Mark, you know anyone in this firm with enough authority to approve that?"

"I just might," he responded with a smile.

"Joe," she went on, "my paralegal is on vacation. How about assigning me hot shot here for the rest of the week?"

"He's all yours," Joe responded with alacrity. He knew his son had just been given a professional compliment of the highest order. "Mark, one more thing. Take Phyllis to the Terrace Room at the Charleston Hotel for lunch and sign my name on the tab."

When the table was cleared, Phyllis retrieved a folder from her briefcase and opened it on the table. "I'm going to give you the short version," she said. "We'll tackle any questions you have when I'm finished."

"I'm all ears," Mark replied with a smile and his hands clasped behind his head as he leaned back in his chair."

"To begin with, all of these properties were acquired by corporations over a period of about a year, and that was about five years ago. These corporations, mostly LLCs, are registered in three different states. Ironically, I handled the sale of one of the smaller parcels. It was the fastest closing I've ever been in. Another local attorney represented the buyer. The one thing I found a little peculiar was the selling price. I'm familiar with land values in that area and this struck me as being much higher than for what it would have appraised,"

"Is that it?" Mark asked.

"Not by a long shot. Here's where it gets interesting. All of these corporations are owned by a land management company called Land Resource Management, in Raleigh, North Carolina." Phyllis took a sip of water and quietly announced as she set down her glass, "It gets better. Land Resource Management is owned outright by a company in Atlanta called Real Estate Wealth Management, REWM for short."

"Sounds like somebody has gone to a lot of trouble to hide their land acquisitions," Mark mused.

"And a lot of land it is," Phyllis noted, "and a lot of money. Oh, I almost forgot," she stated with a hint of cynicism. "The majority partner in REWM; I believe 98 percent," she said after consulting her notes, "is our own Mr. Donald Claiborne."

Mark had been leaning his chair back on two legs during her presentation and nearly lost it. "Finally," he said with a clenched fist, "we might be getting somewhere."

"There is a little more, Mark. On the day of closing for each land sale, a first mortgage was filed in the full amount of the purchase price on behalf of the lender which is a bank headquartered in Raleigh. These land parcels all sold for top dollar and I can't believe they produce enough revenue to amortize the loans."

Mark's mind was spinning and he was thinking out loud. "No bank would intentionally place itself in a negative position. With no down payments, they would have required additional and substantial collateral." After a pause to collect his thoughts, Mark wondered aloud, "It begs the questions; what did Claiborne use as collateral and where does the money come from to make the payments?"

The waiter came by and asked, "Will there be anything else?" Mr. Bradley.

"As a matter of fact, there is. We have a special occasion and I would like to offer my guest a toast. For that, I think two glasses of champagne would be in order."

. . . .

After listening to his Son's account of Claiborne's land acquisitions, Joe inquired, "When did he begin buying up all this land?"

"Five or six years ago. Why do you ask?"

"It's pretty clear why he wants the land. All of it together forms a perfect protective barrier surrounding the trust property. When Walt Disney bought the land to build Disneyland in Anaheim, California, he bought just enough for the theme park. Almost overnight land speculators swarmed in and bought up the surrounding property and it was turned into cheap hotels, pawn shops, souvenir stores, and low life businesses. Disney swore it would not happen again and when he bought the land to build Disney World outside of Orlando he bought a lot of the surrounding land to protect his investment. I'm certain that's what Donald Claiborne has in mind. He doesn't want a lot of trashy development surrounding his dream. His timing coincides with two other events that happened at about the same time. First of all, Naomi suffered a minor stroke. Even though she recovered fully, it drew attention to the fact that she didn't have much time left. That was also when the courts denied our petition to grant Mary a birth certificate showing Thomas Claiborne as her father. At that point, Donald Claiborne would have felt secure enough to take on the risk of the land purchases."

Joe Bradley called his receptionist and told her he would be in a conference for the remainder of the afternoon. "Nothing better to relieve stress and open the mind than about three fingers of Maker's Mark," he suggested as he opened a paneled cabinet door revealing a small bar with liquor and glasses. "Care to join me?"

With a little fine sipping whiskey to assuage their predicament, father and son sat quietly in thought, contemplating their next move; if they had one.

Finally, Joe spoke up. "Mark, I think Mr. Donald Claiborne is in hock up to his neck. When his father, Jack, died some years ago he provided for Donald's mother with a lifetime annuity and divided most of his liquid assets between his three sisters. Donald received the bank stock. Even though it was worth a lot of money there was very little ready cash. Between his bank income as Chairman of the Board and his land management and investment company, I'm sure he has a substantial income. But he and his wife spend money like drunken sailors; trips to Europe, private schools for their children and they attend just about every social event in Charleston. They run with a fast high dollar crowd. My guess is that he is cash poor and used his bank stock as the collateral he needed to secure the loans to buy all of the surrounding lands and he has been scraping the bottom of the barrel to make the payments."

"Dad, if what you say is true, Donald is on a very slippery slope and he knows it. Who knows what he might do if he suddenly feels threatened?"

"You mean like receiving my letter requesting all the financial information from the Trust for an audit?"

Chapter Twenty Five

Rachel's phone rang at seven o'clock Thursday morning. Mark was talking before she had a chance to say hello. "If you pack your bag now, you can take it with you to school and you won't have to go back home after class."

"The bag is already packed, smart aleck and Mrs. Watson has offered, once again, to stay with Grandmother until Monday. Instead of seven o'clock tonight, I can be there by about 5:30. By the way, I didn't receive an invitation. I guess you just assumed I would be coming. A girl does like to be courted, you know."

"Evidently, you haven't checked your email. Take a look."

Rachel turned to her laptop on the kitchen table and opened her email.

An unopened letter from the previous night read: *"Mr. Mark Bradley requests the pleasure of your company at the beach house for an extended romantic weekend. Hors d'oeuvres and cocktails will be served on the deck at 6:00 PM. Dinner and other activities to follow."*

"Exactly, what other activities did you have in mind?"

. . . .

During an early morning conference with his father at the Bradley Law offices, Mark was at a dead end in his quest to find some kind of documentation that would prove Mary was Thomas and Rachel's daughter. Joe's expression suddenly turned optimistic. He suggested, "Thomas Claiborne was one of the wealthiest businessmen on the South Carolina Coast and he was involved in just about every venture one could imagine. Hard to imagine that he wasn't involved in some type of legal action. Why don't you start looking through the old court records? I wouldn't place a lot of hope in it, but it's better than what you have now, which is nothing."

"It's worth a try," Mark replied.

"All the old records are on microfilm at the courthouse annex. Better take your lunch. It will be slow going," Joe conceded as he left the conference room to tend to the morning mail.

"Slow going doesn't begin to describe this," Mark thought as he familiarized himself with the microfilm libraries and viewing equipment at the annex. In its day, microfilm was a huge technological breakthrough for document storage and retrieval. Instead of many weeks, Mark figured his search would be reduced to days instead of a matter of minutes with modern computer based information storage. Thomas Claiborne's land holdings and business interest spanned three counties, Charleston, Georgetown and Horry. Today's effort would just be the beginning.

Mark wanted to get across the Cooper River before rush hour traffic and was about to unload his last microfilm from the viewer when he ran across a case titled Claiborne vs. Jennings. It was a civil case brought by Claiborne for breach of contract. The court found in favor of the complainant, Thomas Claiborne, and the defendant was ordered to comply with the terms of the contract, forthwith. If the defendant was unable to comply for any reason, the court would determine a proper financial settlement. The only court recorder's note stated that the judge had allowed a diary entry by the claimant as written evidence of the contract. All Mark knew was that there had been a trial and Thomas had won. Other than that, nothing. Perplexed could hardly describe Mark's feeling as he headed for the beach house on the Isle of Palms. "Perhaps," he thought, "a report of the trial might have been published in the newspaper." It would be his first stop on Monday.

Chapter Twenty Six

When her last class ended at five o'clock, Rachel was the first person out the door. Her life had begun to revolve around Mark Bradley and he was just an hour away. She had all the classic symptoms of a person in love; no appetite, a mind spinning out of control, and a stomach filled with butterflies. But there was a sense of foreboding. There was a conversation she knew they would have sooner or later. She simply didn't realize how soon it would be.

As promised, Mark had shrimp in Creole sauce and cocktails ready by the fire pit when she arrived. He spent the first twenty minutes telling her about his discovery of Donald Claiborne's clandestine purchase of the land surrounding the Trust property. "It doesn't get us any closer to proving your entitlement to the Claiborne estate," he said, "but it might help us pressure him into a big settlement in your favor if we wind up suing him for mismanagement of the Trust."

"Mark," she said while moving closer to him in the patio love seat, "I know how determined you are to help me, but for the next few days I'd like to put business aside."

With an agreeable grin, he replied, "As I was saying, I think we should table all these estate discussions until Monday. The night is young. What would you like to do?"

With no hesitation, she replied, "Eat pizza, drink wine and whatever floats our boat for as long as we can keep our eyes open."

"What's your favorite pizza?" he immediately responded while reaching for his cell phone to place the order.

While opening the second bottle of merlot, Mark said, "I guess I've dated a lot of girls. Hell, there were a few times I thought I was in love, but nothing like this. I don't even know how to describe it. What about you? How in the world did someone like you stay unattached? Don't misunderstand, I'm sure not complaining. You must have had men lined up at your doorstep. No one special?" She felt a sudden wave of trepidation wash through her mind realizing the time had come.

"There was someone special, but not as special as you," she replied, trying to sound reassuring if not convincing. "Sounds to me like a conversation during a long walk on the beach in the morning." She fell asleep wrapped in Mark's arms in the early hours of the morning looking forward to a conversation she had been dreading, but now relieved for the chance to set the record straight and hopefully put it behind them.

The summer sun worshipers had long since abandoned the beach until the following spring and the couple walked slowly, on the wet sand with the rows of beach houses and the ocean hidden in a veil of fog. "When I told you last night there was someone special in my life, I said it sounded like a conversation for a walk on the beach. This is the beach, so here goes. During my junior year and halfway through my senior year in college I dated only one man."

"Sounds like it was serious?" Mark gently questioned.

"It was," she quickly responded. "Not at first, but over time it became a serious relationship. After he graduated from college he went into the Army as a second lieutenant." Rachel stopped and turned to Mark. With sorrow written on her face, she continued, "He called me from Fort Rucker where he was going through helicopter flight school. He said he was coming home for a three day weekend and had something special to tell me. That was the last time I heard his voice." She put her hands to her eyes to stop the tears that couldn't be contained. "He was killed the next morning in a helicopter crash."

Mark stood stunned, realizing there was no way to know that whatever he might say would be the right thing. Finally, he spoke while taking her hands, "Randall Davis."

"Did you know him?"

"Everyone at the Citadel knew Randall. I guess he was the cadet everybody wanted to be." Suddenly, a revelation swept through his mind. "My God, it was you. The first time I saw you, I felt like I had seen you before, but it didn't come to me until now. You were his date at the Saint Valentine's Ball. How could I have forgotten? You probably caused a lot of breakups that night. I don't think there was a man who could keep his eyes off you. You were easily the most beautiful girl at the Ball and Randall was the most envied."

"Were you surprised?"

"Surprised that it took me this long to remember?"

Her simple, "no," had to be addressed.

"Or was I surprised that you were dating an African American?"

"Mark, you don't have to be politically correct with me. No one at the dance was color blind. They all saw a black man with a white woman or, as it turns out, a woman who appeared to be white."

They walked on until they sat on the wooden steps that led up to the catwalk over the dunes to the beach house.

"You asked if I was surprised. Hell, just about everybody was surprised. The real question is; did it bother me? The answer to that question is no!"

With a pleasant but probing tone, she asked, "Are you sure? I know there were some people there who thought such a public display of mixed race dating was unseemly."

"I'm sure that's true," Mark replied. "Listen, I might not be color blind, but I'm also not color sensitive. I would be lying if I told you all I saw that night was an honor student and his date having a great time. What I saw that night was a black man and a white woman having the time of their lives and probably not giving a damn what anyone thought. The only thing that bothered me was old fashion jealousy. You were with him and not me, and I know it was a feeling shared by a lot of others." After a pause to reflect, he said, "You know, it works both ways. Randall was a good looking man and, if the truth were known, there were probably other white women at that dance who would have traded places with you in a heartbeat."

They sat quietly for a while until Mark spoke again. "You were awfully quiet when we started our walk. Were you worried about how I would react?"

"Perhaps, a little," she replied. "But truthfully, I hoped; no I thought you would react just the way you did. It's the kind of person you are."

He turned and looked directly in her eyes. "I guess it's the lawyer in me or just my inquisitive nature, but I can't help wondering about his last phone call and what he wanted to talk to you about when he came home?"

She turned and looked out at the vast empty ocean and quietly remarked, "The fog has burned off." Without looking back to him, she said, "When they packed up his belongings they found a new engagement ring."

An understanding smile and look of resolve with an affirmative nod was his reply.

Chapter Twenty Seven

During Friday morning breakfast at the kitchen table Rachel felt like continuing the conversation. "It isn't so much how people react. It's a matter of identity. When I went to live with Naomi after my parents died, it didn't take her long to understand how difficult local school would be for me; a white girl from a black family."

"I can imagine. What did she do?"

"In Washington, I had attended a private school. There were Blacks, Whites, Asians, and Latinos; mostly children of government employees and attaches from foreign embassies. Mixed race children seemed to be the rule rather than the exception, and I loved it there. The school had a boarding division and I went back until I graduated from high school. Grandma Naomi and Uncle Harold came to see me several times a year and I always went home for the holidays and summers."

"You mentioned identity," Mark stated with little show of emotion.

"Mark, it's been going on for hundreds of years. When Thomas Claiborne came to South Carolina, nearly ninety percent of the population was black, mostly slaves. Light skinned young black women, mulattoes or creoles were highly prized." She continued as a look of pure disgust came over her face. "Prized by white masters like a prized hog or cow. Those who were accepted in white society were often rejected by the black community. It was all based on the color of their skin. I can only imagine how Rachel must have felt when Thomas brought her home from France. Reconstruction had ended and life for blacks was pure hell. But at least they knew who they were. Until the day she died, Rachel filled the position of house mistress, and the two of them were forced to keep their relationship hidden within the walls of the house. She couldn't function freely in white society because it was too dangerous and the darker skinned blacks wanted nothing to do with her."

"At least things have gotten better over the years," Mark commented.

"In some ways, they have," she replied. "But trying to understand one's own identity is still a problem. One day my mother dropped me off at school after I had been sick and missed several days. My locker was next to the teacher's lounge. The door was open and I heard one of the teachers mention my name when she asked my homeroom teacher if she thought I would be back to school soon. My homeroom teacher said she had seen my mother drop me off at the front door. The other teacher said, 'I thought she was always driven to school and picked up by her black nanny.' She had to be shocked to discover that the black nanny was my mother. I got along fine in school, but it seemed there were always problems if I dated a black boy. There were times over the years when I found myself in an all-white group of people. On several occasions someone told a joke about blacks or used the term nigger. I didn't know whether to be mad as hell or feel guilty for intruding. Does any of this make sense to you?"

"It does," he quickly replied, "but right now I think it's best for me to be a good listener."

"You've seen all the pictures of my family all the way back to Rachel. The women were all mixed race but they were all recognizably of black heritage. I could easily have been. It was simply a matter of how the genes lined up. Sometimes I think I would have been better off." After a pause, she asked the only question that remained. "Would it have made any difference to you if you could easily tell by just looking that I'm mixed race, as much black as white?"

Mark's instinct was to carefully formulate his answer but he replied quickly, fearing an extended thoughtful pause, in itself, would be his implied response, regardless of the words he might use. "I don't know," he said in a straightforward manner. My belief is that it wouldn't have made any difference at all, but I would rather speak the truth than have you always wonder if I was lying."

Rachel's solemn look began to disappear and was replaced with a huge smile. "Damn, you're going to make a hell of a trial lawyer. Clarence Darrow had nothing on you." She stood up and told Mark to swing his chair away from the table."

"Do what?"

"I said, scoot your chair away from the table so I can sit on your lap and make out with you."

As he pushed his chair away from the table, he said, "I guess that means you liked my answer."

With a look of disbelief, she replied as she rolled her eyes, "At least Darrow knew when to shut up."

Chapter Twenty Eight

Shortly after breakfast Mark's cell phone rang and the caller was Chad Ainsworth. After listening for a moment, Mark responded, "That's great. As a matter of fact, she's here with me now. We'll be over in about an hour."

"That was Chad Ainsworth, the boat man I told you about. He thinks he's got just the boat to replace the one that was destroyed. As soon as you're ready we'll run over to his place and take a look at it."

As they pulled up to a gravel and sand parking area surrounded by weeds Rachel surveyed the backwater marina with skepticism written all over her face.

"I know it doesn't look like much," Mark suggested. With a chuckle, he said, "I guess this is the book you can't tell by the cover."

Chad saw their car pull into the marina and came out of his trailer office to greet them. "I pulled that boat we looked at the last time you were here into the shop and spruced it up a little," Chad called to Mark as he walked to greet them.

"Chad, this is Rachel Devening, the lady who lost the boat."

Chad hesitated as he stuck out his hand to greet his guest, and then wiped it clean of grease and dirt on his pant leg. "Mark, you should have given me a little advance warning," he said while looking directly at Rachel. "If I'd known we were going to be visited by such a pretty guest I would have cleaned up a little. Might even have shaved," he said, again directing his attention and comments to Rachel.

"Chad, it's my pleasure," Rachel responded while reaching out to shake his hand.

"Well, come on over to the shop and take a look." The large sliding doors on the rusty corrugated steel shop were open, but Mark and Rachel hesitated in front of a large remnant of water from an early morning rain that blocked the entire entrance. Rachel was wearing jeans and new tan sneakers and Mark was wearing shined leather penny loafers. Sensing the problem, Chad proclaimed, "Come on Sugar, you can't buy it if you can't see it." With that, he placed his right arm around Rachel's back and with his left hand under her knees picked her up as easily as a bale of light straw and carried her across the water. Inside the building, he stood her on her feet on the dry concrete floor.

"And here," Rachel exclaimed, "I thought Southern men had forgotten all about chivalry," with her focus on Mark as he trudged through the water.

"You know I'm never going to live this down," Mark said to Chad as he walked onto the dry shop floor.

On a trailer in the middle of the shop sat the boat. "You've got to be kidding me. This can't be the same boat," Mark said in disbelief. The entire hull had been polished and buffed. All of the corroded steel fittings had been replaced with stainless steel and a new, bright blue Bimini cover was stretched open over the center console and rear seating area.

"One in the same," Chad replied. "The seats are being rebuilt and, along with all the cushions, will be reupholstered in rolled and tucked white vinyl. On the transom is a rebuilt Merc 100 horse outboard."

"Chad," Rachel began, "it looks like new."

"It will be better than new when we get done with it."

"I'm not sure we will be able to afford it," she replied.

"I think Mark told me you are insured with Marine Mutual?"

"That's right."

"We'll make it work. They owe me," Chad replied with a grin. It'll be done by the end of next week. Just tell me where to deliver it."

As they turned to leave they were faced with the same water obstacle. "I believe it's your turn, Mr. Bradley."

In an instant, she was in his arms and being carried to dry land. When they reached the car Rachel stepped close to Chad. "You are so kind and sweet to boot." She followed with a kiss to hischeekk. "It's an old Irish custom," she coyly remarked.

"Chad, my dad told me you are taking the Sea Breeze to Miami sometime next week."

"A week from tomorrow to be exact. My fiancé is going along for the ride. Why don't you and Rachel come with us?"

"Rachel teaches and I don't think she could get away."

With a pleasantly animated voice, Rachel remarked, "As a matter of fact, I'm free on fall break starting next Friday."

Mark looked first at Rachel and then back to Chad. "Sounds like you just picked up some passengers. I'll call you in a few days to see what I can do to help with provisions and other arrangements."

On their drive back to the Isle of Palms, Rachel asked about the trip. "Why is he taking your dad's boat to Miami?"

"He takes it down every November and brings it back in April. Mom and Dad will go down two or three times during the winter months and stay on the boat. Chad and I have made the trip together quite a few times. It's a great time, but this one will be the best of all."

"How is that?" she remarked with considerable interest.

"This time we will have company," he said as his face turned into a broad smile.

"You certainly will," she answered while squeezing his arm. "We have a long open weekend. Any plans?"

With a loving smile, Mark quickly replied. "I'd be happy to spend it alone, with you."

"Funny how two people can have exactly the same thoughts running through their minds at the same time."

Chapter Twenty Nine

Soon after kissing Rachel goodbye in the driveway on Monday morning, Mark was on his way to the newspaper office hoping to find an article about Thomas Claiborne's lawsuit in the archives.

A young lady from the reception area took him to the large archives room on the third floor. With the date Mark had given her, she went directly to the appropriate storage area. She opened a large cabinet and removed a newspaper on a hanging rod and placed it on a viewing table. "This was the paper published on the evening the trial ended. If you don't find anything in this edition, there may be something in the next several papers. It often takes a few days for court judgments to be printed. Before leaving," she reminded Mark, "please use both hands when you are turning pages and be very careful."

He found nothing in the first paper but before his eyes on the third page of the second paper was an article titled, Court Rules in Favor of Thomas Claiborne in Race Horse Suit. It was an interesting article written in layman's language. Near the end of the article his eyes suddenly lit up and he mouthed a firm and audible, "Yes!"

On his way out he stopped to thank the receptionist who had helped him. "Did you find what you were looking for?" she asked.

"You bet I did."

He drove straight to the Bradley Law firm hoping to find his dad free for a conference. He was in luck and took a seat at the small conference table in his father's office.

"You seem charged up," his dad remarked. "What's up?"

Mark paraphrased the article about the Claiborne suit. "Claiborne had a stable of race horses he had bred from original English stock. He made an agreement with another breeder to provide stud services with one of his stallions for two of the other man's mares. In exchange, Claiborne was to have the first pick of the foals born to the mares. The owner of the mares contended that he was to have first pick and Claiborne would receive the remaining foal. Of the two foals, one was a colt and the other a filly. They both wanted the colt."

"Did they have a signed agreement?"

"No, it was a handshake deal, and the court ruled in favor of Claiborne."

"Without something in writing it sounds like it was one man's word against another. How did the court justify the ruling?" his father asked with growing interest."

With a confident smile, Mark responded," With an entry in Thomas Claiborne's diary. He called it his personal daily journal."

"Diary?"

Claiborne presented a diary from the year of the breeding agreement opened to the page on the date the agreement was made. Thomas had written in very succinct terms that his compensation would be the first pick between the two foals and on that basis the two men had reached a clear agreement and sealed the deal with a handshake. The defense attorney objected, stating that Claiborne could have made that entry at any time; even a few days before the trial. Evidently, the judge had the diary examined and it was determined that it was a permanently bound journal with binding thread and glue and could not have had pages replaced without being unbound which would have done permanent and irreparable damage to the book. The Judge said that the whole matter could have been a simple misunderstanding, in which case there would have been no *Mutuality of Assent* but since Claiborne had proof of his understanding of the deal and the other breeder did not, he found for Claiborne."

Joe pondered the matter for a moment. "This is all very interesting, but just what does a race horse have to do with proving Rachel's family relationship to Thomas Claiborne.?

"Not a damned thing," Mark quickly replied. "But since the Judge admitted the diary entry as evidence, we might be able to establish that precedence was established. Now, if we can find Claiborne's diaries and if we can find an entry identifying Mary as Thomas and Rachel's daughter, we've got a case."

Joe smiled with admiration. "Tell me Son, just where do you expect to find Thomas' diaries?"

With an expression of dejection, Mark replied, "That's a damned good question. I'm going to Georgetown this evening and talk to Naomi. She's the only living person who knew the old man and the only person who might know something about the diaries."

"Well, good luck and, by the way, I have some news for you. I sent the letter to Claiborne's bank as you requested, asking for the additional information needed for an audit of the Trust's books." He leaned over slightly in his chair and retrieved a letter sized piece of paper. "Here's their response; no surprise. Just drop down to the last paragraph."

As attorneys for the bank and Mr. Claiborne, we have reviewed your request carefully and have determined that the annual statements that have been provided to Mrs. Richards meet all legal requirements for such fiduciary reporting. Thank you for your interest.

Mark tossed the letter on the table. "It's nothing more than I expected. I'm going to stay with Rachel tonight and tomorrow while she is in class I'll drop in on Mr. Claiborne for a little chat."

Joe and Mark spent the rest of the morning assessing the situation. Finally Joe said, "If you get lucky with the diaries we could find ourselves in tall cotton. But if not, we need a solid back up plan." Mark's father leaned back in his chair and rubbed his chin in thought before continuing. "It may be about time to make a deal with Mr. Claiborne."

"What do you have in mind?"

Joe spent about 30 minutes explaining his view of the "deal."

"Dad, I'm impressed," Mark offered when his father finished talking. "I'll have to review it with Rachel and Naomi. They will have the final word. If Claiborne bites, it will take some time to work out all the details. In the meanwhile, if we find the diaries and the kind of evidence we're looking for, we can always pull out of the deal and go for the entire estate." As he started to leave, Mark said, "I'll stay in touch and let you know how it goes." At the door, Mark turned and looked back at his father. "Dad, you're a hell of a lawyer. I hope someday I'm just half as good."

It was starting out to be one of the best Mondays Joe Bradley could ever remember.

Chapter Thirty

Dressed in cutoff jeans and a sweatshirt, Rachel was doing her class preparation work at Naomi's dining room table. They had always enjoyed each other's company and Rachel was determined to be with her great grandmother as much as possible.

"How about some coffee on the summer porch, sweetheart," the old woman called from the kitchen."

"Perfect timing, I could use a break," Rachel responded as she headed for the kitchen to help with the coffee pot and cups. Once seated in their customary seats on the summer porch, Naomi, who was never one to beat around the bush, dove directly into the issue that had been most on her mind.

"How are you and Mark Bradley getting along?"

"Grandmother," Rachel replied with a chuckle, "You have so many wonderful virtues, but I'm afraid subtleness is not one of them."

"I guess I've always spoken my mind. Besides, you're the only one I have left and I just want the best for you."

Rachel sat her cup on the side table and crossed her arms in her lap and spoke while looking thoughtfully across the harbor. "I told him about Randall Davis."

"Everything?" Naomi asked.

"Everything, including the engagement ring."

"How did he feel about that?"

Rachel pondered the question for a moment, and then asked, "How do you think he reacted?"

"I know Joe Bradley, and if Mark is anything like his father, it probably didn't faze him in the least. Am I right?"

Rachel acknowledged the old woman's question with an affirmative nod.

Naomi's voice grew stern. "Child, this mixed race business has haunted you for years and, if you will take an old fool's advice, it's time to deal with it. Your ancestor, Rachel, was half white and half black and all of her descendants have been Creole. You just happened to pick up enough of your father's genes to make you pass for white. But what the hell difference does it make?

"Grandmother, a lot of my students are black or mixed race. If it hadn't been for the Claiborne Trust and my white Irish father, I would have been in their predicament; trying to beat almost insurmountable odds in search of a dream. Or, even worse, no dream at all of a better life."

"And it makes you feel guilty."

"Sometimes it does."

"I wish you could have known Thomas Claiborne," Naomi replied wistfully. "For all the hardships he endured trying to make a decent life for Rachel and Mary and all the mixed race children he knew would follow, he never lost sight of the most important things in life."

"And those are?" Rachel replied with her interest piqued.

Sensing she had captured her attention, Naomi smiled and continued on her mission. "Mr. Thomas used to say that life is like a poker game and you've got to play the hand you're dealt. Above all, he used to say, you have to be honest and recognize your circumstances for what they are. And if you don't, you can never rise above them," After a moment of shared silence, she continued. "On more than one occasion he took me by the hand and said, 'love is God's greatest gift to man. The day will come when you fall in love. When you do, make of it everything you can. The ability and willingness to love is what makes life worth living."

The telephone rang, interrupting Naomi's train of thought, and Naomi answered it in the living room.

"I'm just fine, Mark," she replied. She is sitting with me on the summer porch. Just a moment." Naomi covered the receiver. "Rachel, there is a young man on the phone who sounds very interested in talking to you."

When Rachel picked up the phone Mark explained, "I tried your cell phone but when you didn't answer I thought I would try Naomi's land line. I hope you don't mind."

"I don't mind a bit," she cheerfully replied. "I must have left my phone in my apartment."

"Honey, I have several things to discuss with you and your grandmother. If it wouldn't be an imposition, I can be there in about an hour."

"Just a minute," she responded. "Grandmother, Mark is on his way and would like to talk with us if you feel up to it."

The old woman felt a surge of energy. "You tell him we'll crack open a bottle of wine; the good stuff."

Mark laughed and said, "I heard her answer in the background. By the way, you wouldn't happen to know where a fellow could get a room on short notice."

Rachel turned away from Naomi and lowered her voice. "If we are going to be drinking wine, you really shouldn't be drinking and driving. I guess you will just have to stay with me. Besides, the bed is really comfortable and the guest services are exceptional."

"Child," Naomi directed after Rachel hung up the phone, "why don't you go freshen up and change while I pick out a good bottle of wine and slice some cheese and summer sausage for hors d'oeuvres."

Somewhat taken back, she replied, "Is there something wrong with what I'm wearing?"

"Not a thing if you're going fishing or cleaning house or weeding the garden." Naomi looked around the living room and continued, "I don't see any weeds that need pulling in here. Go put on a dress; something casual but . . . you know, sexy."

"Grandmother, he's coming to discuss business."

"Really," the old woman remarked. "I guess that means he won't pay any attention to you at all. We saw to it that you speak fluid French but I can tell there is part of your education that has been severely neglected." She walked to the book shelves and removed a book entitled, Coco Chanel. She handed it to Rachel and said, "No women in the world know how to deal with men better than French women. Put this on your reading list. While you're at it, check out the quote on the inside of the back cover." With that said, she turned and headed for the kitchen leaving Rachel standing in the living room holding the book.

After a speechless moment, Rachel turned to the inside back cover to read the quote.

"A woman is closest to being naked when she is well dressed."
Coco Chanel

"Grandmother," Rachel called to the old woman, "you are wicked."

Naomi poked her head around the passage to the kitchen and replied with a big smile. "Thank you. I know you've been sleeping with him. Catching a man is one thing. Hanging onto him is another matter."

Chapter Thirty One

Dressed in a light wool, dark green A line skirt and a snug camel colored cashmere sweater that conformed perfectly to her breasts, Rachel was standing with her hands on the front porch railing when Mark parked in the street in front of the house. She had hot combed her hair, applied just the right amount of makeup, and put on lipstick that was one shade shy of being too red.

Mark stopped on the last step and looked up at her in awe. "You look like you stepped out of a fashion magazine."

"Score one for Naomi," Rachel thought to herself. "You always seem to know the right thing to say," she replied as she stepped forward to hug him.

"You know I love you and I hope you never get tired of hearing it."

"Never," she replied. "Grandmother was happy when I told her you were coming. She is waiting for us inside."

. . . .

While they shared the hors d'oeuvres and wine Naomi had opened, Rachel and Naomi listened with great interest as Mark related the article he discovered in the Charleston newspaper archives. "Claiborne's personal journals could be exactly what we need. Mrs. Richards, were you aware that Thomas kept a journal?"

"Mark," the old woman reminisced, "from the time I was five years old until the day he died it was my job to bring him his diary and return it to his desk in the study when he had finished his entry for the day. Sometimes he would tell me what he had written and sometimes he didn't. But it was always a special time for me. We always talked and often until it was time for me to go to bed."

"Did he ever tell you how long he had been keeping a daily journal?"

"He started not long after he arrived from England; one for each calendar year from January 1st to December 31st."

Mark cupped his cheeks with his hands and sighed as the obvious question was at hand. "Do you know where the journals are?"

"I wish I did," she replied with sorrow in her voice. "I have the one he was keeping when he died. That was in early January so there are only a few entries. I've wondered a thousand times where they might be. Over the years I've gone over every inch of that house, but there was simply never any trace of them. I'm sorry, Mark."

"It's all right. At least we are certain that he kept them." After a pensive thought, he asked, "Could they have been removed from the house after he died?"

"When Thomas died, my mother locked his bedroom and study. Nothing was touched and nothing was removed. As long as my mother lived, those rooms were only opened about once every two months for dusting and cleaning. I have continued that ritual until this very day. His clothes and the bed mattress were removed years ago but everything else is just the way it was the day he died."

The final rays of the October sun were setting low in the western sky leaving the summer porch where they were seated in full shade.

Mark decided he had taken the subject of the journals far enough for the time being and decided to switch gears. "We'll come back to Thomas's journals another day. But now, I'd like to talk about a plan my father discussed with me earlier today. I think it makes a lot of sense."

Rachel's perfume and mere presence next to him on the settee was intoxicating and concentrating was becoming increasingly difficult. He poured a little more wine into their glasses and pulled another chair to the end of the low serving table. He hoped he could properly disguise his need to move to a less distracting position as he commented while placing a legal pad on the end of the table. "I'm going to sit here where I can illustrate a few of the items for discussion on paper and address both of you at the same time. This is a decision you both will need to consider."

Over the next hour, Mark carefully outlined the plan his father had recommended they propose to Donald Claiborne. When he was finished he looked at both women for a response.

After a silent moment, Naomi expressed her opinion. "I think it's brilliant and I don't think Mr. Claiborne will have any choice but to accept it."

Mark turned to Rachel. "Your thoughts?"

"This is grandmother's call but it's all right with me," she replied with a sense of business logic. "I never would have dreamed of being a partner with Donald Claiborne, but the plan has a lot of merit. No one gets all of what they want but everyone gets something; a lot as a matter of fact."

"Remember," Mark said, "we are going to continue searching for the journals. If we find them, you still might wind up with everything. I'm going to see Claiborne in the morning. If he is interested in the plan I'll give him several weeks to review and amend the plan for your consideration. If there is a change of heart between the two of you by morning, we can modify the plan or drop it altogether."

"I'm sure it will be fine," Naomi replied while extending her hand for Mark's assistance in rising from her seat. "I'm beginning to feel a little tired, but the two of you enjoy the porch as long as you like."

As Naomi disappeared through the dimly lit house Mark moved back to the settee next to Rachel and took her in his arms. "If I ever try a case in court, please don't come to watch. I'd never be able to concentrate."

"You can concentrate on me all you want," she replied between kisses while Mark's hand moved up her leg under her skirt. As he pulled her to him, she said, hurriedly, "Let's go to my apartment."

They circled half way around the house on the front and side porch. Rachel handed him the key. "Here, I'm shaking."

Inside the apartment, Mark backed her gently to the kitchen table. Rachel fumbled with his belt buckle and zipper. As she tugged down on his trousers he put his hands on her bottom and lifted her to a sitting position on the table. In an instant, he was inside her. She took a deep breath with the first thrust and wrapped her arms tightly around him. He began with slow but deliberate movement. After a few moments he began moving faster and, as he did, Rachel spoke breathlessly. "My God, Mark, don't stop. Please don't stop." When, finally, he did stop, they continued to just hold each other in wonder. As she caught her breath and began to return to earth, she commented with a conceding chuckle, "I couldn't do that in blue jeans."

With a confused look, Mark responded, "At least not without a whole lot more effort."

Coco Chanel's book went immediately to the head of Rachel's reading list.

Chapter Thirty Two

The following morning, the three of them were seated At Naomi's kitchen table for breakfast.

"Rachel, you simply look radiant this morning," Naomi casually mentioned as she was preparing to take a sip of coffee.

Rachel sent Mark a quick wink and replied, "I can't imagine why."

"Bet I can," the old woman softly retorted with a grin like a Cheshire Cat.

"Ladies," Mark interjected, "If there is no change of heart, I am going to try to see Donald Claiborne this morning, and, if it's all right with you Mrs. Richards, I'm going out to the mansion house later, and have a look around."

"I wish you luck," Naomi lamented.

"Mrs. Richards, I have one last concern. I know how close you and Mrs. Watson have been over the years, but I would not be comfortable with her knowing about any of the things we have discussed. Unless I am mistaken, other than the three of us, she is the only person who knew you gave me the file boxes and that Rachel and I were going to take the boat to the island. The FBI believes there is at least a 50/50 chance the boat explosion was no accident and there is little question that whoever broke into my parent's beach house was looking for the files."

"I know," she sadly replied. "It would break my heart if she has been involved in this terrible business. I won't say a word to her and will pray it all works out for the best."

Rachel walked Mark to his car. "This is a big day for all of us. I hope you don't run into any unforeseen problems with Donald Claiborne."

"He's not expecting me and our proposal will come as a total surprise. At least I'll be able to see how he acts on his feet with no time to prepare. His reaction alone may tell us a lot."

"Last night when we were making love I asked you not to stop."

"I know," he whispered in her ear with his arms around her.

She gently pulled away to look him in the eyes. "I don't want you to stop making love to me but, most of all, I don't want you to stop loving me."

Georgetown, South Carolina – 1857

The parishioners filed slowly out of the Episcopal Church in Georgetown following Sunday services. Most stopped briefly at the top of the steps by the massive oak door to speak to Reverend Wright and his wife.

Thomas Claiborne was among those in line and, when it came to his turn, he congratulated the cleric for a wonderful sermon and added in a serious tone, "Reverend Wright, I need to speak with you whenever you might have a few moments."

Wright smiled at Thomas and replied while grasping his hands. "My wife and I have been invited to the Russell's for Sunday dinner. I'll send her on in their carriage. After everyone is gone, we can talk. When we are finished I'll go on to the Russell's.

Thomas waited in the back row of the sanctuary while Reverend Wright finished his obligatory greetings. A short while later and closing the door behind him, Wright took a seat several feet from Thomas in the same pew. "Well Thomas, what's on your mind?"

"Father, I need to ask a favor and your blessing."

"This church would not exist were it not for your family's generous support. Tell me how I can help and it will be done."

"Our financial support can have no part in your decision. You must consider what I am about to ask on its own merit and I will gratefully abide by your counsel, yea or nay.

"Fair enough, Thomas."

When the discussion ended, Reverend Wright said, "Thomas, God will approve of what we are about to do, but I am afraid most others will not. This is dangerous business."

"I understand and, as God is my witness, I swear not another soul will know of this until you and yours are safely at rest in the hands of God forever."

In the dark of night in a steady rain, a covered carriage pulled up to the back door of the Episcopal Church. Father Wright held the door open as Thomas Claiborne, Rachel, and their new daughter, Mary entered the church. "Dreary weather Thomas."

"Just as well," Thomas replied. "No one is out."

"Thomas, I have confided in my wife and she would like to serve as a witness and assist in the proceedings."

"Mrs. Wright, your kindness will never be forgotten."

Wright lit one small candle to provide scant but sufficient light for the business at hand yet not alert others to activity in the church. He led the small party to the altar. "Victoria, if you would be so kind as to hold the baby, we can proceed."

He concluded the brief ceremony by saying, "By the power vested in me by the Anglican Communion and God Almighty, I declare you to be Thomas and Rachel Claiborne, husband, and wife."

"Thank you, Father and Mrs. Wright," Thomas replied. "We shall both be eternally grateful."

"Victoria, if you will place the baby in Mrs. Claiborne's arms, we have one more task to complete."

Following the child's baptism, Reverend Wright withdrew some papers from the inside vest pocket of his dress coat and placed them on the lectern.

"Thomas, I have prepared a declaration of your marriage and a certificate of baptism. There are two copies each as you requested. I have signed them and Victoria has signed as a witness. You and Rachel will need to sign them and keep them in a safe place."

With quill and ink their signatures were affixed and the deed was done.

During their return to Claiborne plantation in the carriage through the stormy night, Thomas looked at Mary cuddled in his new wife's arms. "This is the best thing I have ever done," he declared.

"I hope you will love me forever," she responded.

"You know I will."

She did.

Chapter Thirty Three

Mark entered the front door of the Claiborne Management and Investment Company and was greeted cheerfully by the receptionist. "Good morning, how can we help you?"

"My name is Mark Bradley. I don't have an appointment, but I was hoping I might be able to see Mr. Claiborne."

"Mr. Claiborne is out of the office and I don't expect him back until after lunch. Perhaps there is someone else who can help."

"Thank you anyway. I'll try to catch him later."

Mark reversed his plans for the day and decided to spend the morning at the Claiborne mansion hoping to develop some notion of where Thomas Claiborne had kept his journals.

. . . .

Donald Claiborne answered the phone at his desk in his home office. "I thought I asked you not to call me here."

"I wouldn't have but I just saw that Bradley fella pull into the mansion drive."

"Keep an eye on him and don't call me back unless you think it's important."

Stan Watson stood in his kitchen listening to the dial tone and staring at the receiver in disgust. He picked up the weed eater in his tool shed and headed across the road to the Claiborne mansion property. He could trim the weeds along the sides of the lane running between the live oak trees to the house and keep watch on the visitor at the same time.

Mark let himself in through the front door with the key Naomi had given him. He began by touring the entire house to refresh his memory of the floor plans. Although most of the furniture was gone, a few pieces remained in the study and none of the furniture in Thomas's bedroom had been moved since he died so many years before. He looked through the desk where Thomas had kept his current journal. According to Naomi, Thomas ended each journal on New Year's Eve and a new blank journal awaited Naomi to fetch for the old man from his desk on New Year's Day. Mark moved slowly through the bedroom and the adjoining study lightly tapping on the walls as he went to see if he could detect a change in the sound that might indicate the presence of some type of hidden opening. He repeated the process on the floors of both rooms. As he expected, his effort was in vain. He pulled a chair into the middle of the study and sat wondering what he might have missed. Unless they had been destroyed or stolen, the journals had to be on the property and they had to be close.

Mark locked the front door on his way out and was startled by Stan Watson as he turned to start down the stairs. "Good morning, Mr. Bradley. Were you looking for anything in particular?"

"No, Stan, I love these fine old homes and thought I would come out and take another look around."

"You know I live just across the road. If you ever decide to come back, let me know so I won't think there's a trespasser."

"I'll keep it in mind, Mr. Watson." Mark wished him a good day as he climbed into his car. This was the second time he had encountered Stan Watson. On both occasions, he wasn't particularly friendly and he seemed to appear out of nowhere.

Chapter Thirty Four

Mark parked his car across the street from Claiborne's office on Front Street a few minutes after noon where he could watch the front door through his rearview mirror and unwrapped a sub sandwich he had picked up at a local deli for lunch while he waited.

Just before one o'clock Mark watched Claiborne enter his office. He waited no more than two minutes and walked into the office. "I was here earlier this morning and you said Mr. Claiborne would be in after lunch."

"I do remember and he just came in. I'll check to see if he is available." She quickly reappeared from a hallway that led to his office and said, "I'm terribly sorry. Mr. Claiborne is preparing for a meeting and won't be available for the rest of the day."

"That's quite all right," Mark responded. He started to leave but suddenly turned and proceeded down the hallway and through Claiborne's office door.

Claiborne was caught off guard and the receptionist followed Mark into his office. "I'm sorry Mr. Claiborne. I told him you were not avail . . ."

"That's all right Susan, I'll deal with this." Standing at his desk and looking directly at Mark, he said, "I don't appreciate you barging into my office, but since you're here, tell me what's on your mind." Claiborne paused and exclaimed, "You're the man I met who was having lunch at the sidewalk café with Rachel Devening."

"Please, Mr. Claiborne, let's not insult each other. You know exactly who I am and why I'm here."

"If you're here about that audit material your father requested, our attorney replied in writing."

"I read the letter. It's about what I expected. If at some time in the future we decide to pursue the matter further we won't send another letter. We'll get a subpoena. Actually, I'm here to discuss a different matter. I've come to make you a proposal."

"And what would that be?"

"I believe your receptionist said you were preparing for a meeting this afternoon. You better have her call the people and reschedule. This is going to take a while." Donald thought about it for a moment, then called Susan on the office intercom and told her to reschedule his meeting and hold all calls.

Mark looked around the office and was leery of hidden cameras and listening devices. On the back wall of the office was a glass door that opened out to a boardwalk on the river. He stepped to the door, opened it, and said, "It's a nice day. Let's talk out here."

Claiborne hesitated before joining Mark on the boardwalk. The two men sat side by side on a bench looking over the water. Mark looked at Claiborne and said, "Just like two old friends sitting together telling fish stories."

"Fish stories my ass. I've rescheduled my entire afternoon for you. If you have a proposal, let's hear it."

The Deal

Mark began to speak looking straight ahead at the river. "As it stands right now, when Mrs. Richards passes away you will inherit the entire Trust as Thomas Claiborne's closest living relative. Everyone knows Rachel Devening holds that position but to date, we have not been able to produce sufficient evidence to compel the court to issue a birth certificate for Mary, Thomas, and Rachel's daughter.

"Let's assume the inheritance is yours and imagine a scenario of what you would do with the land. On the beach side of the island, I can imagine eighteen miles of multimillion dollar ocean front estates. On the Intracoastal side, somewhat less expensive homes but nothing under a million dollars. Probably five or six exclusive resort hotels like Four Seasons, Hyatt, and Hilton. The entire island would probably be developed as a gated community allowing access only to homeowners and resort guests. Perhaps there would be a small retail district that would rival Rodeo Drive in Beverly Hills. You would probably dredge out the large cove on the mainland side for a world class marina that could accommodate the biggest private yachts in the world. Also on the mainland, I can see upper class neighborhoods surrounding golf courses by designers like Jack Nicklaus. By the time you're finished, Donald, you will probably wind up building an entire town. A town occupied by the rich and famous. I can't begin to imagine the wealth the development projects would generate, notwithstanding the maintenance contracts your company would hold in perpetuity." Finally, Mark turned and looked at Donald. "Am I on the right track?"

"Keep talking," Claiborne replied without changing expression.

Mark knew he had scored a bull's eye and with a quiet but deep breath prepared to lower the boom on Mr. Claiborne's dream.

"The only problem with this scenario," Mark observed, "is that it is never going to happen."

With that, Donald rose from the bench, took several steps, and turned to look directly at Mark. "Would you mind telling me what you mean by that remark?"

"Not at all," Mark replied in matter-of-fact fashion. "To begin, if Rachel prevails and is fortunate enough to inherit the Trust, she won't allow that kind of development. Secondly, if, and most certainly, when the Trust is yours; you will feel like the entire legal world is coming down on you. Rachel Devening will immediately file suit contesting your lineage among Thomas's descendants. If the suit fails, it will be followed by one appeal after another until it could even wind up in the State Supreme Court. Rachel's proof of her relationship with Thomas is all circumstantial. It would be up to the court to decide if a mountain of circumstantial evidence would be sufficient to find for Rachel. Naturally, Harold Sanders would immediately recuse himself from the case. Even so, when the other Justices become aware that Rachel is Harold's niece, it's likely that human nature will take over and your chances of winning in the highest court will go from near certainty to no better than 50/50. All of this will take a lot of time and, in the meanwhile, the court is certain to issue an injunction preventing the Trust to be turned over to you until the case is concluded."

"I would expect as much Mr. Bradley." Claiborne replied in a distinctly condescending manner, "I've had some of the finest attorneys in the country preparing to try this case for the past five years. I still haven't heard your proposal, but if this is all you have, you have wasted my time and yours as well."

"No time wasted here, Donald," Mark instantly replied, trying to refrain from appearing smug, "we're just getting started."

"You are certainly aware that the State of South Carolina will be the executor of the will. What you may not know is that Rachel has promised both the University of South Carolina and the State Parks and Recreation Department sizeable chunks of the Trust land if she prevails. You are also aware that because of the female lineage between Thomas and Rachel, DNA will not support her case. But there are other methods including genealogical statistical analysis, forensic anatomy analysis, and more. The means to develop this evidence is all contained within the University system. As executor, it will be up to the State to look at all the evidence and award the Trust accordingly. The University wants at least a portion of the property to establish a marine biology and research center and the Parks Department wants a portion of that beach to establish a state park so bad they can taste it. They will invest all of the brain power at their disposal including the law school to prepare expert testimony in favor of Rachel."

"Accordingly, The Trust might be awarded to Rachel. Even if it's not, you will have an uphill battle. The minute you begin to file applications for all the permits necessary to develop the property as you envision, a whole raft of government agencies will come after you with everything they've got. We're talking about the Environmental Protection Agency, the Department of Natural Resources, the Army Corps of Engineers, The State Watershed Department and . . . well, you get the idea."

Mark didn't have any first-hand knowledge that any of these actions would materialize, but everything he described was plausible and he knew it was all coming down hard on Claiborne.

"Finally, if by some miracle you manage to win all of these battles, your greatest enemy is time. I'm sure you thought Naomi Richards would die five years ago following her stroke. That's when you created all those companies to buy the land surrounding the Trust property. But she didn't die and you have been paying interest on the loans and property tax ever since. I'm sure the banks that loaned you the money to buy the land are first in line to finance your grand development plan. But it has been five years and Mrs. Richards is in remarkably good health. She could live another five or six years or more. The banks will tire of granting loan extensions, if they haven't already, and at the first sign of trouble they will bail out like rats leaving a sinking ship. On the way out the door, they will call the notes and if you can't pay, they will foreclose. Whatever you used for collateral will be lost and I think I know what that is."

Donald Claiborne's belligerent attitude began to give way to a wave of depression as the hard reality of the matter that he had tried for several years to avoid, began to set in.

"The proposal, Mr. Bradley, if you don't mind."

Mark sensed Donald was beginning to weaken. He stood up, put his foot on the bench, propped his arm on his knee, and looking directly at Claiborne, began to spell out the proposal.

"You and Rachel will have to join forces. If you agree with this plan, Mrs. Richards will notify the court that she is abandoning her position of entitlement in the trust. This would have the same effect as her death and the Attorney General of South Carolina will be directed to carry out Thomas's will. Courts always try to honor the wishes of the deceased and in this case, either you or Rachel would easily qualify. In order to avoid contesting the award, you and Rachel will each acknowledge the possibility of the other being the rightful heir and will petition the court to award the Trust equally to both of you as Tenants in Common. When the intended use of the land becomes known to all of the parties who have been preparing to fight you tooth and nail, they will become your allies and will endorse the plan."

"And what is the intended use of the land, Mark?" Claiborne asked with just a hint of genuine interest.

"The eighteen miles of beach would roughly be divided into three parcels. Over the years, the Army Corps of Engineers has used much of the northern end to marshal equipment to construct the protective jetties for the entrance to the Intracoastal Waterway. That land no longer has any ecological value that would be lost through residential and commercial development. This would be the largest parcel and would be used for a somewhat smaller version of your plan."

"And the rest of the beach land?"

"The State Parks and Recreation Department would receive the middle portion to establish a state park so all people; not just the wealthy, can enjoy one of the most beautiful beaches on the entire East Coast. The University of South Carolina would receive the Southern tract, which is a veritable treasure chest of fauna and marine life, to establish a world class marine biology research center.

"Who winds up in charge," Donald asked.

"Both your interests and Rachel's interest will be deeded to a newly formed corporation. Both you and Rachel will own fifty percent of the common stock and share all proceeds equally over the years. Rachel will own fifty one percent of the voting stock and you will hold 49 percent."

"But that gives her the final decision over everything."

"That's right, but the articles of incorporation will describe in some detail how the land is supposed to be used."

"I can't say I'm happy about the prospect of reporting to a woman."

"There may be some things that are negotiable but this is not one of them."

"I will need some time to think about it. There are several problems I'll have to deal with. How soon do you need an answer?"

After a moment of thought, Mark replied, "I'll be out of town over spring break. I'll call you when I return to see what your thinking is. If you decide to accept, we will begin drafting the agreements and notifying all of the interested parties."

"Fair enough, Mr. Bradley."

"One last thing . . . Rachel Devening's safety. There isn't a grand jury in the country that wouldn't consider the deaths of Rachel's parents and her Aunt Jane, homicides. The FBI is still investigating the boat explosion and even though the forensic evidence is not yet conclusive, they strongly suspect attempted murder."

"You don't think I had anything to do with it," Claiborne replied defensively in a raised voice."

"It's not important what I think, but if the FBI had enough to make a case they would have only one person of interest."

"They have already been here," Donald replied. I have his card in my desk. I think the name is Frank Zeller. It's no surprise to me that I would be considered a prime suspect, but I can assure you, I've done things in my life I regret but attempted murder is not one of them."

"One thing's for certain, Donald."

"And that is?"

"If any harm comes to Rachel, whoever is responsible better pray to God that the police get to him before I do."

Claiborne stood speechless with a stunned expression on his face.

Mark extended his hand. "I appreciate you taking the time. Hopefully, when I get back we can formalize an agreement."

Instead of going back through Donald's office, Mark walked a short distance down the boardwalk and turned toward the street and his car. Sitting in a booth in a riverside bar and grill behind a dark stained window was a man who had watched the entire meeting between Donald Claiborne and Mark Bradley. He hadn't been able to hear them, but he knew they had to have been talking about the Trust.

Luke Bratton was one of the problems Donald Claiborne would have to work out.

Chapter Thirty Five

"How did your meeting go with Donald Claiborne?" Joe Bradley asked as soon as he picked up the telephone."

"Better than I thought it would," Mark replied. "I threw everything at him but the kitchen sink. I think he's convinced that we could hold off the final disposition of the will long enough for the banks to begin foreclosure proceedings against the land Donald owns around the Trust property."

"Where did you leave it," Joe asked.

"I told him I would contact him when we get back from fall break."

"Are you still planning on leaving Saturday morning?"

"Bright and early Dad. We are going to stock the provisions on board Friday afternoon, spend the night on the boat in the marina, and leave at first light."

"I'll probably talk to you again before you leave, but if not, have a great time and a safe journey." After the call ended, Joe reclined in his office chair and pondered their position. He may have been the architect of the plan but Mark was the perfect man to carry it out. He was confident that when the entire Claiborne matter was resolved that his Son would be capable of leading the age old family law firm into the next generation.

Naomi was in her normal cheerful mood as she welcomed Mark at the front door. "Rachel isn't back from work, but please come in and tell me how your meeting went," she exclaimed with anticipation.

Just inside the foyer, Mark took her hand and said in a confident manner, "I'll tell you the same thing I told my dad a few minutes ago; I think it went well."

"Rachel shouldn't be long. Why don't we have some tea on the back porch while we are waiting for her?"

A few moments later Naomi came into the summer porch carrying two cups of hot tea on a silver tray. "Some folks like cream or sugar but I've got some special flavoring you might enjoy."

"By all means, Mrs. Richards. Whatever you recommend is fine with me."

She retrieved a small decanter filled with a dark liquid from the sideboard in the dining room and poured about one ounce into each cup.

"It's dark Bahamian rum," she said with a chuckle. "Not for the weak of heart, but good to the last drop. It's got some bite to it. Best to sip it."

A few moments later, Rachel came in the front door and joined the tea drinkers on the sun porch. "Free for two weeks," she announced as she sat next to Mark and kissed him on the cheek."

"We've been waiting until you arrived for Mark to tell us about his meeting with Donald Claiborne," Naomi said, "and having a little special tea. Honey, the water is still hot. Fix yourself a cup and we'll hear all about it.

Mark went through the entire story recalling as much as possible. He concluded with, "If he is short on cash, as we believe, I can't see how he has any choice but to accept. Besides, half of his development dreams are worth more than any hundred men could hope to make in a lifetime."

"You mean any hundred men or women." Rachel interjected with a soft jab to his side."

"I stand corrected," he replied in submission.

They heard the front door open and close and Claire Watson appeared. "Stan and I were on our way home and thought I would look in on you. But it looks like you have plenty of company. I'll be back around nine in the morning." Looking at Rachel she said, "I'll be staying here with Naomi until you return from spring break. You just have a good time and don't worry about us. Stan agreed to stay with me in the upstairs bedroom in case we might need him at night."

"Claire," Rachel responded, "I don't know how either of us could ever thank you enough for all that you do."

"Sweetheart, if you had any idea of all that your great grandmother has done for us over the years, you would know that thank you is not necessary."

As Mrs. Watson turned to leave, Naomi gently confronted her. "Claire, someone broke into Mr. Bradley's home near Charleston several weeks ago. Mark and the police are certain that they were looking for the boxes of personal family files that Mark took with him. Only four people knew about that: Rachel, Mark, myself and you. Is there any chance you might have mentioned it to someone?"

She placed her fingers over her lips and her cheeks were suddenly flushed. "I did," she replied in a quivering voice. After a moment she said, "Excuse me, I'll be right back," as she turned and walked toward the front door.

Chapter Thirty Six

Stan Watson was waiting for his wife in their car when she appeared on the front porch and told him to come into the house.

"There are some things you need to know," she said when they came into the summer porch. They appeared a bit awkward standing in front of the others and Mark quickly rose and gathered two chairs together for them to sit.

After taking her seat, Claire said, "I told Stan, and he . . ."

"And I told Luke Bratton," Stan continued in a subdued voice.

"Pardon my interruption," Mark exclaimed. "But why would you do that?

Claire wiped away tears that were running down her cheek. "He didn't have any choice Mr. Bradley. He'd lose his job if he didn't. It's been going on for a long time." As a quick afterthought, she said with resolve, "This has to stop and now is as good a time as any."

Naomi, Rachel, and Mark all exchanged glances and Mark replied, "Claire, rest at ease and tell us all about it."

She took a few deep breaths and began. "Some years ago, before Jack Claiborne died, our son was in a car accident in Charleston."

"I remember that well," Naomi offered.

"He was hurt bad Mr. Bradley. He was unable to work for almost five months. Between medical bills that insurance didn't cover and no income, they were afraid the bank would foreclose on their house. He's a good man and a good husband and father. We had to try to help him."

"Claire," Naomi said, "when I asked about your son from time to time, you always said things were working out all right. You never told me this part."

"What did you do, Mrs. Watson?" Mark continued.

"We tried to borrow some money on our house but the bank wouldn't loan it to us, even though it was nearly paid off. Naomi had given us the land years ago. We borrowed the money for the materials and Stan did almost all of the work himself. It's not a big fancy house Mr. Bradley but we love it."

"How did you get the money?" Mark asked.

"Stan was working for Jack Claiborne's land management company and he loaned us the money. He paid off the small balance on the mortgage and loaned us $20,000.00."

"Did he take a mortgage on the property to secure the loan?"

"Yes."

"What were the terms of the loan, Mrs. Watson?"

Noting a confused look on her face, he restated the question. "How many years were you given to pay back the loan?"

"I didn't even think to ask. We were both so relieved to get the money. He said to just continue making the same payments we had been making to the bank. After a long pause, she continued. About a year later we received a letter from Jack's company telling us that the balance on the loan was due."

"Did the note you signed have the words, Due on Demand, after a certain date or at least words to that effect?"

She solemnly nodded.

Stan Watson continued the explanation when he noticed his wife was struggling. "Jack told us he could foreclose on the house at any time he wanted unless we could come up with the money. He knew we couldn't. He said he would be willing to accept small monthly payments, enough to cover the interest in exchange for regular information."

"Information?" Mark asked.

"He wanted to know everything that was going on at Claiborne Plantation. He wanted to know who was coming and going and what they were doing. Anything I learned was to be reported to Luke Bratton. He was especially interested in Rachel's mother, Margaret, and her Aunt Jane. It's about the will, Mr. Bradley. It's always been about the will. Jane would have stood to inherit the Trust if she could ever have proved she was direct kin to old Thomas Claiborne. Since she died and the devil finally took Jack, Donald will get it unless Rachel can prove the same thing. It's common knowledge but most people pay it no mind. It's been this way for years."

"I know, Stan," Mark agreed.

"Most of what we told Luke over the years was worthless information," Mrs. Watson said. Sometimes we had to tell him things we couldn't hide."

"Like the boxes of family history files?"

"Good example. He was watching the house and demanded to know what was in the boxes. He's probably watching this house right now and you can be certain he's going to want to know what's going on," she replied in disgust.

"Did he know Rachel and I were going to the island the day the boat exploded?" Mark asked, looking at Stan.

"Miss Devening asked me to fill the portable gas tank for the boat and put it in the Jeep at the big house. Luke Bratton saw me filling it up at the station. All I told him was that I was supposed to put the tank in the old Jeep. I'm sure he figured the rest out by himself."

"Stan, do you think Luke Bratton was the one who broke into my house?"

"I'd bet money on it. He made me go with him to follow Miss Devening the first day she went to see you at the house on the beach. He knew exactly where you live."

"Do you think Bratton was responsible for blowing up the boat?"

"The man is a mechanical and electrical wizard. I'm sure he knew where you were going and where the boat would be. You figure it out. When you started showing up I think he was afraid you might find some proof that Rachel here is a dec . . . desid . . ."

"You mean descendent?"

"Right . . ., descendent of Thomas Claiborne."

"You said he was afraid. You mean Donald Claiborne was afraid I might find something."

"I suppose. But Bratton seemed to have a personal interest. Some years ago I was getting ready to bush hog weeds in the fields around the Plantation house and Bratton sent me on another job. I knew I was supposed to keep the weeds down and I told him I'd better check with Mr. Claiborne. Well, he got maddern hell and said 'I tell Claiborne what to do and don't you forget it."

"Did Jack and Luke seem to get along.?"

"Not so's you'd notice."

"How about Donald and Luke.?"

"I know for a fact Donald can't stand him."

"Then why does he put up with him."

"That's the sixty four dollar question, counselor. I swear I don't know."

Chapter Thirty Seven

"Naomi, I'm so ashamed," Mrs. Watson said. "I know how put out with us you must be. I'll see if my cousin, Anne can come stay with you while Rachel's gone."

"Nonsense," the old woman barked. This is all on the Claibornes and Luke Bratton. We're going to put an end to it right now. How much is the balance on the mortgage on your house?"

"It's still about the same, about $20,000.00. Seems like every time we get a little bit ahead the interest rate goes up."

"You've been paying all these years and the balance hasn't gone down," she exclaimed looking first at Claire and then Mark.

"I'm sure it's legal but it's not right," Mark conceded.

"Rachel, go in my bedroom and get my checkbook. Write a check to Stan and Claire for $20,000.00 and give it to me to sign."

The Watsons were stunned. "Mrs. Richards, We can't ask you to do that," Stan said.

"Never you mind; we'll just call it a bonus for years of hard work by both of you. You just take this check and pay off the loan."

"Naomi," Mark said, "it's a wonderful gesture, but Claiborne and Bratton will both know where the money came from. I'm afraid they might think we have found the evidence we need to prove Rachel's right to the Claiborne inheritance. If Bratton really did try to kill us, this might set him off and this time he might not miss. My father is still your attorney of record. Allow me to give the check to him. He will deposit it in the firm's real estate escrow account and will pay off the loan when we believe it's safe."

"Naomi nodded her approval to Rachel."

"In the meantime, Mr. and Mrs. Watson, I'm sure Luke Bratton will demand to know what we have been talking about. Rachel and I and a couple of friends are going to take my parent's boat down to Miami over fall break to a marina where they keep the boat during the winter months. It's called the Blue Ocean Marina. The marina is gated and outsiders can't get in without a pass. I'm sure we will be safe. We should arrive around noon on Monday."

"You want us to tell him that?"

"Sure, just like always. He'll think the system is still working as usual."

As the Watsons were preparing to leave, Naomi startled Stan with a question. "I have always believed Jane's death was no accident. They said she was knocked unconscious when she fell on the rock jetty and drowned when the tide came in. Do you think it's possible that Luke Bratton killed my granddaughter?"

With a look of sadness on his face, Stan replied, "Yes mam, I don't think there's any question."

For a moment, the silence in the room was deafening.

Finally, Mark spoke, looking at Rachel and Naomi, "Ladies, I'm going to walk the Watsons to their car."

Outside, Stan spoke to Mark. "When Rachel's parents died in that plane crash when they were on vacation, Luke Bratton was out of town for several days. If there is anyone who would know how to rig a plane to crash after takeoff, it's him. I didn't want to say anything in front of Rachel."

"I understand," Mark replied

Mark recalled that Rachel had told him their small charter plane took off early in the morning. If it had been tied down on the tarmac all night, he would have had plenty of time to work it over without being seen.

After Stan got in his car, Mark leaned down and spoke quietly, "I think we ought to turn the tide on Mr. Bratton. I wonder if you would like to do me a small favor?" After listening to the request, Stan smiled and said, "Consider it done."

Chapter Thirty Eight

Mark ordered pizza for dinner so the ladies wouldn't have to cook. Soon after they were finished eating, Naomi remarked in wonderment, "This has been a day for the record books. I missed my nap today and I'm going to turn in early. I'm sure the two of you won't miss my company." With a coy smile on her face, she added, "I know I wouldn't if I were you."

When Naomi was gone, Rachel looked at Mark and said, "I'd like to have a glass of port wine on the summer porch, turn the lights off and watch the sun go down."

"And," Mark replied.

"And then, I'd like to get close and personal. What say you?"

"I'd say it's amazing how great minds think alike."

During breakfast the next morning the subject turned to Thomas Claiborne's journals. Naomi asked, "Did you see anything at the plantation house that gave you any notion where Thomas might have put the journals?"

"Not a clue," Mark answered. "About the only thing I've learned about Thomas is that he was a good and honest man, he was a good businessman, and his behavior was consistent and highly predictable. All of that doesn't get me one bit closer to the journals."

"I'm sure they are still there," Naomi commented. "I know when he died my parents guarded that house like Fort Knox. I don't believe there was ever a time when both of them were gone at the same time. Nothing came in or out of that house without my mother knowing about it. They weren't as concerned about the whereabouts of the journals as they were for the safety of the house and the family members who lived there. They were the worst times for black folks in the South. We couldn't vote or shop in white stores or send our children to white schools. The Jim Crow laws pushed us all down hard. If all that wasn't enough, there were plenty of beatings and lynchings, and almost no one was ever held accountable. No sir, if those journals had been found my mother would have known. After my folks passed away, my husband and I continued to look after the house just like they did. If those journals ever existed, and we know they did, they are still there somewhere."

"I just keep trying to get inside his mind. Can you think of anything we haven't talked about?"

Naomi's mind drifted back to her childhood and the wonderful times she spent with Thomas. "From my own experience, in addition to everything my parents told me about Thomas, there were three things he cared about more than anything."

"Those were?" Mark replied.

"God, family, and the land. For years he attended two church services every Sunday. He and Rachel attended nine o'clock services at the black church he had built here on the plantation. Afterward, he would ride into town and attend eleven o'clock services at the Episcopal Church with his son Robert and his family."

"You mentioned earlier that Thomas and Robert got into a terrible fight when Rachel returned to South Carolina."

"They did, but time heals a lot of ill will and Thomas loved his white Claiborne family as much as he loved Rachel and Mary and his mixed race family."

"You mentioned the land?"

"Claiborne was one of the few plantations that survived the Civil War. Most of them went broke when there was no longer any slave labor to produce rice. The majority of Claiborne land was above sea level and couldn't be used for rice. He converted most of that land into the production of lumber, corn, and beans and produce. He even planted huge peach orchards and raised cattle. He always said if you take care of the land it will take care of you."

"Anything else Naomi?"

She thought for a moment and continued. "Every Monday morning he posted all of his receipts and expenditures from the previous week. And then," she said, the inspection tours."

"Inspection tours?" Mark asked.

"At the end of every month he traveled to all of the outlying plantations to inspect the land and the crops and all of the buildings. He'd be gone for three or four days and on the last day of the month he inspected everything on the home plantation. He checked the big house and all of the houses nearby where his black sharecroppers lived. The last thing he always inspected were the graveyards; the black cemetery where Rachel is buried and the white cemetery up closer to the house where early Claiborne family members are buried and the mausoleum where he is buried with his wife, Katherine, and their first son. My parents told me he never missed inspecting the cemeteries. He regarded them as holy places and, my word, he saw to it they were taken care of so well. After completing his inspections he always spent the next few days issuing orders for all the necessary repairs."

"Naomi, I appreciate all of your help. The more I hear of Thomas Claiborne, the more I like him. I'm sure the journals would tell us a lot more about him if we could ever find them."

Shortly after the Watsons arrived around 10 AM, Mark and Rachel left for the beach house on the Isle of Palms. On the way South on highway 17 they talked about their plans for the trip. They would pick up Mark's clothes and go on to the Marina to make sure the yacht was prepared for departure the following morning. "I'm so excited," Rachel said with enthusiasm. "I've never sailed on a yacht. And Miami and South beach . . . , I just know we're going to have a great time."

"Sounds like fun," Mark replied. But Miami will have to wait for another time."

"Another time?" she responded with alarm. "What do you mean?"

"We're not going to Miami. We, my love, are going to Freeport in the Bahamas."

"The Bahamas," she shouted. "You're kidding."

My dad changed his reservation for the winter to a marina in Freeport. At the end of our trip, we will catch a short flight back to Charleston. I've already bought the tickets."

"It's a wonderful surprise, but I'm a little confused. You told Naomi and the Watsons that we were going to Miami."

"Did I really?" he replied. "I think I'm too young for dementia. I must have forgotten."

"Forgotten, my ass," she said impatiently, "sometimes I just have to drag things out of you. What's up?"

"I think there is the possibility that Luke Bratton will show up at the Blue Ocean Marina looking for us. My father is a friend of the marina manager and he will call Dad if anyone shows up at the marina looking for Sea Breeze. Yesterday, I visited the mansion at Claiborne Plantation. After that, I spent quite a long time with Donald Claiborne and then the rest of the afternoon and evening at Naomi's house on Front Street. After the Watson's long stay, if Bratton was watching us as closely as Mrs. Watson suggested, he must be wondering what in the hell is going on."

"What reason would he have to follow us to Miami?" The answer came to her before the question was completed. "You're not suggesting," she stated with panic beginning to surface, "that he would try to kill us."

"Where better than in a strange place a long way from home? Another accident, perhaps. If he does show up we won't be there, but I think it would confirm Stan Watson's belief that he tried to kill us and probably killed your parents and Aunt Jane as well. What other reason would he have for showing up?"

"None that I know of," Rachel concluded with a frightened look beginning to spread across her face. "You don't think he's stupid enough to show his face at the marina?"

"I'm beginning to think there isn't much stupid about Luke Bratton. My guess is he will be in Charleston to watch us leave and somewhere near the entrance to the marina in Miami to watch us arrive on Monday. Once he confirms we have arrived, he'll have nearly a week to . ."

"To do what?" Rachel demanded.

Mark looked at her and shook his head. His serious demeanor turned to a smile and he said, "I know one thing for sure. We're going to have a great time in Freeport. Don't you worry. I will deal with Luke Bratton if the time comes."

Chapter Thirty Nine

They finished stowing their belongings aboard Sea Breeze about four o'clock. "Chad said he and his fiancé would be here around five. Would you like a beer while we wait for them or some of my dad's Maker's Mark bourbon?"

"What the heck," she replied, "we're on vacation; a little bourbon and water would be just fine."

After settling in the stern seats with their drinks, Rachel asked, "What do you know about Chad's future wife."

"I'm ashamed to say, not much. In fact, I don't even know her name. "Hopefully," he chuckled, "he will introduce her by name and get me off the hook."

After a few relaxed moments and in a sincere and thoughtful manner, Mark asked, "How is your inner struggle with your mixed race background going?"

"That's a good question," she replied with a smile. "The truth is, since we met, life has been such a whirlwind that it simply hasn't crossed my mind that much. Grandma Richards talked to me about it and her message was to the point . . . get over it. I guess my problem was being someone I didn't appear to be."

"You know," Mark replied, "I think almost everyone is not always who they appear to be. Take the Stantons. All these years they were under so much pressure and hiding it as though they didn't have a care in the world. And how about Donald Claiborne? My dad speaks highly of him as a developer and land manager. Even if we had subpoenaed all the trust records, I doubt we would have found much of anything out of order. By all accounts, his dad was a real bastard and I'm beginning to think a lot of Jack's reputation rubbed off on his son. I seem to recall that our strongest criticism of him was that he used to hit on you when you worked in the bank. I guess I can't blame him for that. Seems as though I'm guilty of that myself," he commented with a disjointed smile.

"I swear, Mark Bradley, sometimes I don't know whether to hit you or kiss you."

"A kiss would be my choice."

"Mine too," she said as she put her arms around him for some serious necking. After coming up for air, she said, "I guess you're right. I do have to give Donald credit for one thing. Naomi always got her monthly reports in the mail as long as Jack was alive. They couldn't stand each other. When Donald took over the Trust management, the reports continued to come in the mail but about every three months, he would hand deliver it and stay to answer any questions she had. I guess my thinking about him better change if we are going to be business partners. Do you really believe he will take the deal?"

"I do. I don't think he has any other choice. When our meeting began he was defensive, but the longer it went on the more reasonable he seemed to be. I almost found myself starting to like him. I'll tell you one person I'd like to know a lot more about is Thomas Claiborne. I'll bet we would both be surprised at what we might learn about him from his journals. Unfortunately, I'm beginning to think it's a lost cause."

Chapter Forty

They were both startled by the sound of screeching tires sliding to a stop in the marina parking lot. They watched with curious interest as a black woman wearing baggy blue jeans, a white shirt, and a blue bandanna got out of the driver's door, walked around the front of the van, and opened the panel door on the passenger side. She pulled a child's red wagon out of the van and began loading it with paper bags filled with groceries. With her wagon filled, she paused to look down the concrete piers. Mark and Rachel caught her eye and she started down the pier toward the boat. As she approached, she called out, "I'm looking for the Sea Breeze. Before they could answer she said, "Damn, I must be blind. The name's right on the back of the boat. Looks like I'm in the right place." She pulled the wagon up to the side of the boat and handed a bag up to Mark. She kept passing the bags up to them until the wagon was empty.

"Looks like that's all of it," Mark commented.

She looked at the empty wagon and back to the van and with a disgusted look said, "I'll be damned. I forgot the most important thing." As she started back toward the van she said, "Some of that stuff needs to be in the fridge or freezer."

A few minutes later she fired the engine and roared out of the parking lot. With stunned looks, Mark and Rachel looked at each other and began laughing.

After stowing the groceries and refreshing their drinks, they settled back into the stern seats to wait for Chad.

Thirty minutes later Chad boarded the Sea Breeze with a duffel bag and suitcase. "I fueled her this morning and took her out for a short sea trial. Everything appears to be in shape. I ordered groceries and after they arrive, we'll hang out and get ready to leave early in the morning."

"The groceries were delivered about a half hour ago, and Mark and I put them in the pantry and refrigerator," Rachel said.

"They were?" Chad replied.

"We had to laugh; the delivery lady was a real character. She pulled the bags down to the dock in a wagon. When she handed up the last bag she said she had forgotten something and tore out of the parking lot."

"A black lady driving a rusty old Ford Van?"

"You know her?" Rachel asked.

"She's a real character alright. Looks like you've met Felicia."

"Felicia?"

"My fiancé," Chad replied.

Again, Mark and Rachel looked at each other; this time with thinly veiled shocked looks. Just as that bit of information began to sink in, the old Ford van slid to a stop in the parking lot. Soon the black lady was walking down the pier carrying a cardboard box and a clothes bag draped over her shoulder. When she reached the boat she looked up with a big grin and said, "I've got the good stuff. We are ready to rock and roll."

"Let me give you a hand," Rachel said leaning over the side of the boat.

Felicia handed her the clothes bag and handed the box to Chad. Looking up at Mark she said, "You must be the lawyer. I don't suppose you'd mind reaching down here and giving a lady a hand."

"Pardon me," Mark replied. Reaching over the side, he said, "Put your foot on the side and give me your hand." With one quick pull, Felecia was standing on the stern of Sea Breeze. She reached down and opened the case. It was full of bottles. "Tequila and Rum and everything to go with it," she said. "No way I'm goin' on a sailin' trip without margaritas and pina coladas. No suh, no way, no how."

Rachel sensed something familiar about this folksy and exuberant woman and asked, "Chad, aren't you going to introduce us to your fiancé?"

A little embarrassed, Chad began, "Rachel Devening and Mark Bradley, I'd like you to meet Felecia Adams."

Mark extended his hand. It's a real pleasure, Felecia." Glancing down at the liquor, he said, "It looks like we're going to have a real good time."

"You got that right, lawyer man," she responded with a laugh.

Suddenly, Rachel realized why this woman seemed familiar. She stepped forward to shake her hand and said, "I believe it's Doctor Adams. I can't tell you how delighted I am to meet you."

Felecia knew she had been found out and surrendered with a smile. "You got me, honey, dead to rights. I thought I might be able to leave all that behind me for this trip."

"Don't worry, Doctor Adams," Rachel said as she returned the smile. "If it will help you feel like a regular sailor we can let you take some extra turns at KP duty."

With an astonished look, Mark said, glancing at Rachel, "I guess I'm a little confused."

"Mark, Doctor Adams is a full professor of African American History at the College of Charleston and, unless I'm mistaken is also an adjunct professor of history at Harvard. On top of that, she is also the author of a new book, about slavery and reconstruction in South Carolina, that I believe just made the New York Times best sellers list."

Mark stood speechless. "What's the matter, lawyer man, cat got your tongue?" Rachel teased as she bumped him with her hip.

"I think it did there for a minute," Mark sheepishly replied.

Felicia turned to Chad. "Sweetheart, you make the best drinks. Why don't you fix us all one? I ordered pizza like you asked and it should be here by the time we're finished." She turned back to Mark and Rachel and said, "I put these old clothes on over a new outfit, but I guess it's time to be dressed for a sailing party. It's all white and I didn't want to get dirty hauling the groceries," she said as she unbuttoned her shirt, unzipped her baggy jeans and let them both fall to the deck revealing a white halter top and short flared white shorts. She slipped the bandanna from her head and shook out her hair looking like she just stepped out of a Vogue fashion shoot.

Mark looked at Rachel and commented, "Weren't we just talking about people who are not who they appear to be?"

"I believe we were," Rachel agreed.

"Did I miss something?" Felicia asked.

"Just a conversation we were having," Rachel replied. I'm sure we will get to know each other so well during this trip, you will undoubtedly hear all about it."

Rachel handed Felecia the clothes bag she had laid over the back of a deck chair.

"What's in the bag?" Chad asked.

"Wait till you see," she replied with excitement. She opened the bag and pulled out a dress. "This is the quintessential little black dress and it doesn't leave much to the imagination. Would you hold this dear?" she asked Rachel as she reached back into the clothes bag. "Before this trip is over, I'm going to wear that dress when Chad takes me to the most expensive and romantic restaurant in Miami and you Captain, are going to wear this."

Out of the bag came a white mariner's captain suit with white trousers and a white jacket with brass buttons, epilates on the shoulder, and captain's stripes.

"Aw honey, I don't want to wear . . ."

"You most certainly are going to wear this suit and this as well," she said as she pulled out a white captain's hat replete with a black leather bill adorned with leaf shaped yellow insignia.

Mark whistled and exclaimed, "Wow, what's all this?"

Felicia proudly answered, "Chad has been working on his Coast Guard Captain's certification for nearly five years and received his license last week. This man," she proclaimed with her hand on Chad's shoulder, "is certified to captain any ship that sails the ocean, including one like that," she said pointing to a Carnival Cruise ship in the distance, making its way out of Charleston Harbor.

"Hey man, that's great," Mark said taking his friend's hand. "Oh, by the way, this doesn't mean we have to pay you for this trip, does it?"

England, 1877

Elizabeth was on hand at the port when her father's ship arrived at Weymouth Harbor on the East coast of England south of London. As was his custom, he stopped in England to see his children, Elizabeth and Robert, before sailing on to La Rochelle, France to spend the summer with Rachel and Mary.

The day after his arrival, father and daughter were walking and reminiscing in the gardens of her new husband's family estate. "Father, I wish you could stay more than a week but I know how anxious you are to see Rachel."

"Each year our separation seems to get longer." With a smile on his face, he said, "I think love is in the air with Mary and if she weds I'm determined to yield to Rachel's wish to return to Claiborne Plantation even though I know how difficult it will be."

"I'm so happy for the two of you. I was only four when I last saw Rachel, but I remember her so well. She was a mother to me and I loved her so much. We used to play in front of the house and hang our legs in the pool with the statue. I hope Mary has found a wonderful man."

"I think she has. His name is Alexandre Charbonnet. He is the son of my business associate and I suspect they have been waiting for my arrival to announce their engagement. I only wish Robert was as tolerant as you. He despises black people and I'm not sure why. I guess if we had been able to spend more time together things would be different. I've just acquired a bank in Georgetown and when Robert finishes at the University I'm hoping he will agree to oversee it. Perhaps his sense of commerce and business will help temper his prejudice."

In the parlor on the day of his departure, Thomas handed his daughter a folder. "These are the documents we discussed. There are two sets. I have one and now that you are grown I would like you to have the other for safekeeping. I'm sorry all this must remain between the two of us, but for now, that's t the way it must be. Perhaps one day otherwise good men and women will come to their senses and accept people for the good in them regardless of their color.

Chapter Forty One

At the break of dawn, the throaty sound of the twin engines increased to a finely tuned hum as Chad brought Sea Breeze up on plane at twenty knots and headed through Charleston Harbor for the open sea. The rising sun cast vibrant streamers of coral and blue across the sky and reflected like diamonds from the windows in the houses on the Battery that had stood sentinel at the harbor for over 150 years; testimony to the fact that, even in a rapidly changing world, some things remain the same.

As usual, tourists and early Charleston risers were parked along Murray Boulevard to watch the sun come up over the harbor. Among them was a man with binoculars focused on a yacht heading for the ocean. As the boat passed by he put his binoculars on the seat and checked his watch. Sea Breeze was on schedule to arrive at the Ocean Blue Marina mid-day Monday and Luke Bratton would be there waiting for her.

Chad was in the upper helm while the other three were seated in the cabin having a breakfast of bagels with cream cheese, fruit, and orange juice. Felecia acted like she was on her way to heaven when Mark told her about the change in destination from Miami to Freeport, Bahamas.

"We are barely underway," she exclaimed, "and this trip seems to be getting better by the minute. Chad said we should have really calm seas most of the way."

"Felecia," Mark said with a serious tone but reassuring smile, "We will be hugging the coast for a good part of the trip and should be in cell phone contact most of the time. Other than the four of us, my father is the only one who knows we have changed our destination from Miami to Freeport. If you should talk to anyone on the phone during the trip, we would appreciate you not telling anyone about our change in plans."

"Mind telling me why?" she replied.

"Not a bit," Rachel interjected. "But we better make some coffee. This is going to take a while." Felecia listened with rapt attention as Rachel and Mark unfolded the story of the Claiborne Trust."

As their story wound down, Felecia commented, "Let me get this straight. We could possibly be in some danger if we show up in Miami?"

Mark nodded. "It's very possible."

"Well then, to hell with Miami," she replied laughing. "I've never been to Freeport but I've heard the water is beautiful and I have friends who tell me the nightlife can get wild and crazy."

Chad keyed his mike and his voice came over a speaker in the cabin, "Mark, take the wheel in the cabin and hold the present course. I'm coming down."

Mark slid into the helmsman's chair and took the wheel as Chad came through the cabin door. How about some breakfast, Honey?" Felecia asked as Chad took Mark's seat at the table.

"Whatever you have will be great."

Chad noticed a tablet of stationary and several envelopes on the table. "These yours?" he asked Rachel.

"My grandmother doesn't do well with modern communications, so I thought I would write her a few letters during the trip."

"That's great, but if you leave them out here very long the humidity will wrinkle the paper." He reached over and put them in a cabinet next to the gauges by the helm. "This is a humidity controlled cabinet with a sealed door. If you keep them in here when you're not writing, they will stay good as new."

"Thank you, Chad," Rachel replied in a pleasant and formal manner in deference to his new rank. "I'm no sailor, but it's comforting to know we have a great Captain. By the way, how far will we make it today?"

"We've got really calm seas and I've pushed her up about two knots faster than I expected. We should have smooth sailing and make St. Augustine long before dark. We'll refuel and spend the night at the marina and head on South at first light in the morning."

Throughout the day, Chad and Mark spelled each other hourly at the helm.

Felecia was fascinated with the story of the Claiborne Trust, especially the mystery of the lost journals. "From what you have told me about Thomas Claiborne, those journals could turn out to be a historian's treasure chest."

"I'll be sure to let you know if we find them," Rachel replied. "In the meanwhile, you should come up to meet my grandmother Richards. She's over ninety years old and she has an endless supply of stories about growing up black and living in the low country. Some of it is hard to listen to but she is sharp as a tack."

With Chad and Mark both in the upper helm, Rachel and Felecia moved out to the deck chairs on the open deck at the stern. As they resumed their conversation, Rachel said, "There is one thing I didn't tell you about Thomas Claiborne's mistress after his wife died."

"You mean the woman who had a child with Thomas; the one you were named for . . ."your great grandmother several times over. What else is there to tell?"

"She was a slave."

"No way," Felecia yelled.

Chad hollered down from the helm, "What's the commotion?"

"You're not going to believe this," Felecia called back. "This girl might have an Irish last name but she's a sister."

"What are you talking about?" Chad replied.

Mark couldn't help but laugh and, getting Chad's attention, said, "I'll tell you all about it.

"Finally," Rachel exclaimed to Felecia with her hands held up, "now you've heard the entire story."

"I have to admit, it is the most fascinating story of family history I have ever heard." After a moment to collect her thoughts, Felecia said, "Now tell me about you and Mark."

"I thought I did," Rachel said with a puzzled look.

"No, I'd like to know about you and Mark. I think you know what I mean," she said in a caring tone while taking Rachel's hand.

"I know what you mean." Mark and Rachel's relationship and Chad and Felecia became the subject of girl talk on and off for the rest of the trip.

Chapter Forty Two

With the morning sun lighting the way, Sea Breeze pulled out of the harbor at Saint Augustine and turned due south in the Atlantic headed for Palm Beach where they would spend the second night before their final 80 mile leg to Freeport on Grand Bahama Island.

By the second day at sea, all hands had gotten their sea legs and settled into comfortable routines. Under Chad's watchful eyes, both ladies took hour long turns at the helm and were both declared Able Bodied Helmswomen by the Captain. When Felecia was at the helm in the cabin, she directed a comment to Chad, "Steering this boat is easy. I think you men need to do the cooking and leave driving the boat to the women."

"That would be just fine with me," he countered, "except for two things."

"Which are?" she retorted.

"First of all, the food would probably not be fit to eat, and we'll see what you think about driving the boat if we get into some five or six foot seas."

Rachel snickered with a short response, "I think we'll leave the arrangements just as they are."

Later in the afternoon they pulled into the marina at Palm Beach. There were rows of super yachts all twice or more the size of Sea Breeze and each one grander than the next.

The happy mariners had a dinner fit for a king on the stern deck. Felecia sautéed vegetables in olive oil and white wine. Rachel prepared the salad. Mark fixed steaks to order on the gas grill and Chad made the cocktails. "Here's to great weather," Chad said raising his glass for a toast, "and may it continue."

There was music coming from a super yacht moored several slips away from Sea Breeze and, as the evening went on, the music got louder and the crowd on board began to swell. A man dressed in white shorts and a white polo shirt who appeared to be fiftyish in age stopped near the stern and introduced himself. "I'm John Caruthers. We're having a party on my boat. I apologize for the loud music but why don't you come join us. Mostly middle age and older folks. We could use some young blood."

The four looked at each other and in an instant Felecia stood up and said, "We accept."

Rachel squeezed Mark's hand and said, "Why not, it sounds like fun."

The girls were the hit of the party and, at one point, Mark asked Chad if he thought they would have been invited if the girls were not with them. "Naw," Chad replied, "not likely."

To the relief of some of the wives on board, Chad and Mark were able to steal the girls away from avid admirers, and danced until their feet could stand no more.

While Chad was maneuvering Sea Breeze out of her berth the next morning and the girls were stowing dinnerware from the night before, Mark slipped out of the cabin and called Stan Watson. "Our boy been up to anything?" Mark asked.

"I've been watching him like a hawk," Stan replied. I saw him fueling the airplane yesterday and, on a hunch, I drove out to an old service road near the airport before sunup this morning just in time to see him take off. I don't know where he was going, but he turned right and headed south."

"Thanks, Stan; we'll see you when we get back from Miami."

Mark quickly placed a second call to his dad to give him the news. "The control tower would not have been open when he left," he said, "and you can be certain he didn't file a flight plan."

"Wouldn't he risk being seen landing in Miami?"

"Not really. There are several small airstrips in the Miami area where he could land without being noticed. Then it's a cab ride to the marina where he could find a spot to watch for Sea Breeze coming in from the sea."

The "I'm going to call Frank Zeller and let him know. His people are still working on the boat explosion." After a pause, Joe Bradley said with a worried tone, "I don't like this Mark."

"Neither do I, Dad."

Chad asked Mark to take the helm and Felecia joined him. "I hope you don't mind," she said, "I love sitting up here."

Chad took a seat on the stern deck and called up to Mark, "Take us to Freeport, Mr. Bradley."

Mark winked at Felecia and replied, "Aye-aye, Captain. Any other orders?"

"Don't be a smart ass," Chad called back.

Mark eased the throttle up and set a course for Freeport. I'm really proud of him," Mark said to Felecia. "I know it was a lot of work and a long time."

"I know he said he doesn't want to wear the captain's uniform, but I know he's proud of it himself," she replied.

Rachel emerged from the main cabin and joined Chad on the stern deck. Although the cabin blocked most of the wind, their conversation could not be heard over the steady hum of the engines. "I'm so happy for you and Felecia. She is a real treasure. We have gotten to know each other so well, and I'm sure we will remain friends for years. I'm curious to know how the two of you met."

Chad laughed as he recalled their first meeting. "I stopped to help her with a flat tire on that ratty old van she drives. It took me a while to get her going again and she seemed like a nice lady. She tried to pay me but I wouldn't take any money. Frankly, between the field hand clothes she was wearing and that junker she drives, I didn't think she had two nickels to rub together. She said she was in a hurry but insisted on my name and address so she could send me a thank you note. I gave her one of my cards and she hopped in the van and took off. Next thing I knew, I received a letter in the mail in a formal envelope. It was from the Charleston Historical Society requesting my presence at a cocktail party and dinner to honor Doctor Felecia Adams."

"What was the occasion?"

"I guess it was for her fund raising work for the society. At any rate, there was a hand written note at the bottom of the letter from the director that said, "Miss Adams has requested that you serve as her escort for the evening. Please arrive a few moments early and a suit and tie are required for gentlemen."

"How did it go?" Rachel asked, obviously anxious to hear more.

"It was a great evening but the beginning was a little clumsy."

"Clumsy?"

"When I walked into the banquet hall there were two ladies talking near the front door. One of them asked if she could help me and I told her I was looking for Felecia Adams. The other lady stepped forward and said, 'I think you've found her.' She sure didn't look the way I remembered. My God, she was beautiful." For a moment Chad seemed lost in thought and then turned to Rachel, "I know it makes me sound like a teenager, but do you believe in love at first sight?"

The question brought an instant smile to her face. "I certainly do and it's wonderful."

"Mark?"

"Absolutely, the minute I laid eyes on him."

"Well, I know he's crazy about you."

"Did he tell you that?"

"I've known Mark Bradley since we were in grade school. He has three sisters and we grew up like brothers. He didn't have to tell me. Any time he talks about you, it's in the tone of his voice and written all over his face."

"That's so sweet. He is the kindest and most gentle man I've ever known."

With a grin, Chad replied. "That's his upbringing. Mrs. Bradley is big on respect and proper behavior. Between his mother and sisters, he learned early on how to treat women and all people, for that matter."

"I know he's strong, but I can't imagine he would hurt a fly."

Chad reserved a comment for a moment and finally responded. "He is everything you say but don't be fooled by his behavior."

"Really, what do you mean?"

After another pause to think before speaking, Chad said, "Over the years a few people have taken his mild manners to think he's a pushover." With added strength in his voice and a glance toward Mark in the upper helm, he continued. "Listen, If I was in a fight and needed help, the only person I would want is Mark Bradley."

"Really," Rachel replied with growing interest. "Did he get in a lot of fights growing up?"

"Nope. Just a few and that's all it took. The last time I saw Mark in a fight was at the Citadel during our sophomore year in the locker room after football practice. A black kid on our team who played wide receiver had a bad practice and dropped three passes that probably would have gone for touchdowns in a game. A senior nose tackle ragged him pretty hard and said the kid must have had grease on his hands from all the fried chicken he'd been eating. That drew a pretty good laugh from most of the guys. But then, as he started toward his locker he mumbled something under his breath but just loud enough to be heard."

"What did he say?"

"He called him a clumsy nigger."

"Ouch," Rachel replied with red starting to show in her eyes.

"Ouch is right. Mark stood up and told the guy that his fried chicken remark was kind of funny, even if it was in bad taste."

"The guy started to get his temper up and asked Mark what business was it of his."

"It wasn't," Mark answered, "until you called him a clumsy nigger. That made it my business."

"Right then I knew it wasn't going to end well. Mark told him to apologize. This guy was a lot bigger than Mark and he said he'd be damned if he would apologize. Then he said, 'You open your mouth one more time and I'll rip your ass apart.' Mark told him to do what he had to do. He said, 'take your best shot, but do yourself a favor, don't miss.' That really pissed him off."

"What happened?" Rachel asked as she seemed to be hanging on to every word.

"He missed. Then Mark hit him three times so hard and so fast. It couldn't have been three seconds and he was lying on the floor bleeding from a busted tooth and a broken nose."

"Did he get in trouble for fighting?"

"No. There's an unwritten code. You don't rat on other cadets. Besides, it was the other guy who invited the fight. He just invited the wrong person. "Rachel," Chad said in earnest, "I'm sure Mark wouldn't appreciate me telling you these things, but I just wanted you to know. Anytime you're with Mark, you're in the safest place you can be." As an afterthought, he continued, "I hope it's safe enough."

Chapter Forty Three

A man with binoculars was sitting on a park bench with a clear view of the entrance to the Blue Ocean Marina near Miami. A little after noon, the boat he was expecting pulled into the marina in Freeport. He would have a long wait.

The crew of Sea Breeze spent the afternoon exploring Freeport and sampling local fare. As the sun began to set, they settled in for dinner at a seaside restaurant. Meanwhile, Luke Bratton gave up his watch and checked into a nearby hotel under a false name and paid with cash.

After several hours scanning the marina for Sea Breeze the following morning, Bratton went back to the hotel. He managed to slip into a room where the door had been left open by departing guests. He used the hotel phone to make a local call to the Blue Ocean Marina.

"Blue Ocean," a lady answered after picking up after the first ring.

"This is Jasper Air freight. We have a small package to deliver to a yacht by the name of Sea Breeze. Just wanted to know when she's expected before sending a truck out there."

"She's not," came the reply. "She is normally docked here for the winter but the reservation was canceled one day last week."

Bratton slammed the receiver down and left the hotel through the rear entrance.

The Blue Ocean receptionist stuck her head in the marina manager's office. "Some freight company called asking about Sea Breeze. I told him their reservation had been canceled."

"Thanks, Julie," the manager said as he reached for his phone to call Joe Bradley.

Rachel was sitting on the forward pulpit of the bow with her arms hung over the lower railing and her legs dangling in air as the boat skimmed through the crystal blue Bahamian water while being covered with a fine mist each time the bow nosed gently into the sea. She was surrounded by an endless collage of beauty in nature that was a treat for her eyes and, occasionally, she would look back to the upper helm where Mark was at the ship's wheel. Never before had she felt more at ease in anyone's company. She had never felt more loved and she was beginning to have some difficulty remembering life without Mark Bradley.

A little after 11 AM Mark dropped the anchor in the shallow, clear turquoise water just off a small island about five miles north of the west end of Grand Bahama Island. "All the comforts of home," Chad announced as he loaded several beach umbrellas and a cooler into a small inflatable. I'll pull this in with me. The rest of you can hop in the water and we'll set up on shore."

"Rachel," Felecia summoned, "I can't get the bra strap on my suit hooked. Can you give me a hand?" She asked while holding her top up.

"Sure, turn around and let me fasten it." After a quick look, Rachel said, "I hate to tell you, but the snap is broken and there's not enough to tie."

After a moment to think about her predicament, she called to Chad who was already in the water. "Is there anyone else on this island?"

"You can only get here by boat and we are the only one."

"OK," she announced, "I officially proclaim this a topless beach." With that said she dropped her top on a deck chair and jumped into the water.

"What's the old saying?" Rachel said as she untied her top, "when in Rome."

Back in the marina that afternoon the manager came by Sea Breeze. "Just stopped by to see if you folks need anything and if you're having a good time."

"We're having a great time," Felecia answered. "We even found a topless beach."

With his face beginning to turn red, he replied, "That's funny, I didn't know there were any around here."

"Felecia, you have no shame," Rachel said jokingly as the manager left to continue his rounds.

"You got that right, Honey."

Mark's phone rang and his father was on the other end. "The marina manager at Blue Ocean called. Said they got a call from someone asking about Sea Breeze. I'm going to let Frank Zeller know. When I talked to him yesterday, he said they have new information about the boat explosion. He also said they have begun to take an interest in Luke Bratton."

"Was that all he had to say?"

"He said he wanted to talk to us as soon as you return. He also said to tell you to be careful."

As Mark ended the call he forced a smile to erase the grim look from his face.

"He looked at the others and said, "Dad, just wishing us a good time.

Chapter Forty Four

Rachel and Mark were sitting on the stern deck around seven that evening waiting for Chad and Felecia to emerge from their cabin for their date. When Felecia stepped out of the cabin in her little black dress, even Rachel was stunned. "If that dress was illegal, you'd be headed straight to jail," Rachel exclaimed. "When Chad comes out I've got to get a picture of the two of you together."

"I was hoping the two of you would change your mind and come with us."

"Not on your life," Rachel responded. "This is supposed to be a romantic evening for two. Besides, Mark and I are going to have our own romantic dinner here on the boat. The marina restaurant will serve the entire meal right here."

At that moment, Chad came out of the cabin in his captain's uniform. "Oh my," Rachel said. "If ever there was a time for an old Irish custom, this is it." With that, she kissed him on the cheek. "Killer cologne to boot."

"I have to admit," Mark offered, "You really clean up well."

"It's for Felecia," Chad replied, "she insisted."

"What he means is," Felecia replied with a smirk, "it's a good idea to pay attention to the woman you're sleeping with."

"Touché," Rachel agreed.

"Chad, Rachel, and I got you a belated engagement gift." As Mark handed him a plastic door card, he said, "You have a suite for the night at the Sand Dune Hotel directly across the street from your restaurant. It has a full bar and anything else you need, just call room service." As an afterthought, he said, "We don't expect to see the two of you before noon tomorrow."

"There go two people madly in love," Rachel said as they watched Chad and Felecia leave the docks and amble down the street holding hands.

At eight o'clock two waiters appeared and set up dinner service on the stern table, complete with white tablecloth and linens and two glasses of Moscato to accompany the salad and thinly sliced tuna appetizer. The head waiter lit a candle in a silver holder for the table and said, "Enjoy, I will bring the entrees in about twenty minutes."

"Merci à un serveur. Il fait beau," Rachel said with a gracious smile.

"C'est mon plasir," the waiter replied with a slight bow.

With an approving smile, Chad said, "I didn't understand a word but something tells me I need to learn French."

She reached over and lightly squeezed his leg. "I know just the right teacher."

After dinner, the waiter brought a fresh pot of coffee and Mark poured a small shot of Makers Mark into each cup for an after dinner drink.

"I'm so happy for Chad and Felecia," Rachel said. "They seem like the perfect couple. I know you are going to be Chad's best man and earlier today Felecia asked me to be her maid of honor."

Suddenly, Mark was handed the perfect window of opportunity. "You know," he began with a slow but purposeful drawl, "One good turn deserves another. If we are going to stand up for Chad and Felecia, don't you think it would only be fair if they were to stand up for us? But, of course, that would require a wedding." With that, he pulled a white silk gentleman's handkerchief from his pocket and unfolded it on the table to reveal a diamond engagement ring set in white gold.

Rachel put her hand on Mark's arm and sat speechless. After a moment she rose from the table and following a kiss on his cheek said, "I'll be right back."

She came out of the main cabin and stepped into the moonlight on the stern deck a few minutes later wearing a short white nightgown with an empire top that was not designed to hide her perfectly formed breasts. She held out her hand and said, "Come with me to our cabin. Saying yes is going to take a while."

Chapter Forty Five

Rachel looked up from the letter she was writing to her great grandmother, Naomi, to see Chad and Felecia walking down the pier. Rachel took Felecia's hand as she stepped on the boat. "How did it go?" she asked quietly.

"The food was out of this world. In fact, so good that Chad and I are taking the two of you there tonight."

Rachel whispered in her ear, "That's not what I meant."

"I know what you meant," Felecia replied with a grin. I think the guys are going bone fishing this afternoon. We'll have a Pina colada here on the boat and I'll tell you all about it. Did you and Mark have a nice dinner?"

"It was wonderful. Even had a French waiter. Other than dinner, we just had a nice relaxed evening on the boat."

As Felecia began to withdraw her hand from Rachel, she felt something on her left hand and looked down to see the new engagement ring. "Relaxed evening my eye. Chad, look at this," she said holding Rachel's hand up.

Chad held Rachel's hand as he admired the ring and then reached out to shake Mark's hand. "This is one of those times I would normally make some smart ass remark, but all I can think to say is how happy I am for you both."

When the small charter fishing boat pulled up alongside Sea Breeze, Chad said to the ladies, "I know it's a little late to ask, but are you sure you don't mind fending for yourselves for the afternoon?"

"Lover, Felecia replied, "We'll be just fine. We're going to have some Pina Coladas on the deck and we've got lots to talk about."

"I'll bet you do," Chad replied in a resolute tone.

Felecia made the drinks and brought them to the stern deck. "Who wants to go first?" she asked. "I've got to warn you," she said with a broad smile, "my story about last night is X rated."

"Mine too," Rachel replied laughing.

The evening was filled with great food, dancing to the wee hours to Caribbean music, and conversation that always seemed to return to wedding plans. The following morning, Sea

Breeze pulled out of the Marina and headed for the topless island where they would spend their last two days in secluded paradise. They snorkeled near rock outcroppings in a protected cove, fished, and prepared their catch in a campfire in the evening.

"After all the people and partying," Felecia said, "having this island and the sky and the ocean all to ourselves is the perfect way to end a vacation."

After late night cocktails, while watching the fire burn down to embers, the couples put a lot of beach between them and slept on beach blankets spread on the sand with large beach towels for blankets. Nestled in Mark's arms under a blazing array of stars, Rachel's mind was filled with thoughts and dreams of their lives together. She was never one to wish her life away, but after all these years she hoped the matter of the trust would soon be resolved one way or the other.

She wouldn't have long to wait.

Chapter Forty Six

As they prepared to leave Sea Breeze and head for the airport in a waiting taxi, Rachel suddenly remembered her letter writing materials and called to Mark who was the last to leave the yacht, "Sweetheart, would you get my stationary and envelopes out of the sealed compartment?"

"Just like new," he thought as he retrieved the paper goods. He knew they would have been filled with mildew if not protected.

Just before takeoff Mark called his father who seemed anxious to know their immediate plans. "Rachel still has several days before classes resume. We'll probably spend them together between her place in Georgetown and the beach house on the Isle of Palms. Why do you ask?"

"I've spoken with Frank Zeller several times while you've been gone. He's concerned about your safety and would like to meet with us in our office at ten in the morning if that's all right with you?"

"Sounds serious."

"I think it is," Joe Bradley replied. In the meanwhile, "I've booked a room for you and Rachel at the Colonial Hotel across the street from the office. It's on the concierge floor and the elevator won't stop without a pass key and the fire doors to the exit stairs only open out. I suggest you check in and stay put until our meeting in the morning."

Mark had been shielding Rachel from the actions of Luke Bratton during their trip, but with paradise fading quickly behind them as the plane leveled off on a heading for Charleston, it was time to bring her up to date. She reacted calmly with the thought that perhaps it was an indication that her wish for the whole mess to soon be over was about to come true.

They found Mark's car in the parking stall where his parents had dropped it off that morning and headed for the hotel in downtown Charleston. Just before pulling out of the parking lot Mark pulled over and suddenly stopped.

"Something wrong?" Rachel asked with some alarm.

Mark sat with his hands on the wheel staring straight ahead. After a moment's pause, he turned at looked directly at her. "I know where they are!" he exclaimed with his eyes growing with excitement. "Thomas Claiborne's journals . . . I know where they are. Damn," he said, hitting the wheel with his fist. "Why did it take me so long?"

"Mark!"

"The journals are in the casket with Thomas and Katherine's firstborn child."

Stunned, Rachel replied, "How can you be sure?"

"Listen, if we turn right we go to the hotel. If we turn left, we head to the Claiborne plantation and I'll tell you all about it on the way."

"Turn left," Rachel instantly replied, "and step on it."

"What makes you think they are in the casket and, for that matter, why?"

"Why would you bury a stillborn infant in a casket built for an adult? You wouldn't. Besides, there was a carpenter and blacksmith on the plantation. They could have crafted a baby's coffin in no time. We know Thomas was ingenious. He probably realized that a lead lined coffin would protect the journals from the humidity and a locked mausoleum would keep them secure. You can bet that the coffin was already built to be used if a family member died unexpectedly when the child died in birth. Thomas probably took note of all the available space and decided it would be a good place to store his journals. Makes sense . . . , doesn't it?"

Still reeling with surprise, Rachel asked, "I guess it makes sense but what made you think of it?"

"The sealed compartment on Sea Breeze. Chad told you the intense humidity would destroy your stationary and that you should keep it in the sealed document compartment. And then, for some reason, I recalled you telling me in the mausoleum that the caskets were all made of cypress wood and that they were lined with copper with a lead seal; a perfect place to keep paper journals."

Mark kept searching his memory and continued. "The morning we left on our trip, Naomi talked a lot about Thomas. At the end of each month he inspected all of the plantations. The home plantation was always the last and he always concluded this monthly ritual by inspecting the two cemeteries and the mausoleum on the last day of the month. Don't you see? New Year's Eve is the last day of the month but it is also the last day of the year. Thomas ended all of his journals on the last day of the year. He would store the completed journal for safekeeping and begin a new one on New Year's Day."

It was nearly dark when they pulled onto the lane leading to the Claiborne mansion. Mark stopped the car near the house and they walked down the path to the mausoleum. He had a flashlight and Rachel kept a padlock key on her keyring. When the locks were removed, Mark lifted the heavy iron bars from the flanges and together they slowly swung the heavy door open and tentatively stepped inside.

Mark focused his light on the child's coffin covered with ages of dust and began examining the edges looking for the means to lift open the top. About two feet from each end there was a small finger hold. The battery in the flashlight was weak and the light began to dim. "I keep matches in my purse to light candles at home," Rachel said. There is a candle at the altar that should give us just enough light."

Just as she found the matches, the light from the flashlight went out and they were in total darkness. Suddenly a light shone through the open door followed by a loud and demanding voice, "Who's in there?"

Rachel screamed and Mark's knees buckled. The voice was unmistakable. "Stan, you scared the living hell out of us," Mark said, trying to regain some composure."

"I'm sorry, but I saw car lights driving up the lane from our front window and I drove up here with my lights off to see who it was. What are you two doing here at night?"

"It's a long story, Stan; but first, help me open this casket."

Together, they pulled at the top in the finger holds, but with no luck. It wouldn't budge. "Stan, let's get our lug wrenches and see if we can pry it open." After retrieving the lug wrenches from the trunks of their cars they slipped the flat pry ends into the casket slots and slowly began to apply pressure. Suddenly, nearly a century of corrosion released its grip and the top began to lift up. Mark kept his pry bar in place while both of them got their fingers under the bottom edge of the top. They lifted the top up and leaned it against the mausoleum wall.

Rachel passed Stan's flashlight over the interior of the coffin. At the head was a small permanently sealed box lined in copper. "It's the child's coffin," she said in a solemn tone. The remainder of the casket was filled with neatly arranged rows of leather bound journals and a file sized box made of cypress wood.

"What are all these books?" Stan asked in amazement.

"We think they will answer a lot of questions," Mark replied. "Help us get them to my car."

They all made several trips to transfer all the journals and the wooden box to Mark's trunk.

"Stan, we're going to Charleston tonight but we'll stop in town to tell my grandmother that we have found the journals."

Stan replied with reservation, "Luke Bratton has been in an ugly mood for the last three or four days and I know he's been watching the house. If you don't want to be seen, you should probably go on to Charleston without stopping in Georgetown."

"Good thought," she replied, "I'll give her a call."

They returned to the mausoleum and gently put the coffin top back in place. "Why don't you folks go ahead," Stan said, "I'll lock up and head on to town. After a short pause, he continued, "Mrs. Richards sure is gonna be surprised."

"No one can know about this Stan."

"Don't worry Mr. Bradley, spying on Bratton and making sure he doesn't have a clue about anything that's going on has been more fun than I've had in years."

On the road to Charleston, Rachel called Naomi and told her all about the journals. She was excited and anxious to learn what information they contained.

"I've got to call Felecia. We had a lot of time to talk during the trip and I told her all about the Trust and the journals. I promised to let her know if we ever found them."

With the telephone routed through the car radio, she placed the call so they could both talk. She answered on the second ring. "Felecia, this is Rachel. You're not going to believe why I'm calling."

"Let me guess," she replied with typical Felecia gusto. We're all taking another week off and going back to Freeport."

"I wish," she responded, "but seriously, we found the journals."

It took a moment for it to sink in. "The journals? . . . Oh my God, Thomas Claiborne's journals. Where did you find them?"

Rachel looked at Mark and mouthed a question. Is it all right if I tell her?" Mark smiled and nodded and Rachel began giving Felecia all the details.

When she was finished, Felecia asked, "Where are you going to keep them?"

"I don't know. We haven't gotten that far."

"Those are really old and need to be handled with great care. Why don't you bring them to the Historical Society? It's located in the old Cotton Exchange Bank just down from the hotel where you are staying tonight."

"I know exactly where it is," Mark said.

"Good, pull down the drive on the right side of the building and I'll meet you at the back door. We'll put them in the old vault. Its temperature and humidity controlled. First thing in the morning I'll call our preservationist. He specializes in old documents and he can tell us the best way to handle them."

When they pulled up to the back door of the old bank building, Felecia was waiting with the lights on. In the old vault, Felecia had them arrange the journals on a table in exactly the same order they had been stored in the casket. She put heavy book ends at the ends of each row to prevent any of them from falling open and risking pages being torn. She asked about the separate wooden box. "No clue," Mark responded. "It has a latch, let's open it up."

Inside the box, there appeared to be letters in envelopes neatly stacked along with other documents. Felecia gently lifted one envelope that had the name of the Episcopal Church of Georgetown, South Carolina printed on the front. She couldn't resist her curiosity and carefully removed several papers from the envelope. After looking them over for a few minutes, she said, "I was under the impression from what you told me that Thomas Claiborne and Rachel were lovers and lived together but were never married."

Rachel's expression turned to one of serious interest. "There was never any record of a marriage."

"Well, honey chile, there is now," Felecia replied. "A marriage certificate and a baptismal certificate for a child by the name of Mary Elizabeth Claiborne." Looking back at the documents, she continued, "Father, Thomas Claiborne, and Mother, Rachel Claiborne."

Rachel and Mark each leaned back in their chairs in shock. Finally, Mark collected his thoughts and spoke, "Felecia, would you mind making a copy of those documents?"

When she returned from the copy machine, Mark said philosophically, "This changes everything."

. . . .

Mark and Rachel ordered room service for dinner and talked late into the night about the new developments. The marriage and baptismal certificates would surely be sufficient evidence for the judge to order a post mortem birth certificate for Mary and resolve the question of the Trust inheritance once and for all. However; there remained the offer made to Donald Claiborne and the threat posed by Luke Bratton.

"Where is that little nightgown you wore in Freeport?" Mark asked as he turned down the lights in their room.

"It's in my suitcase. Why do you ask?"

"It's been a long day and I thought you might like to get a little more comfortable."

"How thoughtful of you," Rachel replied in a tone laced with playful sarcasm.

Chapter Forty Seven

A little before ten o'clock the next morning, the newly engaged couple walked into the Bradley Law Firm and were directed to the conference room where Joe Bradley and Frank Zeller were waiting for them.

After a few words about their trip to Freeport, Mark could tell Frank Zeller was anxious to get down to business.

"A few days after you left on your trip I received a call from Donald Claiborne. He said he was concerned for your safety and wanted to meet with me and insisted on coming to Charleston. The meeting was all about Luke Bratton. He said Bratton had nearly turned violent during a brief meeting. That would have been the day after you were supposed to dock in Miami."

"If he followed us to Miami, and we are almost certain he did, he would have been mad as hell when we didn't show up," Mark added.

"Mad, and dangerous," Frank replied. "Claiborne seemed to be in a mood to talk and I asked him to tell me everything he knew about Luke Bratton."

"Why would Claiborne be concerned for our safety?" Rachel asked.

"No one would stand to benefit more from your death, Miss Devening, than Donald Claiborne. In the event of your death, he would no longer have to worry about the possibility of you being able to prove your direct relationship to Thomas Claiborne. Perhaps he was just trying to divert attention away from himself. Or, he might simply be genuinely concerned. I sensed that he was sincere."

Zeller began to lay out everything they had learned about Luke Bratton. "To begin with, we have good reason to believe he was involved in the plane crash that killed your parents," he said looking directly at Rachel. We have an agent in Barbados who concentrates mostly on drug trafficking to the United States. Two days ago he talked to the owner of the air charter service where your parents booked their flight to a neighboring island. He said your parents booked their flight in person two days in advance. A short while later a man came in to inquire about a flight and the owner said he wasn't very specific about where or when he wanted to go; just gathering information. Our agent showed him a picture of Luke Bratton. He said it looked like the man, but after all these years he couldn't be certain. Our agent noticed a manifest of scheduled flights on a chalkboard behind the counter and wondered if the Devening flight might have been posted there for anyone to see. He confirmed that the flight would have been posted with date and departure time and that the man, who, by the way, didn't leave a name, would have been certain to see it. The plane left early in the morning and exploded in midair over a deep trench in the ocean."

"Grandmother Richards believes my mother and Aunt Jane were both killed because they were in the same position I've been in for some time; heir to the Claiborne trust contingent on being able to provide sufficient evidence to prove Mary Claiborne was actually Thomas and Rachel's daughter."

"Frankly, Rachel, we agree with your grandmother. We can't prove it, but we believe both of their deaths were homicides and that Luke Bratton killed them both. We also believe your boat explosion was no accident. Our forensic people have continued to look at the fuel line and have found reason to believe that the slit in the line was intentional; most likely from a razor blade or utility knife. They are certain about one thing; if someone cut the line, the angle of the cut is almost proof positive that the person who did it was left handed."

"Mr. Zeller," Rachel stated with alarm.

"I know," he replied, "Luke Bratton is left handed."

For a moment there was nothing but silence.

"Donald went on to tell me something that, at first, I found hard to believe. But the more I thought about it, the more it seemed to tie everything together. He said Luke Bratton showed up in Georgetown about twenty years ago. He said that his father, Jack, and Luke quickly developed a close relationship and that Luke began working for his father's company. I asked him what his job was with the company. He claimed Bratton never had a job title and that the money he was paid by Jack and later, himself, was nothing more than extortion or blackmail."

"Blackmail?" Mark's father questioned.

"Donald told me that Luke had copies of documents that would prove that Thomas Claiborne and the housemaid, Rachel, were married and that they were the parents of a child, Mary."

"Mary Elizabeth," Rachel said

"Mary and proof of her relationship to Thomas have always been the sticking point in establishing the rightful heir to the Claiborne Trust. Evidently, Luke Bratton threatened to reveal the documents unless the Claibornes paid him. And they have been paying him extremely well ever since."

"Mark asked, "What kind of documents, Frank?"

"Donald wouldn't tell me. He claimed that Luke Bratton showed them to him for the first time a short while before his father died. He said they were official church documents but that's all he would say."

"Why wouldn't he tell you what they were?" Mark asked.

"He told me that you had offered him a deal to share the Claiborne Trust. He said he had decided to accept your offer but didn't want to reveal the nature of the documents until the deal was executed in writing."

Mark pulled an envelope from the inside pocket of the windbreaker jacket he was wearing and slid it on the table towards Frank and said, "Do you suppose the documents were anything like these?"

Frank looked over the papers and then handed them to Joe. Both men appeared stunned. "Where did these come from?" Joe asked.

"We found them last night," Mark answered and settled into an explanation. When he was finished he said, "These are both marked *original-copy one of two*. That would suggest there was at least one more copy.

"Frank," Joe asked, "Where did Bratton come from and how did he get his hands on his documents?"

"Good questions, Joe." I wish I had some good answers. Nobody seems to know. Donald did say that Bratton expects a large payoff when he inherits the Trust."

They all sat for a moment wondering where it was all headed.

"Finally," Frank spoke. "We're pretty sure Luke Bratton killed Rachel's parents and her Aunt Jane. We're convinced he rigged the boat to explode, which would make him guilty of attempted murder. But," he continued after a thoughtful pause, "we can't prove any of it. Donald told me he confronted Luke about the boat explosion. He didn't tell him he had set the boat to explode but he did tell Donald that if the Claiborne Trust was ever awarded to Rachel, he would kill him." Frank just shrugged his shoulders, "Another felony but no proof."

"One thing is certain; Luke Bratton is a dangerous man. He knows something is up and I think he's going to try to strike at his first opportunity. Unfortunately, Rachel, you're his primary target, and Mark; I don't think he would hesitate to kill you to get to Rachel. I wish we could pick him up but we don't have enough evidence to charge him with anything. We have collected Luke's fingerprints from Claiborne's airplane and we are going to send them along with pictures of him to the FBI crime lab in D.C. Who knows? There could be old warrants out for him. I've asked my boss for additional manpower to put a tail on Bratton and to provide protection for the two of you. As it is, we are thin on budget money and resources out here in the field, and I'll be surprised if we get the help. Rachel, you need to stay away from Georgetown as much as possible until we can deal with Luke Bratton. I know you won't like this but I've taken the liberty of speaking with the Dean at the college. He is placing you on paid administrative leave for the remainder of the semester. Mark, if she has to go to Georgetown, you drive her and don't travel after dark. In the meanwhile, all I can say to both of you is, be careful."

"Frank," Joe said, "I gather from your attitude that you don't think Donald Claiborne was involved in any of this."

"We think his dad was probably involved up to his neck in the deaths of Margaret and Jane. But we have no reason to believe Donald had anything to do with the boat explosion or Luke Bratton following you to Miami. Donald is a good businessman and even though I'm sure greed has played a part in some of his business dealings, I don't think he would stoop to murder."

Chapter Forty Eight

When the door closed behind Zeller as he left the conference room, Rachel looked at Joe and spoke with warm sincerity. "Mr. Bradley, there is something we intended to tell you yesterday afternoon after we got back to Charleston. But then, Sherlock Holmes here came up with this wild idea about the journals being stored in a casket and we got caught up in this whole affair."

Joe smiled and said, "It wouldn't have anything to do with that ring on your finger, now would it?"

She blushed and held out her hand for him to have a closer look. "It has everything to do with this ring," she responded, beaming.

"I could not be happier for the two of you and I know Mark's mother will be delighted." They could almost sense another thought forming in Joe's mind as he spoke. "Speaking of your mother, sometimes a little bit of harmless subterfuge is well suited. How about I call her and tell her I've made dinner reservations for the four of us at the yacht club tonight and you can tell us all about your trip to Freeport? Then, when the moment is right, you can announce your engagement. Of course, I will deny any prior knowledge."

"That's sweet, Mr. Bradley."

"Rachel, would you mind if we dispense with Mr. Bradley and shorten it to Joe?"

Rachel rose from her chair and gave Joe a long hug followed by a kiss on the cheek. "That would suit me just fine."

"Dad, we need to go to Georgetown to see Rachel's great grandmother. We want to tell her about the engagement and bring her up to date about the journals and the news about Mary Elizabeth Claiborne."

"I agree. The judge is almost certain to order a birth certificate issued for Mary and that will give you, Rachel, clear sailing as the sole heir to the Trust."

"You're right, Joe, but we have made Donald Claiborne the offer to share the trust. I know we can withdraw the offer, but I believe the final decision should be left to Naomi."

"Once again, I agree. Naomi is a wise woman and I know she will make the right decision. Incidentally, I would go directly to her house and then head straight back to Charleston before dark. I don't think Luke Bratton is foolish enough to do anything in broad daylight on Front Street in Georgetown. Keep your room at the hotel for the time being. It's about the safest place for you to stay."

"Won't that get a little expensive?" Rachel asked.

Joe smiled as he replied, "Remember, our work has all been pro-bono, but given the circumstances, I don't think we would be out of line to bill the Trust for an extended stay at the hotel."

Rachel smiled and nodded approval.

. . . . . .

"Isn't this wonderful," Naomi exclaimed when they told her about the engagement. "Claire, Stan, come in here and look at this ring."

After showing the ring to the Watsons and filling everyone in on how Mark proposed, Naomi said, "We have to begin making plans. Rachel honey, you're going to have to take me to Charleston to buy a new dress."

"It's a date, Grandmother."

When the excitement began to subside they gave her the details about their discovery of the journals and Thomas and Rachel's marriage certificate from the church and Mary's baptismal certificate. Finally, they explained the options regarding the Trust inheritance. "Grandmother, we can simply withdraw the offer to Donald Claiborne or we can let it stand. We think the decision should be up to you."

The old woman suddenly seemed as though the weight of the world had been placed on her shoulders. "As you both know," she said looking at Mark. "I enjoy an afternoon glass of wine. It relaxes me and helps me think."

For half an hour the matter was discussed between the three of them. When there seemed to be little left to talk about, Naomi took her last sip of wine and began to speak. "I was only ten years old when Thomas died, but my memory of him is as strong as it has ever been. I adored him. I thought he was the most wonderful person I had ever known." She paused to dry a single tear from her cheek. "He loved his family; his white family and his black family. He had no way of knowing what would eventually happen to his land and how all of this would work out. But his one stipulation was that the Trust should go to his nearest descendent. I think he would be overjoyed to know that it would be shared by someone from each of his families and I'm certain that he would approve of the intended use of the property." With a satisfied smile and look of resolve, she said, "I say, let the offer stand."

"Mrs. Richards, Rachel, and I discussed it on our way up here and we both thought that would be your decision. We both think it's the right thing to do."

As soon as they left Naomi's house and headed for Charleston, Mark called Donald Claiborne on his cell phone. "Donald," Mark began, "Rachel and I are on our way to Charleston. We need to get together to discuss the offer we made at your earliest convenience."

"I've just finished looking over some of the Trust property south of Georgetown. If you have time now I can meet you at the T W Graham café in McClellanville. We can talk about it over coffee."

As soon as the coffee was served, Mark propped his elbows on the table and said, "Donald, since we last met we have acquired written documentation that will prove that Mary was Thomas and Rachel's daughter and that our Rachel is the legitimate heir to the Claiborne Trust."

Donald leaned against the backrest in the booth and looked like someone had knocked his wind out. "I guess that does it," he said with a slight stutter. "I'm broke. Everything I own was used as collateral to secure the loans to buy up the land around the Trust property. I'd say thank you for the coffee," he said as he straightened to leave, "but right now, thank you are words I don't think I can manage."

Mark reached across the table and held Donald's arm on the table. "I didn't say the deal is off. Mrs. Richards approved the deal in the first place and it was her decision to let it stand."

With a bewildered look, Donald replied, "I don't understand. Why would she do that?"

Mark and Rachel spent the next twenty minutes explaining Naomi's rationale. Finally, Mark said, "Besides, it's a smart business decision. You are already managing all of the Trust property and, by all accounts, doing a good job. I know you have spent years creating your image of the development opportunities. The University of South Carolina will be well served. The State Parks Department will be well served and the county will benefit from a huge boost in property tax revenue. As I see it, you face only one problem."

"And that is?"

With a broad grin, Mark continued, "Do you think a proud Claiborne can actually work for a woman?"

Donald was momentarily confused. "Remember," Mark said, "You will be the Executive Vice President but Rachel will be the Chief Executive Officer."

With a sigh of relief, Donald replied, "It will require some effort but I'm sure I can manage just fine."

As they turned south onto Highway 17 from McClellanville, Rachel called her uncle Harold Sanders. It was a long and exciting conversation.

Entering the hotel, Rachel said, "Dinner is not until eight. I'm going to see if I can get into the hotel beauty salon and do a little shopping."

"OK, but keep my number first on speed dial and keep your finger on the call key."

"It's still daylight and the streets are packed. I'll be just fine." After securing a six thirty appointment to get a short trim and style she headed for the dress shops with Naomi's advice and Coco Chanel's book in mind.

For Rachel, cleavage was a natural asset and she chose a burnt orange dress that simply accentuated what nature had provided. With matching heels and dark auburn hair, Mark Bradley's fiancé was dressed to the nines and ready to spring the news to her intended in-laws.

Joe Bradley could have won an Oscar for his portrayal of the surprised father when Mark and Rachel announced their engagement.

Chapter Forty Nine

Following a travelogue of Mark and Rachel's adventures in Freeport, Joe felt confident in taking the conversation to the next level. "Rachel, how does it feel to know that you will soon be running a huge development corporation?"

"I haven't thought about it that much. I'm still entranced with the idea of being Mrs. Mark Bradley."

"Hear- hear," Joe quickly responded, "That calls for a toast."

After a round of toasts, Joe remarked, "Mark, there seems little left to do with the business of the Claiborne Trust. We should be able to wrap up the agreement and operating contract between Rachel and Donald Claiborne in several weeks. After that, your office at the law firm is waiting for you and I am anxious for you to get started."

Mark sat listening with veiled apprehension as his father spoke.

"Your mother and I have been longing for the time when we can have some adventures of our own and listening to your stories about Freeport has only increased our interest. It will take you a while to get up to speed, but I'm looking forward to the day when I can step aside and you become Managing Partner of Bradley Law."

Mark quickly but carefully considered his response and decided to jump in. "Dad, it's a wonderful opportunity; in fact, the chance of a lifetime, but I'm afraid I've accepted another offer."

"Another offer," Joe responded in bewilderment.

"I've been offered the position of Executive Counsel and Corporate Director of Internal Affairs for Claiborne Devening Development Corporation."

Joe leaned back in his chair as he exhaled his last ounce of steam.

Seated next to Mark's father, Rachel took his hand. "I'm sorry Joe, but I need him more than you do."

"Dad," Mark quickly followed up, "you have a number of very talented attorneys and one, especially, who is as good and probably better than I'll ever be, and capable of taking over as Managing Partner whenever you are prepared to make the move."

"And who would that be?" Joe replied with interest.

"Phyllis Agan."

"Phyllis Agan, but she's a wo . . . Joe Bradley curtailed his comment feeling the piercing eyes of two women preparing to pounce. "She certainly is a very capable attorney and worthy of consideration."

Mark's mother interjected her feelings. "Joe, you are a real sweetheart and I think you need to get on with it; the sooner the better."

The next morning Mark walked into his father's office to face the music. "You know you kind of blindsided me last night," Joe began.

"I didn't mean to, Dad, but I didn't want you to be under a false impression last night and learn the truth today. You've taught me better than that. Besides, Phyllis Agan is hands down the best candidate for the position."

"I know, but I'm having some difficulty coming to grips with Bradley Law being managed by a woman."

"I know it's a big change but consider; can you imagine Donald Claiborne working for a woman or, for that matter, me working for the woman who is also my wife? It's the way of the world."

Sensing his father beginning to weaken, Mark didn't let up. "I've heard you tell with immense pride the story about your father taking you and Harold Sanders to the yacht club for lunch. Your father was forced to face his own prejudice squarely in the eyes. He surely thought enough is enough and did the right thing. Before that incident how many black clients had Bradley Law represented?" Before Joe could respond, Mark answered his own question. "I venture to say none, yet today, and for many years, Bradley law has been a trusted advocate in the black community. Dad, I know that you are not prejudiced against women. You are simply facing a big detour from tradition." After a long pause to allow his words to sink in, Mark, with great love and affection for the man sitting in front of him, closed the deal. "Dad, no son has ever been more proud of his father and I know the day you make Phyllis Agan Managing Partner will always be one of my proudest memories."

Joe responded with a grateful nod and picked up his telephone to speak to his receptionist, "Will you please tell Phyllis Agan that I would like to see her in my office, and please hold my calls."

Mark gave him a smile and thumbs up as he left the office.

"Phyllis, please come in and have a seat," Joe said when she arrived and then continued with a big smile. "We have something to talk about."

Chapter Fifty

Claiborne Plantation 1885

Rachel placed several covered pies in the wagon and climbed onto the wooden seat next to Jacob, a trusted Claiborne worker of many years. "It's hard to believe," Thomas said, "that the work is nearly none."

"It's taken a long time but the women are going to give the inside a good cleaning while the men put the final coat of paint on the outside. Now don't be late. Dinner is pot luck at twelve o'clock straight up and it will be some of the best eating you've ever had."

Thomas stepped up on the foot hold and gave her a kiss. "I wouldn't miss it for the world. Jacob, drive slowly and try to avoid the chuckholes."

"You know I always do with Miss Rachel."

With everyone on the plantation, it was always, Miss Rachel instead of Mrs. Claiborne. In the early years the secret of their marriage, a white plantation owner and a mixed race former slave woman, bothered Thomas and Rachel, but after time it seemed unimportant. Everyone knew that no stronger bond had ever existed between a man and a woman. "God knows," Thomas thought to himself as he watched the wagon carrying his wife, disappear down the lane. "That's all that matters. That's all that's ever mattered."

As the noon hour approached, Thomas saddled his favorite horse, Silky, and headed for the site of the new school and church. The mare wasn't the fastest horse in his stable but she had the most comfortable ride and could run at a steady gait all day long.

Following the war, Thomas had given Rachel's brother, Johnathon, a small but fertile piece of land to farm. He had done well at farming and pursued his lifelong dream of becoming a teacher and minister. They were erecting a building that would be used as a school for black children from the surrounding area during the week and a church on Sunday. This was the last day of construction and the next day the sanctuary would be filled for their first Sunday services.

It was being built on the King's Highway outside of Georgetown. Prior to the war and reconstruction, education for blacks had been against the law and hadn't gained much support in the years since. The location stirred some consternation among the white community. A good many felt that a black church should not be in such a plain site for all travelers on the main highway to see so close to town. Thomas paid their concern little heed as Silky turned onto the main road and he urged her to her steady traveling gait.

About a mile before reaching the church, he heard what sounded like shots being fired in the distance. Then he saw black smoke billowing in the sky and instantly pushed the mare into a full gallop. When the church came into view it was completely inflamed with the roof beginning to fall. Just past the church was the grizzly sight of Pastor Johnathon swinging from a tree with his hands tied and a noose around his neck.

Suddenly, the screaming of a familiar voice, "Master Thomas, Master Thomas, over here." Thomas pulled the mare up to old Jacob and jumped off. "This way," the old man urged.

Behind a small group of pine trees lay Rachel on her back. "She's hurt bad Mr. Thomas but she's alive." Thomas knelt over his wife to check her breathing. She was unconscious and her breathing was laborious but steady. "What happened here?" Thomas demanded.

"The ladies was puttin' food on the table when a bunch of men came riding in shootin' and hollerin'. They surrounded all the folks and the one in charge told 'em to tie up Pastor Johnathon. One of the dinner tables was under that tree for shade and they stood him on the table." Jacob paused to catch his breath. "They put that rope around his neck and threw it over that big limb. Miss Rachel, she ran screaming tryin to stop 'em and the boss man swung his big horse around and knocked her to the ground hard. They lit torches and threw 'em into the church. He yelled at the folks and said the same thing would happen to them if they tried to rebuild it. Then the big boss looped a rope around the leg of the table and tied it to his saddle horn. He pulled the table away and left Pastor hangin'. The folks all took off. Horses, wagons, and some jus' runnin'."

"Jacob, did you recognize any of them?" Thomas yelled.

"Not at first Mr. Thomas. De had their faces covered. But after the folks took off, the boss man, the one who knocked down Miss Rachel pulled the cloth off his face and de left a gallopin'."

"Did you recognize him?"

"He's dat Mr. Chambers who run the general store in Georgetown. It was him alright. I wasn't feelin so good in the heat and laid down by these trees to rest before it all started. They neber seen me. As soon as de left I pulled Miss Rachel away from the church."

Thomas climbed on the mare and directed her next to Pastor Johnathon. He cut the rope and draped the body over the horse. "Help me get him to the ground, Jacob." Together they laid him in the shade of the tree where he had been hung and Thomas covered his face with a tablecloth he retrieved from the food and dinner items scattered on the ground.

Rachel seemed to drift in and out of consciousness and Thomas suspected that she had broken ribs. They loaded Thomas's wagon with a thick bed of pine needles and gently lifted her into the back of the wagon. "Jacob, you drive her home and don't hit a single bump. When you get there tell the house people to get her bed from upstairs and set it up in the library."

"I'm on my way, Mr. Thomas," the old man said as he climbed into the seat and took the reins of the draft horses.

"I'm going after the doctor and I won't be long," Thomas said as he pulled himself into the saddle. A heel in the mare's hindquarter sent her off in a gallop.

The doctor lived on the edge of town and as soon as Thomas arrived he explained what had happened and told the doctor he was needed to see to his housemaid, Rachel.

"Thomas, I'd do anything for you but you know I can't help black folks. My life wouldn't be worth two cents if it got out."

"Doctor," Thomas sternly replied, "nobody is going to find out and you don't have a choice. Get your bag ready while I saddle your horse."

When they arrived at Claiborne Plantation, Thomas unsaddled the mare while the doctor went in to look after Rachel. He gently put his arms around the horse's neck. "We had quite a journey today old girl and you were solid as a rock. Rest well old girl; we've got another journey tomorrow." Thomas called to the stable hand and told him to wash down the mare and feed her.

"The best I can tell, Thomas, is that she has at least two fractured ribs and a bruised lung," the doctor said as they walked out on the front porch. "I've taped her chest to restrict movement and you will need to keep her as still as possible. She's going to be in a lot of pain, but she should be all right in time." He pulled a bottle of syrup from his bag and handed it to Thomas. "It's morphine. Just a little for pain when she needs it and no more."

"Doctor, I'm very grateful and no one will ever know you were here."

"I wish I could come back to check on her but I can't."

"No matter doctor; she's just a housemaid." Thomas put his hand around the doctor's shoulder as he walked to the rail where his horse was tied. "Perhaps you and your wife would like to come to dinner next Sunday after church?"

"I think we can arrange that," the doctor replied. After all, Claiborne has a reputation for some of the best food in the state."

Over the next several months the doctor and his wife accepted several invitations to Sunday dinner.

. . . .

The next evening Thomas saddled the mare and headed for Georgetown. As the sun fell, he rode through the alleys to the back of the general store. He waited until the oil lamps were extinguished inside and knocked on the back door. When Chambers opened the door, he was surprised to see Thomas. "Mr. Claiborne," he exclaimed, "please come in. I was just closing for the night but we are always open for you." Inside the store, Chambers lit a candle and turned to Thomas, "Now what can I get you?"

Thomas pulled out his revolver and placed the muzzle against the storekeeper's head while leaning to blow out the candle at the same time. "That won't be necessary."

"My God, Thomas, what are you doing?"

Thomas grabbed his arm and swung him around. Holding the gun in his back with one hand he pulled a looped strip of leather from his pocket with the other and placed it around Chamber's hand. In one swift move, he had both hands firmly secured behind his back. "You're coming with me," Thomas ordered while grabbing him by his collar and leading him out the back door. Chambers kept a horse in a small stable behind the store and in short order Thomas had him saddled and pushed Chambers up into the saddle. "We're going for a little ride in the country and if you make a sound or even breathe hard, you'll be dead before your body hits the ground."

Once out of town, Chambers said, "Good Lord man, what's this all about?"

"It's all about you getting shot if you say another word."

Several miles from town they turned off the main road onto a seldom used path that led deep into the marshes. When they arrived at a grove of Cypress trees in about six inches of water, Thomas jerked Chambers off his horse and tied his feet together. He dragged him to a tree and set him down with his back against the trunk and tied him with a rope he carried on his saddle. He circled the rope around Chambers and the tree until it was used up and secured the loose end.

"Thomas," Chambers yelled, "are you crazy?"

"Crazy mad I guess."

Thomas bent down on his haunches and looked Chambers in his face. "You asked what this is all about. Now I'm going to tell you."

Thomas told him about finding the aftermath of Chamber's raid on the church the day before.

"Jesus, Thomas, that darky pastor was told any number of times not to build that church. He just wouldn't listen. We didn't have any choice. And that housemaid of yours I knocked down. She was in the way and just kept screaming."

"I guess I can understand how she felt," Thomas calmly stated, "the Pastor was her brother."

"Hell, I didn't know that, but how can you take up for them in spite of your own kind? And the housemaid, what's she to you but just another useless darky?"

Thomas repeated his question. "What's she to me? She's my wife."

Chambers was stunned. "Your wife! How was I to know?"

Thomas rose and removed the bridle and saddle from Chamber's horse and threw them into the marsh. He slapped the horse on the back and watched briefly as he disappeared in the night. He climbed into his saddle on the mare and sat for a moment looking at Chambers in disgust. The man who was brave enough to conduct a lynching was reduced to tears and sobbing. "Thomas," he cried, "you can't leave me here. The tide is coming in. I'll drown."

Thomas leaned over in his saddle and replied, "Mr. Chambers, you're going to die tonight, but I don't think it will be from drowning." With that, he nudged the mare and she began stepping carefully out of the watery marsh toward the old lane. As the horse found her footing on solid ground a twelve foot alligator slid into the water and headed for the cypress trees. About a half mile down the lane Thomas suddenly heard horrific screaming that reverberated through the night air. The screaming stopped as quickly as it had started.

They faced a long ride home but the mare was up to it and picked up her traveling gait.

Chapter Fifty One

For the next several days Mark and Rachel worked in the Bradley law offices on the contracts and all the related documents and working agreements necessary to execute the transfer of the Trust. Before the job was finished, most of the attorneys in the office would contribute their own special expertise. Much of the work would require the services of an expert real estate attorney and, to that end, Phyllis Agan appeared in Mark's office around 10 AM on the third morning.

Mark stood to make introductions as she entered his office. "Phyllis, I would like to introduce you to Rachel Devening."

While extending her hand to Rachel, she replied, "It's my understanding that congratulations are in order for both of you."

"Thank you so much," Rachel replied. "Mark has told me a great deal about you. I feel privileged to have you helping us."

With a smile, she responded, "We will certainly do the best we can." She turned her attention to Mark, "Alright hot shot, tell me what we are doing here."

"Before we get started, Phyllis, I understand that congratulations are in order for you as well."

Phyllis reached out and closed the door. "Nobody is supposed to know until it is announced at the annual meeting next month. Of course, I suppose it's understandable that your father would have told you." Phyllis set her tablet on the conference table and took a seat. "I'm not certain I'll ever figure out why your father chose me. I am certain there are about four generations of Bradleys turning over in their graves. I keep coming back to the notion that he had a little help in reaching his decision." After a pause, she looked directly at Mark and said, "Tell me you had nothing to do with this . . . and don't lie. It's not becoming. Besides," she grinned, "you're probably not a good enough liar to ever make a decent attorney."

Mark was stuck for anything to say. "I thought so. Stand up." she ordered.

"What?"

"I said, stand up." Turning her attention to Rachel she exclaimed, "He is going to be yours for the rest of your life but with your permission, the next ten seconds are all mine."

"By all means, Phyllis, please be my guest," Rachel replied while trying to suppress a laugh.

Phyllis wrapped her arms around Mark and kissed him squarely on the lips using every bit of her ten seconds. "Now, Mr. Bradley, let's get down to business."

After dinner that evening, Rachel told Mark that she needed to go to Georgetown. "I've got to see Naomi. I know she's worried about me and she will be filled with questions about Thomas' journals, and our trip to the Bahamas, and she will be blown away when I tell her we are engaged."

"I understand," Mark agreed. I'll take you up to Georgetown in the morning and come back for you late in the afternoon.

They left Charleston early the next morning to beat the morning traffic. A sign at the entrance to the Arthur Ravenel Bridge indicated that the right lane on the northbound side would be closed at 10 AM for repairs. "That will be a traffic nightmare," Mark said.

The radio was tuned to a local news channel and the commentator was giving an update on a late season tropical storm that was predicted to hit the South Carolina coast north of Charleston in about two days. The concern was that it would make landfall at high tide causing severe damage along the coast from the storm surge.

As Rachel had expected, Naomi was thrilled to see her and besieged her with questions. Laughingly, Rachel said, "Grandmother, I'm going to be here all day. Pick a subject and I'll tell you everything I know. But first, let me show you this," she said holding up her left hand for her to see the engagement ring.

"Oh my," she said as she examined the ring. With tears forming in her eyes, she said, "I was beginning to think I'd die without seeing you married. You deserve to be happy, sweetheart."

"I know you two ladies have a lot to talk about and I have to get back to the office. I need to see Stan before I leave."

Naomi pointed to the stairway. "He's upstairs trying to fix a leaky faucet in the bathroom."

Stan had his tools spread out on the floor by the vanity when Mark walked in. "Stan, I don't want to take you from your work, but I have to get back to Charleston and I want to make sure Rachel doesn't leave the house for any reason until I return this evening."

"I'll sure keep an eye on her," Stan replied.

Rachel was waiting at the bottom of the stairs to kiss Mark goodbye. "You don't leave this house for any reason . . . understand?"

"You worry too much," she replied, "but I have no reason to leave."

On his way back to Charleston Mark was entranced with the chain of events that had brought him to his current station in life. Two months earlier, marriage had never entered his mind. His future had been well planned; graduate from law school, gain experience at Bradley Law in preparation for the day when he would take over the firm, and, in all likelihood, court and marry a proper young woman well-grounded in Charleston society. Things couldn't have turned out any different or better. Rachel Devening was independent and self-minded but she also displayed a love of humanity and the determination to stay the course in any endeavor of her choosing, especially marriage. This young Creole woman had captured his heart and his sense of dedication to her was unlike any emotional force he had ever experienced. Mark Bradley was a happy man.

Chapter Fifty Two

The paperwork required to execute the agreement between Rachel and Donald Claiborne seemed endless; the contract, articles of incorporation, memorandum agreements, real estate transfers, and always, just one more thing. Just before noon, Mark took an incoming call from Chad Ainsworth. "Had lunch yet?" Chad asked.

"No, but I'm hungry and I damn sure need a break. What did you have in mind?"

"I brought the Southern Screamer over to the marina to show to that couple who are flying down from Maine to look at her but they won't be here for at least an hour. Why don't you come on over and we'll get a couple of loaded Coney dogs from the street vendor."

"God, that sounds good. I'm on my way."

For nearly an hour the two friends who, inexplicitly but willingly, had surrendered to the prospect of marriage, dined on the best kept secret of epicurean perfection in the food capital of the South and compared notes that might help them navigate the transition from bachelorhood to married life.

. . . .

Rachel and Naomi's conversation was interrupted around eleven by the sound of a weather alert coming from the television. The center of the storm track led directly to the beach island in the Trust property. "Thank the Lord," Naomi remarked, "There's nothing out there that can get hurt or damaged."

"Except," Rachel suddenly realized, "my seagrass beds."

"I'm sure they will be all right," Naomi said with a yawn. "But if I'm going to be all right I've got to get my nap."

Rachel remained glued to the television until a storm update predicted that it would soon be updated to a category one hurricane. The projected storm surge on the island would easily wipe out her seagrass beds and destroy the discovery of a new species and over a year's effort to protect the plants and the basis of a dissertation for a doctoral degree. She left a note where Naomi would see it when she arose from her nap and headed out the back door to the garage.

She backed out of the rear entry garage into the alley and then onto the side street. At the stop sign on the corner, she turned onto Front Street and toward the highway that would take her to Claiborne mansion where she would transfer to the old jeep and head for her boat docked on the Intracoastal Waterway.

If anything, Luke Bratton was persistent and this time it paid off. He pulled out of an old lane hidden by trees and began to follow her.

Satisfied with his plumbing repairs which had been much more time consuming than he had first imagined, Stan Watson gathered up his tools and descended the main staircase. The house appeared empty. His wife, Claire, had been gone with their car all morning and Stan assumed Naomi was taking her mid-day nap. "Perhaps," he thought, "Rachel had walked around the front porch to her apartment." A piece of paper on the kitchen table caught his attention. It was a note from Rachel to Naomi telling where she had gone. The note ended with the words, "Don't worry. I'll be back in a few hours." She had indicated the time on her note. Stan reached for his cell phone to call Mark Bradley.

"She went where?" Mark yelled into his phone. "You've got to go after her."

"Claire has our car. Even if I could go after her, she's been gone nearly a half hour. I could never catch her.".

Mark ended the call and started running toward his car with Chad chasing him. "Rachel's gone out to that island where Luke Bratton blew up the boat and tried to kill us," he explained out of breath as he reached his car, "I've got to get there."

"Whoa," Chad said while grabbing Mark's arm. The Ravenel Bridge has lanes closed for repairs and the town is loaded with tourists. You'd be lucky to get across the bridge in an hour. There's a lot faster way," Chad yelled as he started running back toward the docks.

Chad fired both engines in the Southern Screamer and pivoted the bow toward Charleston Harbor. He was running seventy five when they passed a marine speed limit sign of twenty five attached to a buoy in the main canal. As soon as the engines warmed up to racing temperature and the Southern Screamer had her sea legs Chad was prepared to open her up.

A couple pulled up to the marina in a rental car just in time to see the boat head into the harbor. "That's the boat, Vickie," the man pointed out to his wife. "He must be giving it a warmup run before he takes us out."

Rachel threw about a dozen buckets and old newspapers from a storage shed at the mansion and started back down the lane. At the gate, she turned left and headed for their dock on the Intracoastal. "There's only one place she could be going," Luke thought as he watched her turn from a hidden vantage point several hundred yards up the road. He kept his small fishing boat on a lift at a dock on a small piece of property he had owned for years. He knew he could be there in ten minutes.

Chad pulled out of the harbor into the Atlantic and turned north on a heading for Claiborne island. "Hurricane's on the way," he yelled to Chad in order to be heard over the powerful racing engines, "but she's two days out and right now we've got calm seas." Chad checked his trim setting and the engine gauges. Again, he yelled at Mark, "Hold onto your ass. This baby's gonna fly." He shoved the twin throttles forward until only the props were in the water.

Chapter Fifty Three

After tying up at the rebuilt dock on the Intracoastal side of the island, Rachel carried an armful of buckets and newspapers up the beach to her seagrass patch. As soon as she had two buckets full of seagrass with the fragile roots wrapped in wet newspaper she carried them back to the boat and then headed back for more. Dark clouds were moving in from the sea and she hurried hoping to beat the rain.

Luke Bratton tied his boat to an old fallen tree behind a tall stand of sawgrass and watched Rachel through binoculars as she stowed her first buckets in her boat and headed back on the island. He opened a watertight compartment and pulled out a pistol with a magazine that was about half full. He stuck a full magazine in his pocket and the pistol inside his belt. He crossed the narrow island and followed her to the seagrass patch with what little sound he made covered by the wave action on the beach and the wind that was beginning to build.

He hid behind a mound of sand waiting for her to come out of the patch with two more buckets in hand. In his hand was a five pound sea crusted rock and in his mind was a final resolution. "All this bitch had to do was keep her nose out of the Trust," he thought, "and she could have lived to play with these stupid weeds for the rest of her life."

Rachel finished packing her seagrass plants into two buckets and decided one more trip would be enough as she lifted a bucket with each hand and started her trek to the boat. As she trudged past the sand dune where Bratton was crouched he grabbed her from behind. She screamed and managed to struggle enough to see his face and his rock laden hand coming down on her head. As Bratton began to drag her out to the beach by the water's edge and the rock jetty a gentle rain began to fall.

The Southern Screamer made short work of the fifty miles from the mouth of Charleston Harbor to Claiborne Island. At the speed they were traveling the soft rain was pelting the small windshield like bb s and it became difficult to see. Chad slowed the boat as they approached the area where the rock jetty jutted out into the sea and Mark was able to scan the beach with his hand held over his eyes. Suddenly, his worst nightmare came into view. "It looks like Luke Bratton and he's dragging something up by the jetty. Christ, it's got to be Rachel. Get me as close as you can."

Chad applied enough throttle to get over the last breaker and headed for Bratton. Luke turned at the sound of the engines and was stunned to see the boat closing in on the beach. Chad dropped the boat into reverse to keep from grounding her on the beach and Mark jumped out on the port side. Bratton dropped Rachel's arms and pulled out his pistol. Chad ducked below the side of the boat when he saw the pistol come out and in quick·succession three or four bullets penetrated the side of the boat with one of them coming into the cockpit area at floor level and ripping through the sole of Chad's right shoe.

"Watch out Mark," Chad screamed, "The crazy son-of-a-bitch is shooting at us. From his position in the water near the bow of the boat, Mark watched Bratton shoot and then pause for a few seconds. He was waiting for an opportunity to rush him and when Luke paused Mark came out from behind the left side of the boat and sloshed through the water until he hit the sand and began running. Bratton was momentarily shocked by Mark's attack but he quickly regrouped and aimed and pulled the trigger. Mark saw him aim the pistol and he hit the sand and rolled trying to avoid the shot. The gun didn't fire. Bratton discharged the empty magazine and reached in his pocket to retrieve the new one. Mark came up out of his roll and reached Luke just as he was ready to fire again. Mark tackled him around his neck and as they were falling he snapped his head around. An audible crack immediately rendered Bratton completely limp.

Mark left Bratton in the sand and ran to Rachel. She was unconscious with blood streaming from her head but she had a pulse and was breathing. Mark lifted her off the beach and waded out to the boat. Chad took her from Mark and laid her across the stern seats. "What about him?" Chad said looking at Luke Bratton lying face down in the sand.

"He's dead," Mark angrily replied.

"Are you sure?"

"I didn't break his neck to let him live."

The engines had been running at idle and Chad told Mark to crawl out on the bow as far as possible to lift the stern up far enough for the props to turn clean in the water. With two quick shots of reverse Chad was able to turn the boat and begin applying some throttle.

As they cleared the breakers and began to pick up speed, Chad yelled, "I'm going into the city docks in Georgetown. Call 911 and tell them to have an ambulance waiting."

Mark tore off his shirt and held it against her head to suppress the bleeding and held her close all the way in until the EMTs climbed on the boat at the docks and took over.

After he finished the 911 call he hit his dad's number on his speed dial. It was hard to hear over the engines and managed to tell his dad that Rachel had been hurt and they were on their way into Georgetown.

"Can you tell me what happened?" his dad yelled into his phone.

"It was Luke Bratton," Mark yelled back. You'd better get up here. I'm going to need a lawyer."

"What about Luke Bratton?"

"He's dead. I killed him."

"I can barely hear you. Tell me again."

He heard him the second time and immediately headed for his car.

Donald Claiborne was in his office when he heard the sirens and walked out on the docks to see what was happening.

As they were loading Rachel into the ambulance, two police officers approached Mark to ask what had happened.

He pointed to Chad and said, "I'm going to the hospital but he can tell you."

Chad gave the police a guarded description of the events and when he was finished one of the officers asked, "This man you say attacked the woman; where is he now?"

"Last I saw," Chad replied, "he was lying in the sand on the beach. I think he's hurt."

When Joe pulled onto Highway 17 he scanned the contact list on his phone and called the sheriff. "Joe Bradley, it's been a while."

"Dave, I'm driving north on 17 way over the speed limit. If one of your deputies sees me, tell him my son's fiancé has been taken to the hospital in Georgetown. I'll understand if he stops me; just tell him I'm not armed or dangerous."

"Hold on Joe, I'll be right back."

A moment later the sheriff was back on the line. "Joe, about five miles up the road you will see the blue lights flashing on one of our cars. He's on the right side of the road waiting for you. Flash your headlights when you see him. Pull in behind him and he will escort you to the emergency entrance at the hospital."

Joe found Mark and Chad in the emergency waiting room at the hospital. "How is she?" he asked.

A nurse came out and told us she is stabilized and they have called a brain trauma specialist, a neurosurgeon by the name of Doctor Spencer. That's all we know.

A few minutes later a uniformed police officer came in and said, looking at the three men, "I'm the chief of police, Howard Curtin, and I'm looking for Mark Bradley and Chad Ainsworth."

Chapter Fifty Four

Mark stood up and said, "I'm Mark Bradley."

Chad and Joe stood and introduced themselves. "Gentlemen, we have a young woman in serious condition and a man who's dead with a broken neck. I'm going to ask the two of you to come down to the station and see if you can help me understand what's happened."

"Excuse me chief, I'm Joe Bradley, Mark's father. I'm sure both of these men will be glad to talk with you, however, the young woman you mentioned is my son's fiancée and we are waiting for her to be examined by a specialist. As soon as that happens I'm sure they will be glad to tell you anything they can."

"Mr. Bradley," the Chief retorted. "I appreciate the fact that you have a personal interest but, in all due respect, I've got a dead man on my hands and my business is with these two men." Looking at Chad and Mark, he said, "All right gentlemen, let's go."

"Excuse me chief, I do have a personal interest. But I also have a legal interest, I'm their attorney," he said as he handed his card to the Chief. "Let's step away for a moment. I need to have a few words with you."

Out in the hallway, Joe continued, "The only way these men are coming down to the station before the doctor shows up is if you arrest them, and right now you don't have enough evidence to arrest anyone. False arrest is not a pretty situation, Chief. Why don't you wait with us and as soon as we get the doctor's report I'll bring them both down to the station." He reluctantly agreed.

Felecia Adams came running in. When she spotted Mark in the waiting room she ran to throw her arms around him. "Oh Mark," she cried, "is she going to be alright?"

Mark's reply was monotone; almost as though he was in a trance. "We don't know; there is another doctor coming to look at her."

After consoling Mark she turned her attention to Chad. "Honey, are you OK?"

Chad forced a meager smile. "My best friend's fiancée has a brain concussion, I got a new shoe shot off my foot, my boat's got four bullet holes in it and the Chief of police is trying to decide whether or not to charge us with murder. Other than that, everything is just fine."

She turned to Joe and said, "Mr. Bradley, can you tell me what in the hell is going on here?"

Before Joe could answer, a tall middle aged man with thick glasses and dressed in street clothes walked in. "Pardon me, I'm Doctor Spencer. I'd like to speak to Rachel Devening's next of kin."

Mark jumped up from his chair. "I'm her fiancée, how is she?"

"The emergency room doctor and his staff did a terrific job getting her stabilized, but I can't discuss anything more about her condition except with a next of kin."

Joe Bradley interrupted, "Doctor, I've been Miss Devening's attorney for over five years and I hold a complete personal power of attorney. What can you tell us?"

They all took seats around a reading table while the Doctor explained. "She's had a serious brain concussion. They've been running brain scans since she was brought in. I haven't had time to do a thorough analysis but, so far, I haven't seen any serious abnormalities. Our biggest concern was brain swelling, but we seem to have that under control."

"Is she awake?" Mark asked.

"Right now she is in an induced state of sleep and we expect her to be awake in the morning. We can help the process along but, essentially, the brain will heal itself and sleep is the best thing for her.

Felecia anxiously spoke up. "How long will it take her to recover?"

"That's probably the most important question and the one that is nearly impossible to answer. She could be relatively free of symptoms within a week or two or she could have lingering effects for several months or longer. We know she will endure some severe headaches and periods of depression. She may also have difficulty with thinking and attention skills and communication skills. We will start running some basic skills tests tomorrow. For now, she has been moved to intensive care and she is doing well. I'm sure you folks want to stay with her but my advice would be to get a good night's sleep and come back in the morning."

"I think that's good advice, Doctor." Turning to the Chief, Joe said, "We are ready to go to the station. I'm sure these men are anxious to dispense with this matter."

At the station, the lead detective recorded each of their statements. Before he began the chief collected Mark's blood soaked shirt and the shoe Chad claimed had been hit by one of the shots.

When they were finished Chief Curtin spoke in a deliberate tone to Joe. "Mr. Bradley, we will be in the process of gathering evidence for the next few days. If I can have your word that your clients will remain in the State of South Carolina and will appear at this station for further questions with a two hour notice we will take no action this afternoon."

"You have my word, Chief."

Chad rode back to Charleston with Joe while Mark and Felecia checked into rooms at a local hotel to stay close to Rachel.

Chapter Fifty Five

The next morning Felecia went to the hospital to sit with Rachel while Mark stopped by Naomi Richard's house to bring her up to date on the doctor's report.

The IC nurse accompanied Felecia into Rachel's room. "We have stopped her sedative and she should be rousing in a little bit. She won't know where she is and will probably be incoherent at first. If she starts to wake push this button and I'll be right in to check on her."

For nearly an hour Felecia sat in the dimly lit hospital room listening to Rachel breathe peacefully. Suddenly, she began to softly moan and Felecia stepped to the side of her bed. Several times Felecia asked if she could hear. Finally, Rachel opened her eyes and recognized Felecia. "What are you doing here?" she asked.

"You're in the hospital, Honey. You've been here all night. Can you remember anything?"

"My plants, that's all."

Felecia reached over and pushed the call button.

In less than a minute the IC nurse came in and said, "Looks like she's awake. Rachel, I'm going to ask you a few questions." She started by asking her name, how old she was, and where she lived. After a few moments, the nurse turned to Felecia. "She is certainly coherent. Doctor Spencer is in the hospital and asked to see her as soon as she is awake. I'm going to page him and he should be here in just a few minutes."

Mark saw Felecia waiting in the hall outside Rachel's room. "How is she?" he asked with some trepidation.

"She's awake and talking. The doctor is with her."

"She is much better than I expected," the doctor said when he stepped out of her room. She has dozed back off on her own and I expect her to do that for the rest of the day. She'll awaken for a little while and then fall back to sleep. Tomorrow, we will put her through a battery of tests to check her recognition, memory, speech, and motor skills."

Mark and Felecia took turns staying with her on three hour shifts over the next twenty four hours.

By the beginning of her third day in the hospital, she was sleeping less during the day and carrying on rational and often lengthy conversations. Her mood swings ranged from periods of minor depression to joyful banter. During one of her better moments she said to

Felecia, "The bikini top with the bent clasp in the Bahamas; didn't you try it on before buying it?"

"I'm sure I did. Why do you ask?" Felecia curiously remarked.

"I've wondered several times how the clasp could have been broken while it was packed in your suitcase. I recall it looking like someone bent it over with their thumb. Of course, you wouldn't have done it on purpose just to add a little spice to the day and see if I'd have enough nerve to take mine off."

"Rachel Devening," Felecia retorted with feigned anger, "You're just terrible. I can't believe you would think I'd do something like that on purpose."

"At this point, Felecia, how many people know you better than I do?"

"Not many, but . . . all right, smartass. It just seemed like a cool thing to do."

Rachel's head began to throb from her uncontrollable laughter.

"What's all this laughter about?" the nurse asked as she came into the room."

"It was just something that happened on our trip to Freeport in the Bahamas," Felecia answered.

"Sounds like the two of you had a good time, Rachel, you'll have to tell me all about it."

"I'd love to," Rachel replied as Felecia just stood and rolled her eyes.

Chapter Fifty Six

On the sixth day Chief Curtin called Joe Bradley and asked Joe to bring Chad and Mark to the Station. They settled on two o'clock that afternoon.

Mark was with Rachel in the hospital when Joe reached him on his cell phone and notified him of the meeting.

"I've been worried sick about this," Rachel said.

"Sweetheart, Bratton tried twice to kill us both. If I hadn't gotten to him, he would have killed us all. All you have to worry about is getting better."

The Chief came into the waiting room a little after two and invited the men into a private conference room. Ray Shuster, the District Attorney, was waiting for them in the room. His presence only heightened Mark's concern. Following introductions, they all took seats and Chief Curtin began to speak.

"Gentlemen, we've put this investigation on a fast track and we would like to bring you up to date. First of all, we found Luke Bratton's boat and we also found several loaded clips in the boat that fit the gun we found on the beach. We are satisfied that the gun belonged to Mr. Bratton."

"Secondly, we recovered three of the four bullets that hit the boat including the one that tore through your shoe," he said looking at Chad. The ballistic tests indicated they were all fired from Bratton's gun."

"According to Naomi Richards, Rachel went to the island to salvage some plants she had been working with. We found two buckets of plants in her boat and two more near the spot where she was digging. The buckets in the sand were dumped over and the ground around them was disturbed; much like one would expect in the event of a struggle."

"Both you and Luke had blood on your shirts but the stains were not the same. Your shirt, Mark, was covered with blood in a manner one would expect when holding someone close with an oozing wound. The blood stains on his shirt were different. They were splattered. We believe we could prove Bratton struck her on the head with a rock causing the splatter stains. Most important, we found about a five pound rock covered in crustaceans with blood stains and some small pieces of scalp flesh near the buckets and we were able to match the rock to the cuts and impressions on Rachel's head."

"Luke Bratton was an auxiliary policeman; mostly parking duty a few days a week. I confess I didn't know him that well. Ironically, Frank Zeller of the FBI and Donald Claiborne both stopped by and provided us with some interesting background on Mr. Bratton."

The District Attorney spoke up. "Fellas, I received a call from a reporter with the Charleston Newspaper asking if she could interview us about Luke Bratton's death. I have prepared a written statement and the last two sentences will be of greatest interest to you." He began to read aloud, "Following a thorough investigation into the death of Luke Bratton we have concluded that he attempted to kill Rachel Devening and that at the time of his death, he was engaged in an act of attempted murder and that Mark Bradley of Charleston, South Carolina acted in self-defense."

"Chad," Chief Curtain said, "I have released your boat. You're free to pick it up any time."

"That's great. The couple who came down to look at it had planned to stay for a while and they are still in town. With a little luck, I can patch the holes and get it sold."

As the men began leaving the conference room, Chief Curtain asked Mark to remain for a few minutes. Joe Bradley wheeled around prepared to protest but Mark said, "It's all right Dad."

When they were alone the Chief said, "There's just one thing that bothers me. You said that you left Luke's body in exactly the same place where he died."

"That's right, I didn't move him."

"Luke died instantly and one would assume that at the moment of his death, he would simply have dropped the gun. Yet, when we found his gun it was over ten feet from his body. How did it get there? You said in your statement that you never touched the gun."

"That's right."

"It's anybody's guess and we will never know for sure. But one thing about it; it's a pretty fair indication that Luke Bratton was not in possession of the gun when you snapped his neck."

"And," Mark replied

"And, that brings me to my final question. Were you aware that Luke Bratton no longer had his pistol when you killed him?"

The scene was little different than a poker player calling his opponent with a million dollar pot on the table. The two men sat and looked each other squarely in the eyes for over a minute without speaking. Finally, Mark answered the question, "Well Chief, let's leave it like this. It happened so fast I just can't recall." After a pause, Mark continued, "But there is one thing about which I was absolutely certain. This was the second time Luke Bratton tried to kill Rachel Devening. There wasn't going to be a third time."

With pursed lips, Chief Curtin nodded his head. After a moment to reflect on Mark's comment, the stern look on the Chief's face turned into a warm smile. "I understand that you and Rachel are engaged to be married. Afterwards, I don't know where the two of you are going to live but there are a number of folks, including me, who are hoping you will choose Georgetown."

Chapter Fifty Seven

On the day Rachel was released from the hospital The Watsons, Felecia Adams and Naomi were all waiting at Naomi's home to greet her. At the front steps Mark gently picked her up and carried her up the steps to the door.

"Mark, you don't have to do that. It makes me feel so helpless."

"Doctor's orders, no steps, besides," he said with a grin, "I can use the practice."

During Rachel's stay in the hospital, Felecia spent every available moment pouring through Thomas Claiborne's journals at the Historical Society and frequently called Rachel with her latest discovery. Inside the house, Felecia handed Rachel a stack of manila envelopes with a year written on each beginning with 1854. "Our restoration expert is making copies of each journal as he goes through them. These are the first ten copies. I'll bring more as they become available." Looking at Naomi and then back to Rachel, she said, "These journals constitute one of the most valuable historical discoveries in the entire country. In fact, I'm certain a lot of history books will be rewritten because of them. Thomas wrote about agriculture, politics, the war, reconstruction and so much more than just personal information."

"Mark," Rachel asked, "would you please give Felecia the paper you prepared?"

Mark handed her an envelope. "Felecia, this is a legal agreement between you and Naomi. It states that although Naomi and then Rachel will retain ownership of the journals, they are to remain under your care and that you shall have exclusive publication rights for any portion of the journals that are published as well as the publication of any information contained in them and shall be entitled to any and all royalties."

Felecia gasped and reached out to steady herself and take a seat. "Do you realize that these journals could be the basis of an entire career and more?"

Rachel reached out and took her hand. "We want the words of Thomas Claiborne to be analyzed and interpreted with great care and his memory honored. There is no one more capable or anyone we would trust more than you."

Naomi stepped forward and handed a carefully wrapped package to Rachel. "We haven't begun to discuss a wedding dress, but I think you should look at this." Inside the wrapping was the dress Thomas had given to Rachel. "Thomas showed it to me many years ago. It was his first gift to her. It's simple but elegant and I think it might make a fitting wedding dress."

Some days later Rachel took the dress to Claire Watson at her home. "It would make a perfect wedding gown and Naomi would be so excited to see me wear it, but its 150 years old and I'm afraid it's just too fragile. After looking the dress over, Claire agreed. "But I could make one just like it that even the original dressmaker wouldn't know."

Rachel's eyes lit up. "You're the best seamstress I know." Remembering Joe Bradley's admonition that, "sometimes a little bit of harmless subterfuge is well suited," she said, "I can hardly wait to see it but Naomi doesn't have to know."

. . . .

As the weeks and months went by, Rachel and Mark were occupied with the transition of the Claiborne trust to the new Development Corporation and planning sessions with the State Department of Recreation and the Science Department of the University of South Carolina for the establishment of the new State Park and the University research center. Plans for a spring wedding were underway and Donald Claiborne began letting contracts for the complete restoration of the Claiborne mansion and submitted an application for the house and surrounding acres to be placed on the National Historical Register.

Felecia continued to send copies of the journals as they were released by the restoration expert. In early December Rachel received the copy from 1885. When she finished reading Thomas's account of the brutalization of his wife and the lynching of her brother, and the death of the storekeeper she was mesmerized with the comparison of Thomas holding his injured wife and Mark holding her in the boat after his encounter with Luke Bratton on the beach. She suddenly realized the emotional burden Mark might bear for the justice he exacted on Luke Bratton for years to come. She firmly placed the book on a table and went to her car to drive to their newly finished corporate offices on the south end of Front Street. When she walked into his office, Mark stood and said, "What a pleasant surprise." She put her arms around him and gave him a long kiss. "Always remember one thing, Mark Bradley, you are a good man and don't ever forget it."

A week after Rachel came home from the hospital; Joe Bradley called and said that the background investigation of Luke Bratton had been completed and that Frank Zeller wanted to meet with the interested parties. Rather than ask Naomi and Rachel to travel to Charleston, plans were made for Frank to come to Naomi's home to discuss their findings.

On the day of the meeting at Naomi's home the interested parties included Naomi, Rachel and Mark, Justice (Uncle) Harold Sanders, Joe Bradley, Donald Claiborne, Chad Ainsworth and Felecia Adams.

After a few minutes of reintroductions everyone took a seat and Frank began. "I wasn't sure we would get any results when we sent out his fingerprints to law enforcement around the country but the calls started pouring in. I'll try to make this brief but Luke Bratton had a long history of criminal activity before he showed up in Georgetown years ago including murder, attempted murder, robbery; the list goes on.

To begin with, his name wasn't Bratton; it was Lucas Merriweather. He was born in England in 1948 to a family of wealth and privilege. Instead of growing up in the lap of luxury and opportunity, he was a spoiled troublemaker from the beginning. He was enrolled in one private school after another only to be suspended by all of them. About six months after he was married he murdered his wife in a domestic dispute but before the authorities could arrest him he disappeared. Not much later he was arrested under a different name in Liverpool for several robberies. Somehow, he managed to get released on bail before the authorities realized he was wanted for murder and disappeared once again.

At this point, we lose track of him for about two years. Then he was identified by several witnesses and his fingerprints as the only suspect in a string of robberies in and around Boston. He was living in an apartment with a woman. A couple in the next apartment heard yelling and a gunshot and when they opened their door our man came running past them from his apartment leaving the woman shot and bleeding. His next stop was Georgetown."

"Why would he come here?" Naomi asked.

When we went through his house after he died we found a metal file box filled with old papers. There were a number of old letters, many of which were written by Thomas Claiborne years ago. There was a copy of Thomas Claiborne's will and two documents that he used to blackmail Jack Claiborne, and after his death, Donald, from the time he arrived in Georgetown. The documents were a copy of a marriage certificate between Thomas Claiborne and Rachel and a baptismal record for their daughter, Mary. At any time he could have used them to prove that Rachel's Aunt Jane, and then Margaret and finally, Rachel, were in line as the legitimate heirs to the Claiborne trust."

"But how did he get these papers, Frank?" Harold Sanders asked.

"We can only assume they were handed down in a family from one generation to the next until they fell into the hands of Mr. Merriweather.

"The name Merriweather seems to ring a bell," Mr. Zeller, Naomi said. "It's been many years but I'm certain I've heard that name before."

"I'm not surprised, Mrs. Richards. You see, Lucas was a direct descendant of a woman by the name of Elizabeth Merriweather. That was her married name. Her maiden name was Elizabeth Claiborne, Thomas Claiborne's oldest child.

Not a word was spoken for a moment and one could almost hear brains churning out data like a computer.

"Folks, if you check the line of descendants of Thomas Claiborne in both of his families, as I have done at least a half dozen times, you will find that at the moment of his death and for many years before, Lucas Merriweather would have been the sole legitimate heir to the

Claiborne trust. But he could never have claimed his inheritance without his criminal background catching up with him.

A prolonged silence was finally broken by Harold Sanders, "If I understand correctly, Luke Bratton, excuse me, Merriweather's self-appointed mission in life was to protect the inheritance status of Jack Claiborne and then Donald with the intention of receiving a big payoff when the will was probated. His biggest concern was that someone else might come into possession of documents proving that Mary was Thomas and Rachel's daughter. His solution was the elimination of Rachel's mother, Margaret, her sister, Jane, and finally, Rachel herself."

Frank Zeller replied with resolve, "That pretty much sums it up, Justice Sanders."

Epilogue

In Early June, on a glorious South Carolina day, Claiborne estate was the site of two ceremonies, both proclaimed celebrations of life. An altar and several hundred chairs were set up on the green in front of the mansion. At the front of the altar, a coffin rested on a bier.

Donald Claiborne escorted Naomi Richards to the altar. One can only imagine the thoughts that ran through her mind as she looked out over the crowd including people standing. "I'm the only person alive who knew Thomas Claiborne," her words resonating through the loud speakers. "He loved this land and all the people for whom it was home over so many years. Today let it be known that Thomas was a good man who judged people by their character and not the color of their skin. When he died in 1924 the hatred for blacks here in the low country was so profound that he felt he could not risk the safety of others by being buried with his wife, Rachel, who originally came to Claiborne plantation as a slave. It was something that the white community would simply not have tolerated for a prominent land owner and businessman."

"Thomas kept a daily journal and I would like to read one of his final entries; written three days before he died. "If ever there comes a time, and I pray there will, when white men and women and children and black men and women and children can find it in their hearts and sensibilities to live together in peace and harmony, my most fervent wish is to be buried next to the woman I have continued to love more with each passing day on earth and will join in eternal love in the house of the lord, my wife, Rachel Claiborne."

After a closing prayer by the attending minister, the coffin was loaded by the pallbearers onto an old wooden wagon drawn by a single mule. The coffin was conveyed to the old slave cemetery and interred next to Rachel. A new headstone had been placed with the inscriptions; Thomas Claiborne, Loving Husband and Father, and Rachel Claiborne, Loving Wife and Mother.

After a thirty minute break following the reinternment ceremony, a voice from the loudspeakers called people to their chairs as the wedding was about to begin.

The groom and his best man, Chad Ainsworth, and the bridesmaid, Felecia Adams Ainsworth, were standing at the altar when the wedding march began. The entire assemblage turned to see Rachel in her ancestor's dress, on the arm of her Uncle Harold Sanders, emerge through the front door of the mansion and proceed down the grand entrance stairs and the center aisle leading to the altar.

It was a large gathering made up of people of different colors; white, black and brown. Those in attendance would long recall that there were two beautiful women at the altar and that the Maid of Honor was Black and the Bride was white . . . or was she?

. . . .

As the small plane made its final approach to the airport in Freeport, Bahamas; the newly married couple spotted Sea Breeze in the marina below. They intended to spend their honeymoon cruising in and out of Freeport and would spend the rest of this day putting provisions on board.

The next morning, as they approached the small island they had named Topless Beach, Rachel retrieved a new two piece bathing suit from her suitcase. With her bottoms on, she picked up the top and saw a tag attached to the clasp. The tag read, "I didn't think you would need this," signed, *F A*. The clasp was broken.

Rachel clinched her teeth and thought, "I'll get you for this one." But in an instant, she began to smile when she realized how much delight this bit of treachery must have brought Felecia. "You're right," she thought, "I don't need it".

After several hours of snorkeling, Mark laid beach towels under an umbrella for them to catch a short rest. His eyes were soon closed and he was on the verge of dozing off.

Rachel got to her feet and said, "I'm not that tired. I'm going to walk up the beach and look for some shells for Naomi."

"Uh-uh," came Mark's sleepy reply.

After a few feet, she turned back and said, "There is something I've been meaning to ask you. If it's a boy, I'd like to name him Thomas and if it's a girl, I think Naomi would be nice."

"Fine with me," Mark mumbled with his eyes still closed.

Two minutes later, Mark's eyes popped open and he sat up like a cannon had gone off in his ear. He scrambled to his feet and began running down the beach toward Rachel. He stopped short of breath, about fifty feet from where she was standing. "What did you mean by that?" he yelled.

Thank You! For selecting

<u>Creole Women and the Men They Loved</u>

Please feel free to contact me with your thoughts about the book at
rdosb6008@gmail.com
R Douglas Osborne

Other Books by R Douglas Osborne
Available at Amazon in Kindle or Paperback

A Train of Destiny

An Unexpected Guest

Made in the USA
Monee, IL
21 August 2024

64287285R00125